SOUL
to
SOUL

A MUIRFIELD MANOR ROMANCE

SOUL
to
SOUL

LYNETTE SANDLIN

ARCHWAY
PUBLISHING

This is a work of fiction. All of the characters, names, incidents, organizations, and dialogue in this novel are either the products of the author's imagination or are used fictitiously.

Archway Publishing books may be ordered through booksellers or by contacting:

Archway Publishing
1663 Liberty Drive
Bloomington, IN 47403
www.archwaypublishing.com
844-669-3957

Because of the dynamic nature of the Internet, any web addresses or links contained in this book may have changed since publication and may no longer be valid. The views expressed in this work are solely those of the author and do not necessarily reflect the views of the publisher, and the publisher hereby disclaims any responsibility for them.

Any people depicted in stock imagery provided by Getty Images are models, and such images are being used for illustrative purposes only. Certain stock imagery © Getty Images.

Business card design in Chapter 19 by Michelle Jerla.

ISBN: 978-1-4808-9994-0 (sc)
ISBN: 978-1-4808-9995-7 (hc)
ISBN: 978-1-4808-9993-3 (e)

Library of Congress Control Number: 2020923430

Print information available on the last page.

Archway Publishing rev. date: 3/26/2021

FOR MISTI AND TRACI

CONTENTS

PROLOGUE

Muirfield Manor is a charming bed and breakfast located on the edge of Blowing Rock, North Carolina, and a short walking distance from the town's quaint shops and boutiques. The large front yard can accommodate parking for almost a dozen cars and boasts a small walking bridge that lies over a pond with a miniature waterfall, and stone pavers leading to the front door. There are trails on both sides of the house guiding patrons to the lush backyard and gardens. In the early spring, the gardens behind the manor are often dotted with remnants of snow and sprigs of green peek from the earth, signifying the beginning of warmer weather to come. Birds sing in the trees above and hints of spring hover in the air. Butterflies dance around bushes and bees flutter around newly budding flowers in search of any gold dust that will soon appear.

Libba, with her petite waiflike figure, sits in the middle of the garden on a bright purple mat, legs crossed, and her arms to her chest in prayer. To her right, the east garden, that was once laden of overgrown grass and shrubs and a makeshift flower bed with dead plants, serves as a gathering place for the manor's patrons, boasting plush trees and bushes with several chairs and benches surrounding a built-in stone fire pit. Near the trees lay a garden of stones about the size of tennis balls, created by the destruction of a huge boulder that once sat there before the manor was completely revitalized. A bird bath and several bird houses stand in one corner of the lawn, and above them a large wind chime hangs from low-lying branches sending soft baritone sounds in the breeze. To her left is the west garden, open to the public but mainly occupied by her closest friends and used for cookouts, soccer practice, birthday parties, and soon a wedding.

Libba never imagined life would bring her here. For six years she was married to a man she thought she knew well, only to find out that she really didn't know him at all. The previous year was a difficult one, but somehow led her to Muirfield Manor, and to Cailin Wade. They met by chance nearly a year ago. He rescued her, her knight in shining armor, ultimately rescuing her in more ways than one. They endured so much in the beginning and through it all, she learned what it truly meant to surrender your soul and give yourself completely to another. He taught her that. Libba couldn't say if it was love at first sight, but she knew it was a love to last a lifetime. A bond that not only joined the two of them in love, but also joined them soul to soul.

As Libba sat reminiscing over the past year, the obstacles she faced, and the friends who helped her overcome them, her mind drifted to that day in February when her entire world changed.

CHAPTER 1

THE RESCUE

In one of my earliest childhood memories, I walk into an antique store with my parents and am immediately struck with the smell of old things. Walking around the store, I notice there is dust everywhere. I can hear the creaking floors and see the light entering from a window, shining brightly on the mane of an old rocking horse. I walk up to the horse, touch it, and instantly feel all its memories flow through me, like the horse is sharing with me all his adventures before arriving to this one place. I see his adventures in my mind as clear as I see my mother standing next to me. I ask her to buy me the horse and she does, and that horse stays with me in my room until I move out of my parents' home.

Since my first day in that antique store, antiques have continued to fascinate me. From talking to people and hearing their stories about items brought down from generation to generation, to learning about the traditions associated with a family heirloom, I have been interested in learning the history behind old artifacts. This love of old things is what brought me to work for one of the region's top antique publications.

My name is Libba. I am married to Alec Spencer, whom I met in high school; he sat behind me in history class. We were friends in high school, and neither of us had any interest in the other beyond that. It wasn't until college that we started dating. I would see him on campus from time to time, and one day during our junior year we ran into each other at the student union and shared a snack. Later, he called and asked me out, and we've been together ever since.

Back then, I was so in love with Alec. The only thing I wanted was to marry him and start a family so when we finally did get married, I asked him how soon he wanted to try to have kids. Alec was not as keen as I was to start a family, and we decided to wait a few years. Having just graduated from college and still trying to start our careers, waiting awhile made sense. Alec wanted us to have successful careers so that we could give our children everything they could ever want or need.

When Alec and I met, he was living with Arnold and Kathy Newsome, his foster parents. Though they seemed to be a stable middle-class family, he never talked about his life before living with them and I often wondered if his birth parents were poor or had neglected him; that would explain why he was so adamant about having money and stability before starting a family.

At the beginning of our marriage, we both held multiple jobs and I was having a hard time finding a full-time position. Thinking I could be a stay-at-home mom, I asked Alec again about having children.

"Now? I can't afford to take care of three people, Libba. We need to wait, but I promise, not much longer," he assured me.

Alec got a job working as a project analyst for a firm that provided fiber-based bandwidth infrastructure services. A few months later, I landed my dream job working for a print and on-line publication, *Nostalgia Remembered*. On our second wedding anniversary, I brought up the subject again, but Alec had just received a promotion at work, and he wanted to be settled in his new position before having to take leave to help care for his wife and a newborn baby, so we decided to wait … again.

Our careers seemed to occupy much of our time. We both worked long hours, sometimes only seeing each other briefly before going to bed and again while getting ready for work in the morning. Occasionally, we would meet for lunch, but more often than not, one of us would cancel because "something came up." Alec progressed with his career, as did I. We both traveled wherever our jobs required and I was lucky enough to visit most of the East Coast, finding antiques, meeting shop owners, and attending networking events to promote my company. One would be surprised at how many antique conventions were held throughout the year, but as an account representative responsible for securing ads, I attended as many conventions and trade shows as possible because this is where I met most of the clients that wanted to advertise with us. Not to mention, this is how my firm made much of its profit. So far, I had contracted with more firms than anyone else in the company and my record was stellar.

As a project analyst, Alec thought he went on far better trips than I simply because he got to travel farther and wider. He promised that one day, one day, I would be able to travel with him, but our schedules never seemed to agree.

My office overlooked Blowing Rock Village. From where I sat, I could look around and see people scurrying along from building to building. I liked to people watch. People were so interesting to me. Sometimes I noticed their clothes, hairstyles, weight, and ages—different things. I loved to watch couples and families too, but normally I just liked to read people's body language and expressions. I watched people more than I watched regular television!

But today, I couldn't look outside and let myself get trapped into the people scene, as I liked to call it. I had worked at *Nostalgia Remembered* for five and a half years, and today I had the most important meeting of my career. Today, I was meeting with a huge client, and if I made the deal, I would secure the largest account in my firm's history. I had previously met with the clients on several different occasions, and they trusted me. I was honest and hard-working, and people wanted me to work with them because they felt safe and I worked hard to make sure they were taken care of.

I planned my meeting very carefully, sketching out every possible detail of the presentation, including my personal appearance. I wore my navy Calvin Klein suit that had a nicely fitted jacket with three buttons going down the front. It came with a pencil skirt that I paired with a white pin-tucked poplin shirt, and I even had a manicure the day before. The outfit gave me confidence, which I desperately needed to land this account. As I sat behind my desk trying to get into the right mindset for my meeting, I listened to one of my Spotify playlists softly in the background, closed my eyes, and tried to control my breathing.

"Libba?" a voice came over my speakerphone. "Your clients are here to see you now."

"Thanks, I'll be right there. Please show them to the conference room and make them comfortable."

I had looked at myself one last time in my hand mirror and stowed it back in the top desk drawer when my cell phone rang. Normally I disregarded any phone calls before a big meeting, but today, for some reason, I looked.

It was Alec.

He never calls me at work, I thought. I could let it go to voicemail, but something told me to answer it.

"Hi Alec."

"Hi Libba," he said.

He was silent for a second.

"Is everything okay? I'm about to go into a meeting."

"Libba, I've decided to leave. I have to go," he said.

He hadn't told me he had a business trip. I checked my calendar and sure enough, I didn't have anything written down on the line I always reserved for Alec.

Just then I realized, he didn't say he *had* to leave but that he'd *decided* to leave … to go.

"What do you mean you've *decided* to leave? You haven't mentioned a trip to me. When will you be back?" I asked.

Again, Alec was quiet on the other end.

"Libba, I've decided … to leave *you*. I'm not happy, and I know you're not either. I want a divorce. I'll be gone before you get home from work."

He was silent again, as if waiting for me to say something … anything.

I froze. I opened my mouth, but no words came out. I couldn't breathe; I couldn't think! I stared at the mahogany clock on the wall, but the time didn't register. It was as if time had stopped. I could hear muffled sounds all around me, and then a pain shot through my veins, so deep, so severe, that I wasn't sure what was happening. I felt a burning pulse run through my body, through my face, and hold like a rock in my throat. Slowly, my eyes began to close. The room turned fuzzy and then, my world went dark.

I must have dropped the phone and passed out because the next thing I knew, I was lying on the floor rubbing my head. Trish, one of the marketing specialists that I often collaborated with at work, was kneeling next to me shouting something.

"Libba, Libba. Are you all right?" she asked. "Let me help you get up."

I looked up at Trish, but all I could do was stare. The room was still a little fuzzy, and then the pain shot through my veins once more. I winced.

"Libba, you're white as a ghost!" Trish began to panic. "What happened? Are you all right? You're not pregnant, are you?" She grabbed my arm trying to help me up to my chair.

"What? No! No, I'm not pregnant. I'm fine—I'm fine," I told her, trying to escape her grip. "Just … give me sec."

Trish allowed me to get up but kept holding onto my arm as though I were about to fall again. Admittedly, it was hard to get my balance, but I managed to make it to my chair. My hands were trembling. I tried to hide it from Trish, but I think she noticed.

"You sure you're all right?"

"Yes, Trish. I'm fine. I … just slipped." I didn't want to tell her about the call, but she was eyeing me suspiciously as I grabbed my cell and laid it face down on my desk.

"I can tell the clients that you'll need to reschedule if you aren't feeling well," Trish said, although I could tell she really didn't want to do that. She knew as well as I that we needed this account.

Again, I looked at the clock. It was already after three o'clock. I'd kept them waiting nearly fifteen minutes! I couldn't cancel now; that would be unacceptable and surely cost us the account. My mind started racing. *I can quickly cover everything in my notes—short, to the point, but not rude—make an excuse to end the meeting early and be out of the office and on my way home by four-fifteen!* Trish was still staring at me and I could tell I must still look a bit pale. I grabbed my hand mirror from my desk drawer and confirmed what her stare implied. I dabbed some powder on my face, freshened my lipstick, then turned to look at Trish.

"Better?"

"Much." Trish didn't say anything more. We had worked together for years and she knew I would talk to her when I needed to, I always did. She touched my shoulder. "I've never seen you look … nervous before. Good luck in there."

"Thanks," I told her, not meeting her eyes. It wasn't the meeting I was nervous about.

After my meeting was over, I ran straight through the parking lot to my car. Today *would* be the day I parked all the way in the back just to help close my activity ring! I was almost to my car when my heel broke and I tripped, spilling all my notes and the rest of the contents from my purse. I dropped to the ground and sat there. That's when it hit me, again, like a hot stream of lightning pulsing all the way through my veins. Once more, I felt that burning sensation rush to my face and hold at my throat. The pain was so unbearable that I could hardly stand it … but I refused to cry.

"This is stupid," I screamed, though no one was around to hear me. "Get a grip, Libba."

I took a deep breath and started picking up my things. *He could still be there.* My meeting ended early as I had planned. We discussed everything that needed to be discussed, perhaps not as thoroughly as I normally would have discussed them, but I hit every major topic and then some. I couldn't tell how they felt afterwards or if I had closed the deal or not, but at this point, I really didn't care.

I looked at my watch. If Alec expected me to return home by six o'clock, and I were lucky enough not to get stuck in traffic, I could make it home before five o'clock and maybe talk to him before he left. Maybe I could even convince him to stay.

I threw everything back into my purse, took off my shoes, and ran the rest of the way to my car. The traffic on 321 wasn't nearly as bad as it is after five o'clock when everyone was usually getting off work. I was less than five miles from the house—I was going to make it!

As I turned onto Tower Hill Road, my hands started to shake. I was nervous about what I would say to Alec, but I'd practiced my script several times in my head and I knew I was ready to talk to him.

I had a little further to drive when I heard a loud shriek. It sounded like the wind was howling through the trees, though the trees weren't swaying at all.

The steering wheel shook in my hands.

I really need to get my axel checked, I thought.

I rehearsed my lines one more time in my head. The steering wheel was still shaking and the howling was getting louder.

I rehearsed my lines again, this time out loud, so that I could hear myself over the shrieking noise.

Suddenly, the car jerked to the right. I could hardly control the wheel as the noise grew louder and louder, and then the entire car was shaking. *Not car trouble now.* I pulled off the road and got out just in time to see the back tire deflate and my car literally slump onto one side.

What a perfect time to get a flat.

I've never changed a tire in my life. I looked at my watch again and realized there was no way I would be able to change my tire and make it home before Alec left. If only my tire could have blown while I was still on the highway, I would at least have a chance of catching a ride with someone, but I was surely too far away from the highway to be seen by anyone.

I did what came naturally to me. I picked up my cell phone and called Alec. A woman answered the phone.

"The number you have dialed has been disconnected, no other information is available," the woman said.

I couldn't believe it. His cell was already disconnected.

I did the next thing that came to my mind.

I sat there.

Seconds, minutes, what felt like hours passed, and I sat. I sat listening to the silence and thinking about the past few years of my life. What did I have to show for it? Sure, I had a successful career writing about antiques, going to shows, and closing deals. I had a beautiful home full of beautiful furniture, although who knew what it was full of now. For all I knew, Alec could have taken anything he wanted. I still had my car though, and it was paid for, so there was that.

Besides my co-workers, clients, and Alec, I barely talked to anyone on a regular basis. Geez! I didn't even have any real friends other than Trish, and we mainly just hung out at work.

Trish and I met shortly after I started working for *Nostalgia Remembered*. Trish worked for one of our ad firms and was always fun to talk to over the phone. We became phone friends and sometimes when I would call, I'd talk to her longer than to my client. One day out of the blue she commented that she would love to work for *Nostalgia Remembered* and I told her we were hiring. One thing led to another and in no time Trish and I were working together. Yes, Trish was pretty much the only friend I had.

What had I let myself become? I was a workaholic with only one friend, no personal life or even pets, and now my husband was leaving me. And I thought I had a perfect life.

The sun was starting to go down so I decided I should attempt to change my tire before I ended up spending the night in my car. I grabbed the spare, the jack, and the owner's manual and began to read. I could do this. I could at least get the spare tire on and drive, very slowly, to the nearest garage. I kicked off my heels, hiked up my skirt and slid under the car.

After struggling with the jack for what seemed like forever, I heard country music blasting in the air. I crawled out and looked both ways. In the distance I could see a truck. I waved my arms frantically in the air, but the truck continued down the road, leaving me stranded once again.

I put my face in my hands and stood there fighting back tears.

Cailin sat at his desk flipping through *Nostalgia Remembered*, and admiring the advertisement Mike, his business partner, had placed announcing their newest completed project. It was a small five-thousand square-foot restoration project, but with the many sustainable features that were incorporated into it, the project was getting rave reviews and more clients were calling every day. He looked at the time and decided to call it a day.

"Well, I'm out of here," Cailin said to Mike.

"What, you got big plans this weekend so you think you can leave early?" Mike threw one of his paper basketballs at Cailin.

"Nope, I just can't sit around looking at your ugly mug any longer." Cailin caught the makeshift basketball and banked it off the wall, landing the shot into the trashcan. They high-fived each other in the air from a distance.

Cailin Wade was co-owner of a small construction company that specialized in renovation work and historic restoration projects. Mike was not only his business partner, but also his brother, and best friend.

Cailin and Mike were almost two years apart, although Mike was older and had a son in elementary school. It was Cailin's idea to start the construction company after working for several larger ones in the area. Cailin liked the idea of owning his own business. Larger companies wanted to do big projects like hospitals, which meant of lot of time in cities and a lot of time away from his mountain home. Plus, Cailin wanted to do historic renovations, projects that weren't lucrative for larger companies but were perfect for a small company to showcase its talent, build a name, and turn a profit. And it was something he loved and was particularly good at.

He asked his brother to go into business with him after his brother's wife passed away and left him a widower and father of a three-year-old son. This was three years ago and his son, Noah, was now six. Sharing a business with Mike was the best thing Cailin could ever expect. Mike was very business savvy and running a company was second nature to him. He managed the books, payroll, and personnel, and basically anything associated with running the business while Cailin managed the construction operations. Cailin knew how to build and he knew how to manage a project, plus he never missed a deadline.

Wade Brothers Construction Company was fast becoming

one of the more profitable small companies in the state. They employed over fifty employees and would have to hire a few more if Mike landed the next project he was chasing. Business was great.

"Why don't you bring Noah over after practice tomorrow?" Cailin asked Mike, grabbing his jacket from the coat rack. "I'm planning on driving to Muirfield Manor to do some work on the house and you guys could come over and keep me company."

"You mean help you, don't you?" Mike teased. "I know once we get there, you'll put us to work. Hard work, too. You do realize there are child labor laws and I can't subject my son to such offenses, or it could have devastating effects on him." Mike grinned and they both began to laugh.

Cailin shook his head and started out the door.

"Maybe we'll stop over. I can't make any promises." Mike knew without a doubt that he would go.

Cailin was planning on spending his weekend at Muirfield Manor, the new house he'd recently purchased. Well, it wasn't exactly new; in fact, it was nearly one hundred years old. Cailin bought the house, an investment, in order to restore it with the hopes of turning it into a bed and breakfast. He knew nothing of running a bed and breakfast, or the hospitality industry in general, but he had money and could hire someone to manage it, someone who shared his same interests in the house.

The house possessed such character. If only walls could talk, he'd said to himself the first time he walked into the house. He knew there were untold stories held within the walls of that old house. That's what captured his heart and made him decide to buy it in the first place. Restoring the house, he felt as though the house was talking to him and he could see the families that probably lived there in years past.

Mike stuck his head out the door and yelled to Cailin. "Don't forget to stop by the Stanleys."

"Ah. Isn't it your turn? It feels like I just went over there," Cailin complained.

"Nope. Your turn." Mike was back in the trailer before Cailin could complain further.

He got into his truck and started it. The Stanleys were old family friends. For the past year, Cailin and Mike rotated going over to their house the first Friday of every month, ever since Martha Stanley came home after recovering from a bad bout of pneumonia, which was just after Louis Stanley had broken his hip. Since Cailin and Mike lost their parents, the Stanleys were the closest thing Cailin and Mike had to a mother and father.

Cailin loved the Stanleys almost as much as he ever loved his own parents, but he was itching to get to his new—old—house to see what else he could uncover. He would go by the Stanley's though, not out of obligation, but because he really did care for the couple and he knew he would feel rotten if he didn't. Plus, Mike would ask him the next morning and what would he say? That he forgot? Not a chance.

He turned up his stereo and headed towards Highway 321. He would stay for a few hours, have dinner as always, and then backtrack over the bridge to Muirfield Manor. Maybe he'd have enough time to stop by the paint store before they closed. He wanted to pick up some swatches to compare to the existing color in the parlor room.

Dinner at the Stanley's was always early. They went to bed by eight so there was no fear of staying out too late on a Friday night. He'd told them he needed to stop by the store before they closed because he knew Martha would make sure he left in plenty of time to complete his errands.

Martha enjoyed Cailin's company, but she also felt as though she put him and his brother out and she didn't want to be a burden to either of them. Cailin always reassured her that they enjoyed being around her and Louis, but when the clocked struck six-thirty, she told Cailin to leave so he could stop by the store and then go work on the new house a few hours before going to bed.

Cailin grinned and kissed Martha on the cheek as he said goodbye, and then he was off like a teenager being released on his first date without his parents. He got into the truck, turned up his music, and started singing as he backed out of the driveway. He would have more than enough time to work in his house tonight.

Cailin turned onto Tower Hill Road and noticed a car pulled over on the side. *Looks like someone is having car trouble,* he thought. *Poor guy, he's in the middle of nowhere and it doesn't look like he has a clue of what he's doing.*

Cailin wanted to help but was faced with the dilemma of being a good citizen and helping a stranger in need or getting to the paint store before they closed. Hesitantly, he turned left in the opposite direction of the stranded car, but something made him look in his rear-view mirror. Just then he saw a small figure crawl from under the car. It wasn't a poor guy, it was a poor woman, and she looked so … sad. She slumped her head into her hands and stood there.

Cailin stopped his truck and continued to look at her in the mirror. *I should just keep on going. Why do I always have to be the one to save the day,* he thought. But she looked so pitiful sitting there, no shoes, dirt on her skirt, and her head bent down. He turned the truck around, and slowly, made his way to her rescue.

CHAPTER 2

CHANGES

I was so grateful the truck was turning around. There's no telling how long it would take me just to lift the car high enough to put the spare on. I could hear my mother telling me not to talk to strangers, but at this point, he could be a serial killer and I wouldn't care, as long as he could change my tire so I could go home.

Home ... to an empty house.

But that wasn't anything I needed to think about. Right now, I needed to pull myself together and be grateful that fate delivered me someone who, hopefully, knew how to change a tire.

The gray GMC truck pulled up behind my car and the engine shut off. The truck, with its bold dominate design, had black aluminum alloy wheels, and donned an impressive front end with a wide grill. I don't know much about vehicles, but I could tell this truck had some raw power to it.

The music was still blaring; I wondered if the man was waiting until the end of the song to get out of his truck. Should I walk up to him and introduce myself? Surely, if he were being nice enough to stop and help a stranger, he would be nice enough to get out of the cab.

I started to walk toward him when suddenly the music stopped. I certainly was not expecting what I saw.

The man that got out of the truck looked like a Titan god straight out of some Greek Mythology painting. He was tall, six three or four, with broad shoulders and lean muscles, definitely carved from hard work, not long hours in the gym. His light brown hair was streaked by the sun and was just a little too long, curling slightly around his ears and hairline. A five o'clock shadow highlighted his square jaw and accented the tan he earned, probably the same way he earned those broad shoulders.

He wore faded blue jeans with a soft white cotton shirt underneath a long sleeved, light blue, unbuttoned shirt. His sleeves were rolled up to his elbows and I could see his tanned, well-muscled forearms. His dark beige boots had a bit of red clay around the bottom. He was a rugged man who worked and played outdoors.

"Looks like you're having a bit of trouble with your car," he said. "Would you like me to give you a hand?"

"I'd appreciate that." I smiled, extending my hand to him. "Libba, Libba Spencer," I said introducing myself. Right then, I realized I probably shouldn't have given him my full name, but it was such a force of habit since I often meet people in my line of work.

He smiled at that point and I could tell that he was trying to be kind. I could also tell that being kind probably came naturally to him although for some reason, right now, he seemed annoyed. I hoped I wasn't keeping him from something. After all, it was a Friday night.

"Cailin," he said and shook my hand. "You know, you shouldn't be so fast to give out your last name. Didn't your mother ever tell you not to talk to strangers?"

Yes, she had ... but how often did I listen to my mother. If I listened to my mother in the first place, who knows, I might not be in my current situation.

My mother, both my parents in fact, never approved of Alec. Up until the day my dad died, he had said Alec looked shady, like someone who shouldn't be trusted. Through the years, my mother learned to get along with him, but every now and then she would tell me she didn't know how we had lasted so long and that she still thought one day he would walk out on me. Imagine what she would say to me now. I was beginning to dread having to make *that* phone call. I could hear her saying, *"I told you so"* already. The now-familiar hot pain shot through my veins again, burning my face and stopping at my throat. I felt a bit dizzy and I could tell I was probably going pale.

"Don't worry lady … I promise I'm just here to help you with your tire," he said raising his arms like he was being arrested and lifting his shirt as if to show me he wasn't carrying a weapon.

I don't know what came over me. In an instant, a hot flash like I've never experienced swept over me and my stomach fluttered with warmth. *What the heck,* I thought. I swayed off balance for just a second. Cailin touched me on the arm and when he did, I felt an electric shock pierce right through me tingling my whole body from my temples down to my toes. What a stark contrast to what I felt earlier thinking about Alec.

I looked at Cailin but could only stare into his eyes. Immediately, he tucked his hands in his pockets and the sensation started to fade.

I opened my mouth but wasn't sure what to say. His touch left me speechless.

"I'm sorry," I finally managed to speak. "I've had a bad day and now this …" I gestured to my flat.

Cailin nodded but didn't look at me directly. "Well, let's see how fast I can get this changed so you can be on your way." I thought he said something else under his breath, but I was having a hard time concentrating on anything while my body recovered from his touch. I wondered if he felt the same shock that I had?

We walked over to the car; he bent over and grabbed the jack. I felt badly that his clothes were getting dirty, but he didn't seem to mind.

"Thank you for stopping. I really am grateful."

"U-huh." He straightened slightly and started to loosen the lug nuts on the wheel. He was eyeing me now and I noticed he had the most beautiful cobalt blue eyes I'd ever seen. That took me by surprise … a second time since I'd met him. I brushed my skirt trying to get all the dirt off and trying to avoid his stare.

"Do you think this will take long?" I asked.

"Not too long. You should be home before dark," he told me.

He worked swiftly, like he had done this a million times with his eyes closed. He whistled while he worked, and I noticed the slightest hint of a dimple in his left cheek. I wondered if I should make small talk. He didn't seem to mind the quiet, but I wondered if he thought I was afraid of him. I remembered how he stood there with his arms raised. Looking at him now, he looked like a very polite man—an extraordinarily strong, handsome, polite man.

"Um, so Colin, you don't look familiar, do you live around here?" I was trying not to sound too nonchalant.

"It's Cailin."

"Pardon?"

"My name, it's Cailin, Kal-in not Colin."

"Oh, sorry, Kal-in" I'm sure I was annoying him again.

"No worries. I just like people to pronounce it correctly and no, I don't live around here. I was just in the neighborhood." He flashed his dimples at me then his lips pursed, like he was a child trying to keep a secret.

In the neighborhood? There is no neighborhood around here. What does he mean by that?

As if he could read my mind he continued, "I was visiting some old friends."

In this part of town, most of the houses sat several acres from one another and because you had to travel through the mountains, it could take several minutes by car to get to the next house. No doubt he was on his way home and my troubles delayed him even more. Maybe that's why he was annoyed. He probably had a wife waiting for him at home and instead of being with her, he was stuck with me ... changing a tire. As if I had to know the answer to that one burning question, I looked down at his left hand, but at that moment, he stood up.

"Well, that does it. Do you want me to put this tire in your trunk?"

"That would be great." I opened the driver's door and pulled the latch for the trunk.

He walked to the back of the car. I heard him move some things around, put the tire in the trunk, and then he walked around where I could see him again. He had grabbed an old copy of one of my antique magazines that I threw in the trunk a few weeks ago.

I watched him peruse the pages noticing that his mouth curved up slightly as he studied one page in particular. He didn't seem the type to like antiques, but then I realized he was looking at some construction advertisement.

He closed the magazine and looked at the cover, then gave it back to me.

"Thanks for your help. I really do appreciate you taking time out of your schedule. I hope I didn't inconvenience you too much."

"Not a problem at all, glad to help."

Cailin smiled softly and I felt that flutter in my stomach again.

"If you want, I can follow you to the garage to make sure you get there safely," he said. "There's one about three miles down the road."

"That's okay. I think I'll take care of it tomorrow." I really didn't want to go home, but I also didn't want to keep him any longer than necessary.

He held the driver's door for me and peeped inside. My car was a mess! In my haste to get home I had thrown everything on the passenger side and now there were papers sprawled on the chair and floor. I could feel the heat of embarrassment rising in my cheeks.

I sat down, started the engine, and rolled down the window. He closed the door and leaned against it in a way that looked so familiar, like having this type of conversation was something we had done a million times before. I felt like a schoolgirl saying goodnight on a first date. I think I must have been blushing again because he smiled brightly and chuckled, and then he tapped the door and started to walk away.

"Maybe I'll run into you again sometime," he called to me as he closed the door to his truck. He waved as he drove away, and I noticed he was *not* wearing a ring.

I walked up the steps of my house only to feel the burning pain race through my veins. What would I find when I opened the door? Would Alec have taken only a few things, or would I find an empty house? Would he at least leave me a way to find him in case I needed to contact him about … a divorce? Is this really where my life was heading?

I slowly opened the door and walked in. The house was bare but not empty; in fact, most of the furniture was still there. Our tastes were different, so it didn't surprise me that Alec didn't take many of the paintings from the walls. He took the spare bedroom set, but that was his as a teenager, and he also took the flat screen television and entertainment center, neither of which mattered to me.

I walked into our bedroom; it looked exactly as I left it this morning. He took all his clothes from the closet and drawers, and all his personal belongings were gone from the bathroom as well. The smell of his cologne still lingered in the air.

I walked into the kitchen and on the table sat a brown envelope. It was addressed to me and the return address read Bumgardner and Rose, Attorneys at Law. I knew what this was. Alec was thorough and never left anything half undone. He must have been planning this for months. Once I signed these papers, he would be out of my life forever. The only thing we had to divide was property since we had no children. There would be no reason for me to see him ever again. He would be completely erased from my life.

I now recognized the pain in my veins as rage. Sorrow would cause a pain in my heart and not once had that happened, nor had I shed one tear since receiving that phone call from Alec. It was definitely rage that I felt. *Rage* that he had the audacity to end our marriage over the phone without the decency of telling me to my face. *Rage* that he had denied me a child for all those years so that he could concentrate on his career. *Rage* that my parents were right because he did walk out on me. *Rage* at myself for not knowing why he walked out on me in the first place. I had to assume … it was because of me.

My cell phone rang, and I immediately answered.

"Hello Alec?"

"Hey Libba, its Trish."

"Oh … hi Trish."

"Is everything all right? You left so quickly after the meeting that I didn't get a chance to talk to you. I've been calling and calling—why haven't you answered your phone?" Trish sounded very worried. I knew I needed to give her an answer or she would be pounding on my door before too long.

"Sorry, I just heard it ring."

"Are you okay, are you feeling well? What happened at work, why did you pass out?"

I lamented, "Trish … Alec left me."

"What! Are you serious? When?"

"Yes, I am serious. He called today just before the meeting. He said he was leaving."

"What? Did he say why? Do you want me to come over?"

"No." I cut her off mid-sentence. "I really don't want any company right now. I'll be okay. I'll call you tomorrow, all right?"

"Libba, I should come over, bring some wine ..."

"Trish, please don't. I'll call you tomorrow, promise."

I hung up knowing Trish would be over first thing in the morning. I guess she was the one friend that I did have. I ripped the envelope open and grabbed a pen.

Cailin couldn't believe his eyes. What a delicate, beautiful creature she was. She looked like a fairy with soft sunflower blond curls falling down her back and framing her fine-boned face. All she needed were wings. She was petite and slender and though she dressed in a power suit, she looked so fragile that the slightest wind could break her. She had the most striking hazel eyes and long eyelashes that curled perfectly around her tender eyelids. It looked like she was crying, or rather, holding back the desire to cry. Why was she so sad? Surely not over a flat tire? He felt the urge to scoop her up in his arms and cradle her like a child.

Cailin watched her as he worked on her tire. It was obvious that she had never changed a tire; she was trying to lift the car before even loosening up the lug nuts. She made small talk, which was fine, although Cailin was content working in silence ... and looking at this fairy-like creature.

When he drove up, she seemed so frail standing there with her face in her hands, and then she looked irritated when he was tying his shoes before he got out of the car. She looked terrified and went pale as a ghost when he pointed out to her that she had given him her last name. So terrified that she almost fainted and when he touched her … what was that all about? He could still feel the sting that flowed through him when he'd touched her. He never felt anything like that in his life. Her touch was like a drug that traveled through his body, awakening his entire soul. It was a good feeling though, slightly wild yet intimate and natural. He remembered the way she looked when she got in her car. She blushed like an innocent fairy—an incredibly beautiful, sexy, fairy. His fairy.

Cailin took his time driving to the paint store. He was no longer in a rush to drive to Muirfield Manor and work on his new project; he had a different project on his mind now. In the store, he walked up and down the aisles looking at various paints and brushes, but his mind kept wondering back to Libba.

He knew there was something going on with her, but he didn't know what. She seemed so sad. No, anxious. No, … she seemed scared, especially when he mentioned her getting home before dark. Why would she be afraid of going home?

He hoped she made it home all right. He knew he should have let her leave first and then he could have followed her. No, then it would seem like he was a stalker. He could have asked to follow her home to make sure she got there safely. She probably would have said yes; after all, she gave out her last name. He still couldn't believe she did that; then again, she did say no when he asked to follow her to the garage. He was, however, glad she slipped her last name, because now he knew a little more about the mysterious fairy with the hazel eyes.

He also knew she liked antiques, just as he did, because there were so many issues of *Nostalgia Revisited* magazines in her trunk that she could stock a library. He noticed her name and address on the cover. Maybe he would look her up and pretend to ride by her house the next day, then if she were outside, he would stop, and act surprised to see her. No, that was too childish, not to mention very obvious. He would have to think of another way to see her again.

Maybe Martha knew her. Martha seemed to know everything

about everyone in that area, not that it was a big area, but people talked, and Martha listened; well, she talked too, but that wasn't the point. Cailin decided he would visit the Stanleys the next day and see what he could find out.

Cailin stopped at the gas station on his way home. He had to wait behind a U-Haul truck, and it seemed the guy filling up was taking his time and talking on his cell phone. While he waited, he continued to think about Libba.

Libba? Did the man in the U-Haul just say her name? He rolled down his window to better hear the conversation, but the man had just finished pumping and was starting to drive away. Eventually the man drove off and Cailin was soon on his way home, too.

Cailin felt asinine for trying to eavesdrop on the man at the filling station. To think he had met a woman just a short while ago and he was already, what jealous, curious? Yes, that was it. Cailin was curious and intrigued by his fairy. He simply couldn't take his mind off her.

Once home, he put his paint supplies away and grabbed a beer. He tried to watch the game, but his mind inevitably floated back to Libba. It was no use; he would have to go to bed. That would be the only way to settle his brain, not to mention other parts of his body. Besides, the sooner he went to bed, the sooner he would wake and could talk to Martha to see what, if anything, she knew about Libba.

Cailin climbed into bed and thought of his precious fairy. She came to him wearing a long white gown, her sunflower curls flowing in the breeze. She smelled like lavender and honey. He inhaled deeply and was lost in the scent of her. Cailin reached out to touch her silky blond hair and it was soft, so soft. He put his hand in the small of her back and pulled her close to his chest. With his other hand Cailin cupped her face and leaned into her. Then he closed his eyes ... and drifted to sleep.

CHAPTER 3

COFFEE AND
CRAB CAKES

Cailin awoke the next morning with Libba on his mind. That didn't surprise him as she was his last thought before going to bed. He quickly dressed and hurried to his truck. He planned to pick up breakfast and drive over to the Stanleys to see what he could find out about Libba. Of course, Martha would be happy to see him, but she would also be suspicious once he started asking about Libba. Cailin didn't really talk to Martha about women, or dating for that matter, but today, he didn't care. He desperately wanted to find out more about Libba ... his precious little fairy.

When he arrived, Martha and Louis were returning from their morning walk. Cailin was right—Martha was glad to see him, but she was also suspicious and immediately started with the questions.

"Well, well, what's got you up bright and early on a Saturday morning?" She took one of the bags from Cailin and peeked inside. "Muffins huh? Are you trying to butter me up for something?"

Cailin grinned and kissed her on the cheek. "You know what they say, 'sweets for the sweet'."

Martha served coffee and fruit with the muffins, and Cailin talked jubilantly, making up for the previous night. He waited until they were cleaning up before he brought up Libba. By then, Louis had gone into the living room and appeared to be napping.

"You'll never guess what happened to me when I left here last night," he began, and he had the feeling that Martha knew this was his reason for being there. "I was turning back onto Tower Hill when I saw a car on the side of the road. I stopped to see if there was a problem and it turned out the lady had a flat, so I helped her change it." Martha's brow rose, and she turned to face Cailin. It was not unlike Cailin to help someone in need, especially with car trouble. He was handy with cars, almost as handy as he was with a hammer and nail. "Maybe you know her, her name is Libba, Libba Spencer?"

Martha dried the plate she was holding and handed it to Cailin for him to put away. She grabbed another plate and whispered, "Libba, Libba Spencer, hmm?" She pretended to think and study Cailin. He was embarrassed now. "She told you her last name!?"

Cailin let out a quick laugh. "HA! That's what I said. Martha, you should have seen her face when I pointed that out to her. She went ghost pale—she was terrified! I joked with her and showed her that I wasn't carrying." He raised his arms and assumed the same position as the night before. He was relaxed now talking to Martha about his new interest.

Slowly, he lowered his arms. "She … intrigued me … a lot," he said in a very low voice.

This was the first time he came to Martha to talk about a woman and he hoped she was as thrilled as his real mother would have been if she were alive, yet she didn't want to ruin the moment. She looked at Cailin and for the first time she saw the expression on his face she had been waiting years to see. This Libba Spencer not only intrigued Cailin, but she also captured his heart.

Martha poured them both another cup of coffee and sat down

at the little kitchen table. Cailin sat next to her wondering if he should continue.

"Martha … she looked so sad, and I don't mean about the flat either. There was something about her that made me want to … shelter her, hold her, to make things … better for her. I know this sounds stupid, but I worry for her and I don't even *know* her. I don't even know if I'll see her again."

"Tell me about her. Tell me what happened."

Cailin thought about the night before and told Martha every detail he could remember, which was quite a bit. He didn't tell her about their touch though or how he could still feel her liquid drug running through him. He wanted to keep that part private, but he wasn't sure if he could hide the feeling or not.

Martha listened carefully and studied Cailin's every movement. *Yes,* she thought, *Libba unquestionably captured his heart; he merely hasn't realized it yet.* Martha squeezed his hand, "You'll see her again Cailin; I know you will. Don't worry, fate deals a hand to everyone and it seems it's finally your turn to play."

They sat in silence. Martha admired the young man in front of her. She knew Cailin Wade and she knew if he were determined, he would find a way see Libba again. "But now, you should get over to that old house of yours. I thought you were painting today." She stood up and grabbed their empty coffee mugs, then carefully placed them in the sink.

"Oh, you're right! And Mike and Noah are supposed to meet me there." He grabbed his keys and stood up too. "I'll tell them you send your love."

Martha walked Cailin to the door and watched him drive away. She hoped fate would be kind to him. The Wade brothers already suffered far too much when it came to matters of the heart and it was about time for each of them to find their destiny, especially Cailin. He had waited far too long. Martha went to her room and pulled out a little gray box from the back of her dresser. She had a feeling Cailin would need this soon enough.

Cailin was a little disappointed that Martha did not have any knowledge of Libba, but he was grateful, not to mention proud of himself, that he had confided in her. It wasn't as awkward as he thought it would be. When he arrived at the place where he met Libba, even though he knew she would not be there, he stopped and lingered. He could picture her, her cheeks as pink as wild sweet peas looking up at him with those stunning hazel eyes. Her eyes were a mystery to him, one minute they showed how strong she was and the next how impossibly fragile she could be. He wondered if she had repaired her tire yet. There was only one garage close by. Perhaps ...

Cailin picked up the phone and dialed his brother. He wanted to let Mike know he was going to get an oil change and he doubted he would be working at the house any time soon.

I slept in the next day. After all, I had nothing and no one to wake up for. I stayed up late thinking Alec would call to explain to me why he was leaving, but he never did. I would have to wait until Monday to talk to his attorney, who could perhaps shed some light on the situation.

I made breakfast out of habit but really had no appetite to eat. I decided to go to the garage and have my tire repaired and then call Trish when I got back. I was sure she would have a million questions, questions that I wouldn't be able to answer. I threw on a pair of jeans and an old t-shirt, grabbed my purse and headed for the door.

I drove slower than necessary to get to the garage. When I came to the spot where I had pulled over due to my flat, I parked the car and got out. Instead of reliving the despair I felt when I realized my tire was flat and I would never get home before Alec left, for some reason, I thought about Cailin. I remembered how he looked when he got out of his truck and my stomach fluttered the same as it had the night before. What was *that* all about? Sure, Cailin was handsome but shouldn't I be thinking about Alec? Was *he* with another woman or did he leave me for other reasons, reasons that other men would also find unappealing, reasons that *Cailin* might find unappealing? *Wait. Why am I thinking about Cailin again?* My husband just left me, my life was changing abruptly and dramatically, and I'm thinking about the guy who changed my tire? I thought about the turn my life was now taking. Was I ready for this type of change?

Looking back, I noticed all the signs that our marriage was not what it had once been. We were no longer a couple and probably hadn't been for quite some time. In a way, our marriage was over long ago, I was just so stuck in the same mundane routine that I didn't realize it. We rarely had decent conversations, we mostly talked about work. On the weekends, we ate breakfast together but then went our separate ways working on hobbies that the other had no interest in. I couldn't remember the last time we ate dinner together much less the last time we had sex. Oh my gosh! I couldn't even remember the last time we had sex!

The worst part was that I didn't even miss it.

I was neither sad nor angry. In fact, the longer I analyzed our relationship, the more I could justify it being over. Perhaps I was not the perfect wife he wanted or needed, but neither was he the perfect husband. For the most part Alec was kind, but on a few occasions his anger got the best of him, and me, especially if he had been drinking. It had been almost a year since … well, since he had to apologize for his behavior, but still, you don't forget that kind of rage easily, no matter how hard you try.

I looked at the clock; it was after eleven. Had I really sat here all this time? I needed to get my tire fixed. Maybe I would call Trish and meet her for lunch.

When I arrived at the garage, there was a familiar gray GMC truck in the parking lot. I recognized Cailin standing at the counter inside the waiting room. He turned as I was pulling up. I waved politely and he flashed me a smile, watching me until I came to a stop. I entered the shop and spoke to the attendant about my flat. I didn't have to see Cailin to know he was still watching me with those cobalt blue eyes of his. As I entered the small waiting room, Cailin greeted me.

"Hi Libba. I see you finally made it. I wondered when you would get here."

"I slept in." *Oh, that was a stupid response. Say something else!* "Thanks again for your help last night. I don't know what I would have done without you." *Now that sounds too helpless. Don't be a sissy!* "What brings you here? You seem to know enough about cars that you wouldn't have to visit a garage." *That's better. An open-ended question, a compliment, that's good.*

"Actually, I've been waiting for you. I was beginning to doubt if you'd ever show up." He watched me with a mischief in his eyes that made my insides tremble.

"Oh." I was at a complete loss for words.

He knew his response took me off guard and his face lit in triumph. "Does that shock you?" he asked.

"Yes."

"Well then, that's something for you to think about," he winked at me and walked out the door.

What was with this man!? He *winked* at me ... at ME? What? Did he expect me to follow him to his truck? I looked out the door. Apparently, he did.

Cailin stood propped against his truck with his arms crossed at his chest ... watching me. I leaned my head over the counter to get a better view. *This man is crazy.* I straightened up and turned to the attendant, Natalie, a young girl who looked about eight months pregnant. She stood there with a smirk on her face.

"You should go talk to him," Natalie said as if answering an unspoken question.

"I beg your pardon. I don't even know him. He happened to help me with my flat yesterday, that's all."

"That's Cailin. Cailin Wade. He's co-owner of Wade Brothers Construction Company and one of the hottest, not to mention one of the wealthiest, bachelors in town. If I were you, I'd go talk to him." Natalie looked over my shoulder. "Looks like he's waiting for you."

Yes, he was waiting for me. I hesitated a few seconds, then walked out the door. He was handsome … standing there with his sun-kissed hair. He had shaved since yesterday and didn't look quite as rugged as the day before. It gave his face a deceptively boyish look, but the rest of him was all man. Definitely, all man.

He wore a blue t-shirt that hugged his chest and shoulders but hung loose at the bottom hinting at a tapered waist. His tan arms flexed as he casually tossed his keys between his large, callused hands. His long legs were clad in dark denim and one knee was bent, braced on the truck's runner revealing well-worn tan boots. He wore a pair of black Ray Bans that concealed his eyes making me wish I could see them again to know what he was thinking.

"You have my attention," I said.

"Good." He ran his fingers through his thick mane of hair then stuck his hands in his pockets. He didn't seem as arrogant as he had a few moments earlier. "I was hoping I would run into you here because I wanted to see you again. Would you like to have lunch with me while they fix your tire?"

At that exact moment I raised my hand to adjust my purse on my shoulder. He saw my ring finger. "I'm sorry, I didn't realize you were mar—I would never …"

Automatically I began to fidget with my ring. "No, no …

actually ... well ... it's a long story—part of the reason behind
the bad day yesterday. Remember?" I was sure he remembered. I
had acted like a complete lunatic, yet here he was, wanting to see
me again.

Cailin looked at me like he wasn't sure what to do. I don't
think he expected to find out that I was married, and this had
stumped his game. He no longer seemed confident compared to
five minutes ago; he even looked a little ... disappointed? I didn't
know what to say; I wasn't sure what to do. I was beginning to
feel a little awkward just standing there so I decided to tell him
the truth. I kept my eyes on the ground, too embarrassed to look
at him.

"My husband left me."

"I see."

Did he really?

He shrugged his shoulders and continued with chagrin.
"Well, its only lunch, right? I don't see how that could hurt any-
one. Besides, they have at least three cars ahead of you. Hop in."
He opened the door and hesitantly, I climbed in.

His truck smelled just like a man. It was a little musky with
a hint of nature and leather, *real* leather. The scent of his cologne
wafted in the air and when I inhaled the aroma excited my senses.
The chairs were warm and the rays from the sun prickled my
forehead. It felt as if my body was being wrapped in the essence
of his soul.

It felt natural.

I closed my eyes and leaned into the seat, my head turned automatically toward Cailin and then the sound of his voice brought
me back to reality.

"Comfortable?" he chortled at me as if catching me with my
hand in a cookie jar.

My eyes flew open! *How embarrassing!*

I tried to think of something witty to say, "This is a nice

truck," I said looking around and patting the warm leather seat, "or is 'nice' not the right word to use when referring to such a manly vehicle?"

"You can call my truck manly ... I don't mind." He smiled a wicked smile that I'm sure made me blush, then started the engine and backed out of the lot.

As boldly as I could manage, I looked directly at him and said, "Well then Cailin, you have a nice, *manly* truck." *My gosh, was I flirting with him?*

We both laughed and then my stomach growled. I didn't eat the breakfast I had prepared and now my stomach was politely reminding me.

"So where are we going?"

"You like crab cakes?"

"Yes! I *love* crab cakes. I haven't had them in years!"

"There's a place not far from here that we can go, and we can sit outside if you like. Would that be okay, sitting outside, I mean?" He turned slightly and looked at me as if seeking my approval. I wondered if he asked that to see if I was afraid to be caught with him in public or if he wondered if I enjoyed eating outdoors. I hoped it was the latter.

"That would be lovely."

He took me to a quaint seafood café not far from the garage. There was a small outside seating area that offered a spectacular view of the mountains. The cool air was refreshing. A light breeze carried the fresh scent of homemade cornbread from the restaurant with it. The waitress appeared and we both ordered the crab cakes.

"So, I hear you own a construction company. Must be nice working for yourself." Realization set in as I remembered him thumbing through my magazines. That's why he was looking at the back issue of *Nostalgia Remembered* in my trunk. His company bought ad space in my magazine. My magazine!

"And how did you find that out?" His forehead wrinkled as he thought about what I'd said.

"The girl at the garage told me," I replied and took a bite of my cakes. They were the best crab cakes I'd ever had.

"Yes. My brother and I started a company a few years ago. He's a great businessman and I'm good at construction, so it made sense."

"Do you specialize in anything in particular?"

"Small projects, historical restorations, and other renovation projects." He popped a fried okra into his mouth. "In fact, we just finished a historical restoration. Mike, my brother, wants to submit it for a sustainability, 'Green' award. It's received a lot of great reviews, so I guess we'll see."

"It must be a good project then. That's great news." It was easy to talk to him; if only the flutters in my stomach every time he smiled that wicked smile at me would stop.

"So what business are you in?"

I sipped my raspberry tea. "I'm an Account Manager for *Nostalgia Remembered*. It's a print and online antique publication. I mostly secure sponsorships and ad space, but every now and then I write feature articles for our Gold and Platinum sponsors."

"*Nostalgia Remembered*. I'm familiar with it." He didn't mention the ad. "Is that why you have so many copies in your trunk?"

"Yes, you noticed. I'm a junky! I love old things, *and* old houses."

"Hmm? Looks like we have something in common. I love old houses too, restoring them anyway. That's part of the reason why Mike and I started the business, so we could work on more historical projects, but it's the other work that brings in the bacon."

"Maybe my magazine could do a feature article on the project you just finished. IF you buy a sponsorship, that is." I teased.

"That's an idea. Seriously, but you'll have to talk to Mike about it. Not exactly my area of expertise." He slowly raised his fork to his mouth and licked it.

No, that might not be his area of expertise, but I could imagine what was. *Lucky fork. Did I really just think that?*

"He should give Trish Knight a call." I pulled out a business card, wrote down Trish's name and number, then handed it to him. "He can reach her at the main number or her cell. I'll talk to her on Monday and tell her to be expecting a call from Mike this week. She works in our MarCom department and has access to the editorial calendar so she could get him on the schedule, and I'll see what I can do about getting him a good deal."

The waitress came back and Cailin ordered dessert. He caught me off guard when he asked about Alec.

"I don't mean to pry, but you haven't said anything about your husband. Did you want to talk about it? I mean, he's not the crazy type that will come after me for having lunch with you, is he?" I could tell Cailin was trying his best not to make me nervous or pressure me into saying anything I didn't want to, but I found that I was completely comfortable talking to him.

"Actually, I don't know why he left me. He wasn't happy, I guess." I shrugged my shoulders. "I was on my way home to talk to him, that's when I got the flat. By the time I got home last night, he was gone." I signed. "I think … I think our marriage has been over for some time, I just never really took the time to acknowledge it, and he did."

I couldn't look at Cailin. I stared at my hands and played with my napkin; I didn't want him to see the shame on my face. Seconds passed. Cailin didn't say a word. I looked up and Cailin was watching me with such intensity that I was afraid to move for fear that I would miss something.

As if considering each word carefully, he spoke very slowly and said, "I can't say that I'm sorry for you, Libba. I hate for any marriage to end but if you were happily married, you wouldn't be having lunch with me at this moment and I might never get to talk to you, or see you smile, or look into your eyes. I *want* to know you, Libba."

He took the napkin out of my hand and set it neatly on the table between us. He began to iron the creases with his own hands and paused to think, as if he dared to say the next thing on his mind.

"I know we've just met but I have to tell you, Libba, there's a force pulling me towards you and I'm not sure it's one I'm strong enough to deny ... or one that I want to deny. I don't want you to hurt, but quite frankly, you seem to be taking this better than I think most women would. Especially for someone whose husband left her less than twenty-four hours ago."

He was right. I *was* adjusting well. In fact, I felt incredibly at ease at the thought of starting all over again. He wanted to know me. But did I want that too? There was no telling how I would be tomorrow or the next day or next week. So, what if I seemed to be okay today; tomorrow, I might not even be able to drag myself out of bed. The one thing I did know was that I would need time. Time to recover from losing Alec, though I doubted that would take long, but I needed time to find myself again. There were parts of me that I knew I had suppressed for years—eating crab cakes for one thing—and I wanted a chance to release all of it. Now, I was beginning to welcome the change, I looked forward to it. I almost craved it.

Could Cailin adjust to all this as well? Was he ready for such a challenge because surely that's what it would be? I didn't even know if I was ready for these changes. Cailin seemed like a decent man; he was polite and open, and we already had hit it off well. What I thought was arrogance back at the garage was simply the type of man he was, saying whatever was on his mind, being straightforward, being honest.

"I'm only asking to be friends, Libba, that's all ... for now." Again, he smiled his wicked smile, and I could tell his thoughts were a little *too* friendly.

He dropped me back at the garage and watched me patiently

until I drove away. I agreed to let him call me at the end of the week. I figured I would need the time to sort things out and it would give him time to decide if he really wanted to 'know' me like he said he did. If he called, I would find out.

Once home, I showered, cleaned the house, started the laundry—anything to keep busy. I had so much on my mind and couldn't keep my thoughts straight. I needed to call Trish. It was time for her to bring over the wine. There was a lot to talk about and wine definitely fit into the picture. My stomach growled; maybe pizza, too.

I called Trish and invited her over.

"I know this is bad timing, but do you mind if I bring Mallory? She's been begging to do something with me since her mom has Olivia for the weekend." Trish knew I wouldn't have a problem with Mallory; I liked her, the little bit I knew of her that is. I had met Mallory on a few other occasions, and she was nice, funny, and quite easy to talk to. She was younger than Trish and me, and she was also a single mother. Her daughter Olivia was four years old.

I'd heard that Mallory fell hard in love at a young age but never married the father of her baby. I think she kept in touch with the father, but I knew for certain that she had full custody of Olivia. She was doing a great job raising a child on her own. I admired her for that.

"Okay, but you'll have to bring an extra bottle of wine," I joked.

Trish brought a six pack of Amstel Light beer and two bottles of Stella Rosa wine, and Mallory brought tequila and margaritas mix. I had already ordered the pizza.

"Looks like we're in for a long girl's night," I said as Mallory hugged me gingerly with her free arm.

"I'm sorry about Alec," she said. "How are you doing?"

"So far I'm okay, I think, or reality hasn't quite set in yet."

I jumped on the countertop and grabbed a cookie from the jar. Trish poured us each a glass of white wine. She handed me my drink and set Mallory's on the counter on her way into the living room. She looked around stopping at the entertainment center, or what was left of it.

"Doesn't look like he took much except for the guy stuff," she wiped some dust off a shelf.

"Nope. He took all his personal belongings, his old bedroom furniture, and a few other things but that was it. Unless he plans on coming back—which reminds me, do you think I need to change the locks on the doors? I mean, what if he comes back and tries to take more stuff?"

Mallory picked up her wine and I noticed how perfectly manicured her nails were. "Why would you change the locks? Don't you want him to come back?"

I shrugged, jumping off the counter and walking towards her to get a closer look at her hands. "Your nails look really nice. What salon do you go to?" I asked.

"Why thanks!" she said, stretching out her arms and spreading her fingers so I could get a better look. "Really? Do you like them? I do them myself. They're those Color Street nails, have you heard of them?"

I shook my head, "No, but I'm so behind on everything it seems."

"Well, basically they are colors and nail art designs that adhere to your nails, like stick-ons, but new and improved. I order them from one of my co-workers, Ivey. She sells them, you know, like Mary Kay but for nail stuff. Anyway, you don't have to worry about waiting for them to dry, they don't chip—well unless you're tough on your hands I should say—and they go on really easily, AND they're a LOT cheaper than going to a salon. You just need nail clippers and a file. For me, they normally last about two weeks before I take them off and put on something different."

"I think you change them more often than that," Trish yelled from the other room. "Every time I see you, your nails look different. I swear I don't know how you find the time to do them Mal."

"Actually, they take no time at all." Mallory's face lit up. "Oh, we could do our nails tonight!" She grabbed her purse and started to rummage through it. "I think I brought some with me, let me—"

"You're not getting me to do my own nails," Trish interrupted. "I'd screw them up and have to go to the salon anyway to get them redone."

"I don't know if I'm talented enough to do my own nails like that, Mallory," I took a sip of my wine, then looked down at my own nails. They no longer looked as good as they had the day before, especially after trying to change my flat tire. I had chipped two nails on my right hand and the polish was coming off a few more.

Mallory pulled out a handful of little white packets from her purse. They looked like a stack of greeting cards at first and then I noticed strips of color resembling long nails.

"Don't be silly. They're easy to put on, you just need a steady hand. I'll leave them out in case we decide to have a little fun with our nails." Mallory did a little shimmy, and I could tell she was excited to be hanging out with friends and that she really wanted us to do our nails together.

"Maybe after we eat, we can give it a try. Right, Trish?"

Trish walked back into the kitchen and gave me a deadly glare. "Yeah, yeah, maybe," she said. "And by the way, you didn't answer Mallory's question about the locks, but if you ask me, I think you should change them. Never know if he might try to come back or not, and it would serve him right if he couldn't get in."

"Why don't you want Alec to come back?" Mallory grabbed the napkins and set one next to each plate.

"I don't know. Last night I was a nervous wreck but this morning … I've accepted it."

"Why do you think he left?" Trish grabbed a slice from the box. She didn't bother sitting down to eat.

"Don't know. Passed out, remember?" I grabbed two pieces and sat down next to Mallory.

"You passed out! Trish, you didn't tell me she passed out ... and come sit at the table."

"Geez." Trish grabbed her wine and sat down. "I'd forgotten about that part, it happened at work." She turned to me. "I knew you were on the phone—even though that's so unlike you to take a call before a meeting—but I knew it!" She was pointing her pizza at me now accusingly. "That's when he did it, huh? And you haven't talked to him since."

"Nope, haven't talked to him since. I called his cell last night, but it's already been disconnected."

"Disconnected?" Mallory thumped Trish on the back of her head. "Did you know about that, too?"

"Hey!" Trish rubbed her head.

"Fill me in, Libba. What have I missed?" She sat the napkin on her lap and cut her pizza with a knife and fork.

"There's not much to tell really. Alec called me at work and said he was leaving me. I got a flat tire on the way home and called him, but his phone was already disconnected. I got home ..." I left out the part about Cailin coming to my rescue, "... and divorce papers were waiting on the fridge."

Mallory's jaw dropped.

Trish was shaking her pizza at me again.

"Well, you need to get a lawyer," Mallory began. "I can ask my boss if he—."

"Who changed your tire?"

I knew Trish wouldn't overlook that detail.

They both looked at each other and then at me.

"Okay, so there's a little more I need to tell you guys."

Mallory jumped up and grabbed the tequila. Trish grabbed another slice of pizza. Yes, it was definitely going to be a long girl's night.

CHAPTER 4

ADVICE

Two full weeks passed since Cailin met Libba. Since then, he had worked alone in his house taking comfort in the solitude of labor. He needed the time to think. Working in his house settled his mind and helped him to escape the psychosis that his life seemed to be encountering. He had decided not to use his heavy equipment on the floor and found a calming rhythm in every stroke as he sanded the floor by hand. This would take more of his time but, in the end, the reward would be greater knowing that he put his blood and sweat into every wooden board.

He thought about his time with Libba. He certainly did not expect her to be married or going through a divorce or whatever was happening to her. Why couldn't she be a normal, single, good-looking woman? What if this ex-husband of hers came back, what would she do then?

It was a long time since Cailin entertained the idea of dating. For years, he and Mike invested all their energy into the business that neither one of them so much as thought about a relationship. Now, when he finally found someone, someone who took his breath away, he couldn't even see what his future could be like because hers was so unclear. At any moment, her ex could come begging for her to take him back and Cailin didn't know if she would go back to him or not. He hoped she wouldn't but that was selfish, and he felt guilty for even thinking it.

Libba agreed to let him call her but he had not done it yet.

He was afraid.

He was afraid that he might hear her voice only to be told that she was back with her husband and he could not bear the thought of that. The days were long trying not to think about her, and at night, when all was quiet and he laid his head on his pillow, she haunted him in his dreams. She was his fairy with the sunflower curls and the bewitching hazel eyes. And in the morning, he ached with the fear of losing her.

But how could he lose something he didn't have. Libba didn't belong to him; she was married to another man. A man who woke up one day and decided to leave her, or at least that's what she had said. He wondered how a man could fathom the idea of leaving someone like Libba. She deserved better than that and Cailin knew he was better; he would never walk out on her.

Mike pulled into the drive and parked behind Cailin's truck. Before he could even stop the car, Noah was out with his soccer ball running towards the backyard. Mike knocked on the door and let himself in. His brother was quiet far too long and now today, Friday, he had taken the day off work. Mike knew Cailin well enough to see that he was brooding about something. He always poured himself into his work whenever he needed to calm his mind—or body—and since Cailin had not spoken of a girl since he talked about the one he changed the tire for, he assumed it had to be her.

"Time for a break," Mike waved a beer in front of Cailin who was still sanding the floorboard.

"In a minute, let me—"

"Now," Mike ordered.

Cailin looked up at his younger brother. He knew it would be no use arguing. He also knew Mike was coming to lecture him. Mike could always tell when something was bothering him.

Cailin grabbed the beer. "Thanks."

"Are you going to tell me what's bothering you or am I going to have to get you drunk first?"

"There's nothing to talk about. I'm just trying to work, that's all." Cailin knew Mike wasn't going to give up that easily. He stood up and walked into another room where he had set up a few chairs and a television. He grabbed a bag of chips lying next to his wallet and cell phone from the top of the TV.

Mike followed and sat down in the recliner. He snatched the bag of chips from Cailin and waited. Cailin couldn't stand the silence between the two of them, but he knew that Mike, being the most patient of the two, would sit there forever until Cailin decided to tell him what was wrong. He couldn't put the conversation off any longer.

"Remember the girl, Libba, the one I helped with her tire?"

"You mean the one you said was married?" Mike raised his eyebrow in condemnation but Cailin knew he was giving him the benefit of the doubt.

"Yes, that one. I didn't tell you the whole story." He tasted his beer and grabbed the bag of chips from Mike. "I went to get my oil changed hoping to run into her and I did. I asked her out to lunch and that's when I noticed her ring. She said her husband left her the same day I met her."

"You *did* have lunch with her?" Mike was following closely, trying to be unbiased as he listened.

"Yes. She said she was hungry, and her stomach was growling," he chuckled, "so we went to eat. We sat outside. I wanted to make sure we were in the public so I wouldn't try anything stupid with her, if you know what I mean. We had such a good time. It was so easy to talk to her."

Mike heard the tenderness in Cailin's voice.

"We laughed, she smiled, and Mike, she has the most beautiful smile I have ever seen." Cailin looked Mike in the eyes, "She's truly special Mike. She made me feel complete, like a part of me was missing before meeting her. And now, now ... I feel empty without her. That's stupid isn't it?"

"No, I don't think so. Have you talked to her since?"

"No, she gave me her card and said I could call her, but I haven't." Cailin ate another chip. "What if she's back with her husband? I know it's wrong, but I don't want to hear that they got back together."

"Only one way to find out. Give her a call."

"I don't—I don't know if I can handle it. Mike, if she got back with her husband that would tear me apart. And if she didn't ... I don't know if I can date someone going through a divorce."

"Why not? People do it all the time—"

"But I don't."

"Call her!"

"What if she doesn't want to talk to me?"

"Call her!"

"I can't. I'm not sure if I'm ready ... I don't want to be the rebound guy and she has baggage."

Suddenly, Mike was irritated. "Well, I never thought I'd hear you say something like that. I understand your position, but I hope not everyone is as closed-minded as you."

Cailin's jaw dropped. How could Mike call *him* closed-minded? "What?"

"I have baggage too you know." Mike turned to look at Noah, who was playing in the yard. "But I should hope any lady I take an interest in would see beyond that and see what a great life the two of us could offer her. Libba can't help having a life before meeting you. She's not tainted, she's not contaminated, she's just human. You can't expect every woman our age not to have *some* kind of past. You have one—I have one—that's the way life works."

"Your situation is different. You had no control over what happened."

"No, and apparently neither did Libba." Mike was calm again; he never liked confrontation and knew Cailin didn't mean harm by his previous comment. "Look Cailin, it's like this, in every book there's a story to be told. When you finish one chapter, a new one begins. You take the time to read, to find out how the story is going to unfold. You read for the adventure and the adventure brings pleasure." He stared Cailin in the eye, "Aren't you ready for a new adventure?"

Cailin stood there rubbing his brow. "Why do you have to be so profound? Why can't you just say, *'Cailin, give it a shot. If it works it works and if it doesn't, it doesn't'*?"

Mike huffed. "Fine then. All I'm saying is if you love her, go for it."

"Love! Woah! Who said anything about love? I just met her two weeks ago. I don't even know her." Cailin was yelling now, "I'm wondering if I should *date* her, not *marry* her!"

Mike reclined in his chair and grabbed his beer. "Cailin, are you that naïve? Have you never heard of love at first sight? Can't your mind comprehend what your heart already knows? You're falling in love Cailin, and the sooner you figure that out, the better off you'll be."

Cailin shook his head in disbelief. Love, he couldn't love her. He very much liked her, and the thought of lust crossed his mind a time or two or three. But love? Surely not. Cailin didn't believe in love at first sight. He barely talked to her enough to make that kind of judgment call. How could he *love* her?

Mike walked to the TV, grabbed Cailin's cell, and tossed it to him. Cailin hesitated but then swiped and started typing.

"Oh please," Mike groaned. "Texting? Very mature."

"Just be patient." Cailin typed a few words then showed it to Mike for his approval.

May I call you? I miss the sound of your voice. Cailin.

"Sweet. I guess I approve." Mike raised his beer in salute and Cailin pressed the send button.

I didn't think Cailin would be the kind of man to say he would call but then not. In fact, I thought for sure he would have called the very next day, he seemed so eager to go out with me. But that was before he knew I was married. I guess after having time to think about getting involved with someone like me, he decided to bail. I couldn't blame him. I wished I hadn't gotten my hopes up. Every morning for that first week, Trish asked if he called, but day after day, I told her no. Finally, she stopped asking. She didn't want to hurt my feelings by bringing up his name. I couldn't blame her.

I busied myself, meeting with my lawyer and trying to finalize the divorce. Mallory, whom I had found out worked at a law office, convinced one of her associates, Rowan, to cover my case. Rowan was older than I and had practiced family law for a few years. He was a good lawyer or at least I thought so. As I had assumed, Alec was very thorough and there wasn't much for me to settle. Our savings and investments were equally divided, and I got the house in lieu of alimony.

Much to my surprise I landed the big account. My boss even took me out to lunch to celebrate. But no matter what I did to keep myself busy, my mind kept wandering back to Cailin and I knew I would need to come to terms with the fact that he would not be calling. He too, had abandoned me, without a last goodbye.

It was Friday afternoon and nearly everyone had left the office for the day. Earlier, Trish had asked me to lunch but I told her I was going to stay and work. The time was approaching three o'clock as I stood at my window, watching an older couple as they sat on a bench eating ice cream cones. The woman kept touching the man's knee and pointing at things, while the man leaned in closer to her face then turned his head in the direction that she would point. I presumed he couldn't hear that well and that's why he kept getting closer, to hear her better.

Trish opened the door and peeped her head inside my office distracting me.

"Come on Libba, it's Friday and most everyone is already gone for the day. We could go get some coffee and hang out. Maybe go shopping after. I'm worried about you."

I was not in the mood. I did not want to eat. I did not want coffee. I did not want to shop.

I wanted to mope.

I wanted to see Cailin.

"I have work to do Trish, and there's no need to worry about me. I'm fine, really."

"You don't seem fine." She came in and sat down. "By the way, congratulations. I heard—not that *you* told me—but I heard that we got the account. You know the one with Rudolph and Murphy. I guess you didn't scare them away after all."

"I'm so sorry, Trish. I forgot to tell you. Yes, we did get that account. Thanks, and thanks for not being mad at me. I've been a little preoccupied, you know."

"As if I couldn't tell," Trish rolled her eyes. "Libba, why don't you just call him? It's the twenty-first century, women do that these days. It's okay."

"Call who? Alec? Even if I wanted to, I don't know how to get in touch with him. Besides, we're done. Signed, sealed, and delivered the papers yesterday."

"I'm not talking about Alec, I'm talking about Cailin." She handed me a slip of paper with a number on it. "I talked to Leah in accounting. She gave me the information. And don't worry, I didn't tell her I was getting it for you. She has no idea. Just give him a call, Libba. It might make you feel better."

"I can't," I said, crossing my arms over my chest. "I gave him my number and if he wanted to talk to me, he would have called by now. Apparently, he's not interested. Why would he want to get involved with someone like me anyway?"

"Libba, don't be so hard on yourself. He said he wanted to get to know you and—"

"And I guess he changed his mind, didn't he? Because he hasn't made any effort!" My eyes burned just listening to those words. There was a lump in my throat. I couldn't comprehend the pain caused by thinking of Cailin not wanting me. I never shed one tear for Alec leaving me, but now, when I thought of Cailin, my heart throbbed with a need I never knew possible.

A tear ran down my cheek. I quickly wiped it away.

"It's okay, Libba." Trish handed me a tissue. "You've been through so much lately. Divorce is hard. It's okay to cry."

"I won't cry because of Alec," I said with a harshness that could cut through glass. "He doesn't deserve my tears."

"But Cailin ..." Trish looked directly at me and tilted her head, as if daring me to look away.

Another tear ran down my cheek. Cailin was a different story.

"I ache for him Trish," I admitted, my hand automatically reaching for my heart. "Not hearing from Cailin is more agonizing than I could ever imagine. It's like he woke up a part of me that was dormant for years. When I talked to him, I felt so alive, and happy, and I realized that's what's been missing from my life.

"Alec was my security blanket. I honestly don't know if I married him for love or because it was what I thought was supposed to be the next stage in my life. But when I think of Cailin, my heart patters, my stomach flutters, and—oh what am I going to do, Trish? I shouldn't feel this way so soon."

Trish leaned back in the chair and crossed her arms. "Says

who? Who ever said we must wait a certain amount of time between break ups before starting another relationship? Think of
your breakup with Alec as an opportunity, Libba. How does that
saying go? We are all faced with a series of great opportunities,
brilliantly disguised—"

"... As impossible situations," I whispered. "Since when did
you start quoting Charles Swindoll?"

Trish grinned as if up to no good. "I went on the internet
trying to find some wonderful words of wisdom to enlighten you."

"Trish, you're a good friend," I said, shaking my head.

"I know." She held out her hands admiring her manicure, then
with a sense of surety, she spoke again. "Libba, here's my advice.
If you like Cailin, then go for it. Honestly, I never cared much for
Alec, especially after that time he forgot your anniversary and
tried to make it up to you by taking you to that awful restaurant
that gave you food poisoning.

"Remember the day Mallory and I went to your house? Your
eyes lit up when you told us about Cailin and I've never seen you
shine as brightly as you did then ... and this, just one day after
your husband—ex-husband—left you. You need to talk to him,
Libba.

"Plus, call me selfish, but if Alec leaving means we can hang
out more, then good. And if it means you can start dating, good
for that, too. One of us has to. But you have to give me all the juicy
details. I need to live vicariously through someone because my
love life is a bore."

At that we both laughed. I was starting to feel a little better,
when ...

Beep, beep, beep.

I grabbed my cell from my purse and stared at the message.
My hand began to shake.

"What is it?" Trish leaned forward trying to get a better look
at my phone.

"It's a text from Cailin." I blushed. "He says he misses the sound of my voice and wants to know if it's okay to call."

"Ahh!" Trish was bouncing in her chair and screaming with delight! "Yes! Yes! Tell him yes!"

I typed a message and showed it to Trish.

Yes. I've missed yours too. ~L

Send.

Immediately the phone rang, and Trish disappeared, closing the door behind her.

Cailin's parents loved to ski. Whenever possible, they would take off and hit the slopes. They loved the thrill of sliding downhill and the cold brisk air beating against their faces. Growing up, Cailin, Mike, and his parents would travel different parts of the northern territory experiencing the many slopes and collecting shot glasses along the way. His parents had a shot glass, or two, from every mountain they ever skied. One night, when Cailin and Mike were away at college, his parents left on a three-day weekend to go skiing at Snowshoe Mountain. It happened in the middle of the evening on their way home. They were less than an hour away.

Hit and run.

A car crossed the median on 321 and swiped the side of Cailin's parents' car. Tire marks showed they swerved and went over the cliff. They never caught the other driver. That was four years ago. His parents died instantly.

Jared, one of Cailin's old school mates who worked the EMS squad for Blowing Rock Hospital, was the first paramedic on scene. He was also the one to break the news to Cailin and meet him at the hospital on that tragic occasion. Cailin called Mike, who was away with Ellen at the time. He remembered how his hands shook and the dryness in his throat when he dialed Mike's number. It was the hardest call he ever had to make.

Calling Libba seemed to be just as nerve racking for Cailin.

He had sent her a text first to make sure he could call. He desperately wanted to talk to her, but if she didn't want him to call, he wouldn't overstep his boundaries, no matter how much pain that caused him.

Beep, beep, beep.

Cailin looked at his phone. It was Libba. Mike rushed to read the text over his shoulders. He punched Cailin on the arm and howled. Cailin was already on his feet walking away from Mike, dialing Libba's number.

"Hello."

"Hi, Libba."

"Hi, Cailin." She waited a second, "I wondered if you would call."

"Right, I'm sorry about that. I wanted to call but I also wanted to give us both time to think about things."

"And … what kinds of things did you think about?"

"Well, I thought about several things but being the gentleman that I am, I can't speak them to a lady, so let's just say, I thought about letting you date me." Cailin couldn't see Libba, but he was sure if he could, she would be blushing, and her cheeks would be as pink as wild sweet peas just like the day he had changed her tire.

"Oh," was all Libba could manage.

He realized he shouldn't have said that. For all he knew she was still married, and he shouldn't flirt with a married woman.

"Seriously, how have you been? It's been a while since we've talked. How are things with you?"

"Things are good. I've been working a lot, staying busy. What about you?"

"Same here. Working on restoring a house, Muirfield Manor,

just off Main Street." He opened the back door and let Noah in the house.

"Muirfield Manor? Are you serious? I love that house; I've admired it for years! Who are you working for? I heard someone bought it not too long ago."

"Actually, *I* bought it." He smiled as he heard Libba gasp. "I can give you a tour one day, if you like. I mean, if you want to, if it's okay—," Cailin was starting to trip over his own words.

"Um, Cailin, there's something I should tell you," Libba paused. Cailin heard her swallow over the phone. Libba was nervous. He knew this was where she would tell him she had patched things with her husband. He braced himself. "Um, I retained a lawyer."

Cailin was surprised. "You did?"

"Yes, not that I had to, but to be safe. Everything was already taken care of. All I had to do was sign the papers."

"And … did you?"

"Yes, Cailin. I'm divorced, now."

Cailin was speechless. This is what he had been waiting to hear, and now, finally, he didn't know what to say. For the past couple of weeks, he had brooded over Libba, wondering if she went through with the divorce or if he would find out that they were back together. He had even driven by her house several times hoping to get a glimpse of her, or heaven forbid, the ex-husband, but he never saw either of them. Either she was going out a lot or she hid inside her house like a hermit. He hoped she was hiding.

But now Libba was divorced. He didn't want her to be divorced; he would never wish that on anyone. He watched some of his friends go through divorces and they always ended badly. He wondered if Libba's was a messy divorce or if things were a clean break since she had told him they didn't have any children. He wasn't sorry, just like he had told her when they had lunch that day. Her divorce had opened the door for him, and he wanted her.

He had waited too long for someone like Libba Spencer to come into his life. He had his chance, and he was taking it. Libba was finally divorced. He thought of his precious fairy and he wanted to—no, his mind couldn't go there, not yet anyway.

"Cailin?"

"I'm here," or at least he was trying to get his mind back on their conversation. "Sorry, that just seems so quick to already be divorced. I figured it would take a lot of time."

"Yes, normally. In North Carolina, the law requires a year of separation before one can get divorced, but apparently my ex-husband found a way around that by going through some Guam court, so yeah … it's official. I am divorced."

"Great! Sorry. I mean, I understand." Cailin smacked his forehead. *Get a grip, man.*

"So, I guess a tour would be okay then?" Cailin was elated. The dread he felt from not knowing was suddenly all washed away.

"Yes, I'd like that."

"And … what about dinner, tonight, maybe?" Cailin winced, wondering if he'd asked too soon.

"Well, you know, I have been craving crab cakes."

They made plans and Cailin walked back into the bare room, hanging up the phone and grinning ear to ear. Noah and Mike were kicking the soccer ball and practicing for Noah's game.

"Well?" Mike looked at Cailin and passed the ball to Noah.

"She did it. Everything is finalized. Apparently, her ex took care of the whole thing. All she had to do was sign the papers. She's single now."

"And you're okay with that?"

"Yeah," Noah kicked the ball to Cailin. He caught it with his left foot, dribbled it, and then passed it to Mike.

"And *she's* okay with that?" Mike's foot slipped but he recovered the ball and began dribbling it.

"Yeah, we're going out tonight. Our first date."

"Now aren't you glad you called. I hate to say 'I told you so' but—"

"Then don't." Cailin stole the ball from Mike and kicked it to Noah.

"Uncle Cow, has a date, Uncle Cow, has a date!" Noah was dribbling the ball and showing off his new moves.

Cailin looked at his brother. "Thanks, Mike. For everything."

CHAPTER 5

MURRAY'S PUB

I stood in front of my mirror hating the way I looked. This was the seventh outfit I tried on and I still looked a mess. What does a girl wear on a date these days? Dating? I didn't know how to date. I haven't dated in a million years. What was I thinking? I could never pull this off. Dating meant flirting and I didn't know how to flirt, much less how to react when someone flirted with me. Maybe I should call it off.

Hell no! Cailin was too attractive and I might never get another chance with him. No, I needed to pull my act together and figure out how to do this, this, dating thing. *I'm a grown woman,* I told myself. *I can handle dating.* Could I handle Cailin Wade? That was the *real* question.

I decided to wear my uptown weekend outfit. It was a pair of faded wide-leg jeans and I paired it with a white cotton long-sleeved shirt and a rust-colored cotton trench. Of course, that was the first outfit I had tried on, seven outfits ago! It did the job, not too casual, but not too dressy either. It worked whether we went to a movie after dinner or for a walk.

I had no idea what Cailin planned to do after dinner. I didn't ask for fear of looking stupid. I could have asked Trish for some ideas, but she was so excited for me that I didn't want to look stupid in front of her. She called me three times on my way home, suggesting what I should wear, giving me pointers on topics of conversation, and asking me if I planned on having sex. My goodness, that girl had an imagination. I was newly divorced and going on a first date—sex was *not* in my immediate near future. Trish slipped a condom in my purse before we left the office, "just in case," she said. Even though I was on the pill, getting pregnant was not the only thing I needed to worry about these days, she stressed. I knew I wouldn't have to worry about that either, at least not tonight.

We met at The Ridgeline Restaurant at seven o'clock. When I arrived, Cailin's truck was in the parking lot. I checked my face in the mirror, touched up my lipstick, and crossed myself for good luck. Here goes everything.

I walked into the restaurant where Cailin was already waiting for me. He looked so perfect sitting there with one leg crossed and one arm resting across the back of the bench. He wore washed blue jeans and a pair of black leather Tecova boots. His shirt was a long-sleeved gray button up and he wore it with a classic gray herringbone tweed vest. As I walked toward him, his cobalt blue eyes flashed and slowly his gaze followed me up and down. I felt like he was undressing me with his eyes. He smiled his wicked smile and immediately my insides fluttered. I was lost in his trance. The sound of his voice gradually brought me back to reality.

"Hi." In three strides, Cailin crossed the lobby and was standing in front of me. Goodness, he was tall! Then again, I was short, only five-two on a good day, and surely, he was over six feet tall. Even though I wore my tallest heels, I barely reached his neck. I could smell his cologne. It tickled my senses but excited them at the same time. He touched my elbow and a flicker surged though me. "It's good to see you again."

"It's good to see you, too." I craned my head to see him. "I hope you haven't been waiting long."

"Only a few weeks, that's all," he said and smiled. His dimples were irresistible. I tucked my hair behind my ear and looked down. "Do I make you nervous, when I say things like that?"

"No, you don't make me nervous," I lied, looking up through my lashes. "Okay, perhaps a little ... but it's a good nervous."

"Hmm. I'll have to remember that."

The hostess appeared and showed us to our table. I had not been to the restaurant in a long time and I noticed the menu had changed. Cailin made a few suggestions.

"The fried ravioli is good."

"No, I don't think I want that tonight."

"Shrimp?"

"No. I think I'll try the blue crab fritters. I think you've got me hooked on crabs!" *That wasn't the only thing I was hooked on.*

I ordered the crab fritters and Cailin ordered the lobster roll, which was highlighted as a new item on the menu. We both ordered the tomato and cucumber salad served with balsamic vinegar dressing.

"Did I tell you, I'm glad you called?" I asked.

"In so many words you did. I'm glad I called, too." He looked serious. "I thought about you a lot, Libba. I wasn't sure if you had gone through with it ... the divorce ... or if maybe you would wait to see if he would come back."

"I wasn't sure either. It was a hard few days, but Trish and Mallory, my girlfriends, were there for me. Trish never liked Alec and she was *very* supportive of me getting a divorce. And Mallory, well, Mallory just has a good head on her shoulders. She found me my lawyer. An exceptionally good one, I might add."

"I wish I could have been there for you, too." He looked down at his plate and swirled a cucumber in the dressing.

"Yes, that would have been nice—but then, it brought me

closer to Trish and Mallory. I've never had any real girlfriends and
I honestly think I can say they're my best friends now. I needed
that time to get my life in order. Not that it's really 'in order' now,
but I know where I've been, and I know where I want to go, and
I have people in my life." He looked up at me now. "People that I
want to be with, that are important to me. You know?"

"And do I fit into that category?" His eyes held my gaze and
it wasn't until the waitress appeared that I was able to pull myself
away from him.

"Thank you," he said as he turned to look up at the waitress
who filled both of our glasses with tea then walked away.

"Do you like your salad?" I asked.

"Yes, I do, and you still haven't answered my question." He
stole a cucumber off my plate. "Do I fit into the category of people
in your life that you want to be with?"

"Yes," I whispered.

He smiled his wicked smile, again my stomach fluttered. The
waitress brought us our meal and I dove into the crab fritters hoping the food could settle the nerves in my stomach.

Dinner with Cailin was better than I could have imagined. We
talked about his house and Muirfield Manor, and I found out that
he was thinking about turning it into a bed and breakfast when
he was finished with the restoration. He was going to let me tour
it the next day, a plan that ensured I would get to see him after
tonight, so I was completely fine with it.

The night was still early and Cailin asked if I was game for
going someplace just outside of town, a surprise, he said, but I still
wanted to know. He said not to worry, the place was very friendly
and relaxing, and he knew I would like it. It wasn't hard for me to
agree. We decided to take his truck since I didn't know where we
were going. I liked his truck and I very much wanted to ride with
him, plus I figured if he thought my car would be safe enough in

the restaurant's parking lot, then why not? He guided me to his truck, lightly touching my elbow along the way as if protecting me. He opened the door and helped me up, then quickly appeared at the driver's door.

We listened to Hits One on Sirius Radio and my fingers tapped my leg as I enjoyed the music. After the first song, Cailin reached his hand towards mine, but swiftly withdrew when I turned to look at him. His movement caught my eye. I stopped tapping. Should I reach over to touch his hand first or was that too forward? I very much wanted him to touch me, but for the life of me I didn't know what to do. I was so out of practice. I sat still but made sure to keep my hand readily available, just in case. The tension in the atmosphere was nerve-racking. What was he waiting for? *Grab my hand*, I thought, trying to mentally will his hand over mine. *Touch me.*

When the next song was over, Cailin turned to look at me. My hand twitched. I think he noticed. "May I?" He looked down at my hand. *What a gentleman.* Slowly, very slowly, Cailin reached over and placed his hand on mine.

"That's nice," I said.

"Yeah right, my hands are like sandpaper."

"No, I didn't mean your hands—they're nice too," I said whispering on that last part. "What I meant is, holding hands. This is nice."

"Nice, but is it manly?" We both chuckled remembering the first time I sat in his truck.

I thought of all the times I wished Alec had held my hand. But that wasn't his nature. No public display of affection. Like I was a plague or something. He might tolerate a minute holding my hand on the way inside a store, but two minutes was his limit. He would never take my hand first either, not if we were walking around an amusement park, not in the movies, not even if we were walking in a dark parking lot together just to make me feel safe. We never held hands unless I took the initiative, and after so long of being told he'd held my hand long enough, even if it were for just a few seconds, I just stopped trying. When I'd find my hand itching to touch his, I would simply twine my hands together or find something else to fiddle with. Alec never seemed to notice or either, he never seemed to care. But Cailin was nothing like Alec. I knew down to my very core that he was different, and better, than any other man I knew. And I also knew that I wanted to be with him, more than I'd ever wanted to be with anyone before.

"So where are we going anyway?" I asked.

"It's a surprise, remember." Cailin kept his focus on the road.

"I know ... but you could still tell me."

"Libba," he said, turning and raising an eyebrow at me, "if I told you, it wouldn't *be* a surprise."

"I know, I know. I was hoping to trick you. I do love surprises though, so no worries. I won't ask again."

"Good." Still holding my hand, he rubbed my cheek with his thumb, then rested our hands on his thigh, squeezing gently. My insides churned, in a good way, and I had to look out the window to steady my breathing.

He took me to a little bar on the outskirts of town called Murray's Pub. It looked small from the outside and the parking lot was dark, but I felt safe walking, and holding hands, with Cailin. We entered the building, and the place was larger than it appeared. It had an eclectic air about it. There was a long bar along the left wall and to the right were a few private lounge areas separated by gold sheer curtains with bronze tassels. Each lounge had red velvet sofas, plush pillows, and lamps with soft lighting. Looking straight to the back of the room, there was a small stage raised by two steps with several round tables and chairs lined in front of it. A hallway was to the left of the stage and appeared to lead to other rooms.

The place was filled with a mix of people. One couple sat in the middle lounge area, snuggling closely as if in the privacy of their own home. There was a table full of women who looked like they were having a 'girl's night out'. Across from them sat two younger men, who were watching the women and flirting as much as possible. Cailin took my hand and led me to one of the tables near the front of the stage.

Within seconds, a waitress was bringing Cailin a beer.

"Saw you come in and figured you'd like your usual," the waitress said.

"Thanks, Ginny," Cailin said, then looked at me and asked what I wanted to drink.

"I don't like beer," I whispered to him.

"They have sodas … or hard liquor, if you prefer." He smiled devilishly flashing his dimples.

"Then, I'll have a blue margarita. Please. With sugar. Not salt."

"No problem." The waitress, Ginny, weaved through the tables and disappeared.

"What do you think?" Cailin was watching my every move and I couldn't help but feel giddy.

"This place is so cool!" I guffawed like a kid in a candy store.

Ginny reappeared and handed me my drink. Then she looked at Cailin and spoke, "Are we on for tonight?" *The nerve of her and right in front of me. Did she not see that we were on a date!*

Cailin looked at her, then at me, and back at her. He raised his head and she leaned down to him, placing her ear right in front of his lips. She gently touched his shoulder while he whispered in her ear. She whispered something back and then swiftly, she walked away.

I couldn't believe it. How dare she—I hope he told her! Ugh! I tried not to show my jealousy, but my heart was pounding so fast I didn't know what to do. I grabbed my drink, huffed, and tried to pull myself together.

"Everything all right?" *I hoped that sounded casual.*

"Why? Jealous?" There was that smile again. My stomach fluttered. This time, I rubbed it lightly with the hopes that it would behave from now on.

I opened my mouth but could only manage to sip my margarita.

"You *are* jealous, aren't you!" Cailin roared with laughter then grabbed my chair right in between my legs and scooted it towards him. We were sitting face to face and he was so close to me that I could feel his breath on my lips. He lifted his hand and gently moved a strand of hair behind my ear.

I shivered.

He looked me directly in my eyes. "Libba, precious, you have nothing to worry about. Tonight, I'm under your spell." He rubbed my cheek softly. "I'll be right back," he said, and then he disappeared.

More people were beginning to show up and by the time I regained my senses and looked around, I couldn't find Cailin. Moreover, I noticed I didn't see where Ginny had taken off to either.

I sat alone nursing my margarita when a man stepped on the stage and introduced the first karaoke singer for the evening, something about a local favorite who apparently hadn't been there in a while. I searched through the crowd but still couldn't find Cailin. The lights dimmed and the music started. I recognized the tune as one of Tim McGraw's hits.

"Dancin' in the dark."

Nice voice, I thought.

"Middle of the night."

Very nice.

"Takin' your heart."

Sounds familiar.

"And holding it tight."

Oh ... my ... gosh.

I slowly turned to look at the stage and it was Cailin, singing with such a beautiful, flawless voice that it melted my soul. He sat alone on a bar stool in the middle of the stage with the spotlight shining brightly upon him. One foot rested on the floor and the other on a rung on the stool. He held the microphone with one hand and the other rested comfortably on his leg. He was wrong. Tonight, I was under *his* spell.

Ginny came on stage and assisted with the chorus. I felt so lame. Now, I understood why she asked if they were 'on for tonight.' She meant singing. She had a lovely voice, too though not as good as Cailin's, but I was partial to him. Ginny worked the crowd and when she passed in front of me, her lips curved in a half smile as she looked at me, then Cailin, then back at me.

Cailin sat, stared, and sang only for me. For those few moments, there was only the two of us in the room.

> *And who I am now is who I wanted to be,*
> *And now that we're together,*
> *I'm stronger than ever*
> *I'm happy and free.*
> *Oh, it's a beautiful thing,*
> *Don't think I can keep it all in.*
> *If you asked me why I've changed,*
> *All I gotta do is say your sweet name.*

"Libba." He spoke my name with such anguish that it strained my heart.

He set the microphone down and walked toward me. I stood up and stared into his eyes. He placed his hands on my hips, squeezed, and pulled me to his waist. His hold was urgent, almost desperate, and I could all but see the need in his eyes. I steadied my palms under his elbows and braced myself for what was about to happen. He leaned down and softly, so softly, touched his lips to mine.

I knew Ginny was still singing but at the moment all I could hear was the sound of the adrenaline racing through my blood. His kiss became rough, more eager, and his hands braided through my hair. Suddenly, he stopped kissing me and rested his forehead to mine. He let out a low moan. His eyes were still closed.

"Ah, Libba. You have no idea what you do to me?"

"Cailin—"

"Shh, shh. Come with me." He grabbed our drinks and led me to one of the lounges. We sat on the couch. He put his arm around my shoulder and pulled me close to him.

"I never imagined our first kiss would be in front of a bar full of people," he said as he softly ran his fingers down my hair.

"And how did you imagine our first kiss would be?" I licked the sugar from the rim of my glass.

"I don't know, maybe standing on your doorstep, asking if I could come inside." He stroked my hair. I could sit like this forever.

"Umm. I think this was a little more romantic," I said, snuggling into him a little closer. "I had no idea you had such a great voice. Thank you. I like my surprise."

"I hope you didn't worry too much when I took off like that. Ginny told me I would be first up—"

"Ah, Ginny ..."

"She's just a friend, Libba. I've known Ginny since grade school."

"It's all right, Cailin. I'm not the jealous type anyway."

"Yeah, right!"

Just then Ginny walked by and stuck her head between the sheers. "You two lovebirds doing all right in here?" she joked. I blushed, and Cailin laughed and pulled me closer.

Ginny walked in the little lounge, dimmed the light, and lit a candle for us. "Can I get you some more drinks?"

"Sure, thanks." Cailin finished his beer. "Ginny, Libba.

Libba, Ginny." He said pointing his empty bottle to each of us, then handing the bottle to Ginny.

"Nice to meet you, Libba. Hope you're enjoying yourself."

"I am, thanks. Um, Ginny?" This was the first time I spoke to her and if she was one of Cailin's friends, I wanted to make a good impression. "You have a lovely voice. Great job out there. I could never sing in public."

"Never say never. Cailin will have you on stage before you know it." He shushed her away and she was off, like a butterfly fluttering between the tables.

We sat in the lounge talking for hours. I wanted to find out everything I could about Cailin, and he asked me a million questions too. He told me how his parents had died and how that brought him closer to his brother, Mike. He also told me about the Stanleys and how he and Mike took turns visiting them the first Friday of every month. I talked to Cailin about Trish and Mallory. I told him how Trish was single, wild, and such a free spirit, and how Mallory was a single mom and had a beautiful little girl named Olivia. She was doing a great job working and raising a daughter all on her own. Trish, Mallory, and I were all different in our own way, but in just a short amount of time, we somehow knew each other so well we could almost read each other's minds. Ginny took her break with us and shared some of hers and Cailin's childhood stories. They argued and cut up. Each was very adamant about telling their versions of stories. They acted just like close siblings. Ginny and I were fast friends and Cailin seemed pleased with that.

"Remember that time when we almost burned down Martha's house?" said Cailin.

Ginny laughed and turned to me. "We were hiding in her spare bedroom and holding those long matches that you use to light fireplaces with. Well, we were trying to see who could hold the match the longest without burning their fingers. My match fell and started burning the carpet. Cailin quickly blew out his match and started blowing on mine, which was still lying on the carpet. It just made the fire worse! He pulled off his shirt and started beating the flames with it. Mike came in drinking a glass of water and saw the fire. He calmly walked over to the spot and dumped his water on it. It was out like that." Ginny snapped her fingers to show how fast the fire had stopped.

"Oh my gosh," I said. "How terrible! That must have been scary."

Cailin was laughing now. "No, the fire wasn't but the size of a half dollar. I just panicked and overreacted—"

"He has a tendency of doing that," Ginny stated.

"Do not—"

"Do, too! You'll see, Libba. Cailin is overprotective sometimes but he means well." She patted my knee and stood up. "I have to get back to work now. It's been great meeting you, Libba." She turned to look at Cailin, "You hold onto this one. I like her." She winked and was gone, floating through the crowds again. She returned about an hour later.

"Last call," Ginny said, poking her head in between the sheers.

"None for me, I'm driving. Libba?"

"No thanks. I think I've had my limit, more than my limit probably." I half stood up stumbling along the way. Ginny started to laugh.

"I think you need to get her to bed." Ginny was on my side helping me up. Cailin was on my other side.

"To bed? This is our first date!" My words slurred ever so slightly as I tried not to giggle.

"Precious, she didn't say 'take' you to bed—though I'm sure I could handle that quite well—but she did say 'get' you to bed and I think she's right. You need to sleep off some of that tequila."

"Cailin, you'll drive her home, won't you?" Cailin had told

me how very adamant Ginny was with all her customers about driving under the influence and had frequently called cabs and even driven some friends home herself. "Libba, give Cailin your address so he can get you home, hon."

I muttered something incomprehensible. Cailin just nodded his head. I *so* did not want to get drunk on our first date. I should at least try to act sober. I tried waving them away and standing on my own, but I swayed. Cailin put his arm around my waist and I decided not to argue with him about that. If being tipsy meant Cailin would hold me, oh well. Cailin kept his arm around my waist the whole way to the car. As soon as we were inside, buckled up, and on our way, he grabbed my hand and kissed it gently.

I turned to look at him sleepily. "I had a very good time tonight." I put my other hand over his and circled his knuckles softly. "I was wondering—"

"What were you wondering?"

"Well, I was wondering if our second kiss could be like you imagined our first would be."

"I suppose." He smiled and raised an eyebrow at me. "Should I ask to come in?"

"Did I say 'yes' … when you imagined?" My eyelids were getting heavier now.

"Of course, you did."

"Umm … of course I did." He rubbed my hair softly and my eyelids closed.

Cailin gazed at Libba in contentment. Her eyes were closed but he knew she was not asleep. She was resting her eyes and probably trying to sober herself. He didn't mind; she could take all the time she needed. She was so lovely, and the alcohol made her face slightly darker than usual. Her cheeks were red, and when he touched them, they were warm. He rubbed her cheek gently and ran his fingers through her hair. She moaned very low and then shifted in her seat.

He could look at his precious fairy all night, and he planned to do just that. After all, he couldn't leave her if she were not feeling well. Besides, it was his fault; he kept passing her margaritas all night even though he barely sipped on his beer. That settled it, he would have to stay the night and take care of her.

He parked in front of her house. She had left the porch light on and a light was on in the house too.

"Libba, precious," he whispered and stroked her hair. "Libba, we're at your house. Wake up."

"Mmm." She turned and leaned into the seat, opening her eyes slowly and matching his stare. "Already?"

"Yes, come now." Cailin helped her out of the car and walked her to the door. Libba opened her purse and reached for her keys. She jiggled things around but couldn't seem to find them.

"I know they're here somewhere."

Cailin waited patiently as Libba searched her small bag to no avail. She was forced to pull items out of her purse one by one. Cailin couldn't believe how many things one small purse could hold. Libba pulled out a little jeweled pouch he assumed was her wallet, a compact, lipstick, a condom, her iPhone—a condom? Cailin was sure he was mistaken. A condom? Libba? Was she really planning—did she really want to—did she expect he would try—on their first date? Cailin angled himself to get a better look. Indeed, it was what he thought. It wouldn't be Cailin's first time having sex on a first date, but Libba? She didn't seem the type. He never imagined she would—on their first date?

Libba shoved the contents back into her purse, her keys in hand. She unlocked the door and waited. Cailin knew he couldn't walk through that door. If he did, he knew what would happen. He very much wanted to be with Libba in that way, but now, when the opportunity was ripe, he knew he couldn't. Libba was drunk. Well, maybe not drunk but not completely sober. He wanted their first time to be special and if they—tonight—he would feel as though he were taking advantage of her. Cailin certainly did not want to take advantage of his delicate fairy.

"I better go," he said.

"But I thought you were going to come in."

"I know, but now is probably not a good time. You need sleep and if I go inside … well, I doubt you would get much rest."

"That's okay. I'm not tired." Libba tried to hide a yawn.

Cailin put his finger under Libba's chin and lifted her head. "But you need *sleep*, Libba. And maybe a couple of aspirin, too."

Cailin gave a half smile. It was a sad smile. He hated to leave her. He leaned down and kissed her deeply. His fingers pulled the back of her hair slightly, and she parted her lips and pulled him closer. He caressed her back and could feel the passion rip between their bodies. The same wild yet intimate electric surge he felt weeks ago ran through him, awakening his soul once more. Cailin could feel his body reacting with every second that passed. He stepped back to let the cool night air calm him.

"Goodnight, Precious. Sleep in. I'll bring over breakfast in the morning," and with those last few words, he turned and walked back to his truck. As he backed out of the drive, he checked his rear-view mirror. Libba had gone inside. The porch light turned off.

CHAPTER 6

TROUBLE

A lec was an average-sized man standing five feet, ten inches and weighing 170 pounds. Though he rarely frequented the gym, he considered himself healthy because he didn't smoke or use drugs, and he ate well-balanced meals consisting of less meat and more plant-based foods.

But Alec was not as healthy as he appeared, at least not from the outside. Alec had a secret.

Alec had a history of drinking too much and when he drank, he was reckless. While he and Libba dated, she knew he would drink yet still get behind the wheel of a car and somehow make it home. Those were the times she would lie awake in bed and pray that he made it home safely. She tried to make him stop drinking, even pleaded with him, and threatened not to marry him until he controlled his drinking problem. And so, he did. Or so she thought.

After they were married, Libba witnessed firsthand the effects that alcohol had on Alec and saw how different he was under the influence. One day, Alec decided to have a beer while watching a game on TV. He started with a six-pack but went to the Jiffy Mart to pick up more. By the time Libba came home from a day of shopping, Alec had already completed the second pack of beer.

Libba complained about his drinking but he kept on, and the more he drank, the more his temper flared, and he became wild and obnoxious. He lost his temper and accidently hit her—more than a few times. He apologized and Libba forgave him, but after that, she strictly forbade alcohol in the house except for cooking wine.

Alec remembered how he had given her a black eye and bruised her arms. No one suspected any malicious behavior and Alec promised Libba he would never lay another hand on her. Of course, she believed him. She told everyone she had fallen while they were cleaning out the attic. Alec had come close to losing his temper on more than a few occasions, but he was able to control his temper and able to hide his drinking from Libba. Alcohol had not controlled him in a long time. He had not given in to that feeling of power he thought alcohol gave him; that part of him had been buried for years … until tonight.

He ordered another beer and thought about Jennifer. She was the reason he had left Libba. Alec met her on a business trip more than two years ago. He found out they lived only a few hours from each other and one week when Libba was out of town, he drove to visit her. Jennifer was different than Libba. She praised him for what he did; she knew how to take care of a man, and she knew how to pleasure a man. But after two years of being with her, Jennifer gave him the ultimatum of her or Libba. Of course, he would choose Jennifer because she didn't want any pesky children, unlike Libba. However, once he left Libba, things changed. Jennifer changed.

Alec could not understand how he ended up in this situation. He left Libba to be with Jennifer only to have Jennifer break up with him and kick him out of her apartment. He had walked to The Tavern, had a few beers, then stolen one of the employee's cars. Now he was back in Blowing Rock sitting at Ben's Brewery with such distress on his mind because he had no place else to go. At this moment, he hated Jennifer, he hated Libba, and he hated women. Period.

He turned and looked at the trio sitting across the bar. The man on the right kept buying the red head drinks but she was flirting with the man on her left. Women were always stringing men along. Well, it was about time they learned their lesson. He slammed a twenty-dollar bill on the counter and left.

When he arrived at the house, the porch light was on. *She must be planning to stay out late if she left the light on,* he thought.

He could wait.

Alec drove around to the back of the house and parked. He tried to put his key in the door, but it didn't fit, so he busted the window, reached in, and opened the door. He walked in the kitchen and was surprised to find a six-pack in the fridge and tequila in the cupboard.

"Well, well, what do we have here?" he whispered. "I see you've changed the rules about alcohol in the house Libba."

You know how it feels when you get off a roller coaster. For those first few moments directly after, you can still feel the rush of the wind in your hair and the thrill of the ride in the pit of your stomach. That's how it felt kissing Cailin. His kiss was rough yet gentle, passionate yet primal. When he let go of me, my chest heaved ever so slightly, and I had to touch my heart to make sure it was still beating. I didn't want him to leave but he was probably right; if he stayed, neither of us would get much rest, and I wasn't sure I was ready for that type of relationship yet. I had such a wonderful night; it was the best night I could remember in a long, long time. I closed my eyes and I could still hear Cailin singing to me with his flawless voice.

But Cailin was right I needed aspirin and sleep, in that order. I watched him drive away then walked into the house and shut off the porch light. That's when I realized something was wrong. A light was on in the hall and I was sure I had turned off all the lights before leaving. Someone was here. I was sure of it. I was reaching in my purse for my cell when he spoke name.

"Hello, Libba. Where have you been?"

It was Alec.

Slowly, I walked into the living room entry. Alec sat in one of the chairs appearing drunk and disheveled. By the looks of things, he had been drinking a lot. There were several empty beer bottles on the coffee table, and he held another in his hand. I suddenly had a flashback of the last time he was drunk, and a shudder ran through my body.

"What are doing here, Alec?" I tried to compose myself, but I was still feeling the effects of the tequila and my stomach was starting to churn.

"I asked you first. Where have you been, or should I go out and ask your trucker boyfriend? Oh wait, he's gone already, isn't he? What a shame, it's just you and me." Alec stood up, bumping into the coffee table. He cursed, then downed the rest of his beer and slammed it on the table, cracking the glass top.

"Where I have been is none of your business, Alec. I think you need to leave. I'm tired and I have nothing to say to you."

"NONE OF MY BUSINESS! We were married for six years. You go out with another man and it's NONE OF MY BUSINESS!"

I felt the same burning pain race through my veins that I felt the day he called me and told me he was leaving. It burned my face and held at my throat. Now, I recognized this feeling as rage. "You walked out on me Alec, remember? That was *your* choice. Six years must not have meant anything to you because *you* walked out on ME. YOU left me without so much as an explanation. So,

NO! Whoever I go out with is NONE of your business." I was so angry with him that I all but snarled my words.

He walked towards me with a fury in his eyes that I have never seen before. "How dare you talk to me like that, BITCH!"

The back of his hand hit my cheek hard and fast, and I could already taste the blood in my mouth. I knew not to try to fight him, so I turned and walked towards the door. He was quickly behind me, grabbing my arm, squeezing, and yanking me back. With his other hand, he punched the center of my back and then swung me around. My purse flung across the room. I lost my balance and hit the back of a chair.

"Alec, please, don't do this. I promise, I won't tell anyone you were here, just please—"

"You won't tell anyone? What about your trucker boyfriend? You mean you won't tell *him* I was here. I don't care about *him*! TELL him I was here." He grabbed my hair and pulled. I tried to hold onto the chair, but the pain was so great, in my back and in my head, that I had to let go. He slapped me again then pushed me to the floor, this time I slid and bumped into the coffee table.

"How many times have you been out, Libba? I've only been gone a few weeks and you're already hookin' up with truckers. You little SLUT! You're just like every other woman. You tease men and use us to try to get what you want. You disgust me!" He kicked me in the stomach, and I rolled over clutching my belly. Whatever he was yelling I could not understand; the pain was so great. I had to vomit. I heaved and Alec's hand was at my face again. I could taste the bile as I swallowed it back down but not before spilling some onto the floor. As I watched him walk towards the kitchen, the sound of his voice started to fade, and everything turned black.

I must not have been out long because when I came to, Alec was still in the kitchen. I could hear him rummaging through the cabinets and, by the sound of things, he was looking for alcohol.

The pain I felt was excruciating and the taste in my mouth was a mixture of iron and vomit. I needed to get out of the house, quickly, but I didn't have my car. I had left it at the restaurant and Cailin had driven me home.

Cailin. I had to call him.

I spotted my purse in the corner of the room and crawled backwards towards it, keeping an eye on the kitchen door. As quietly as I could manage, I grabbed my phone and dialed Cailin's number.

"Hello."

"Help me."

"Libba? Is everything okay?"

"Cailin! Help! He's here! He's back and he's drunk, and—"

I could see Alec's shadow drawing near. I hid my phone under my purse but didn't hang up. I knew Cailin would still be able to hear but I also knew it would make him get here that much quicker.

"So, I see you're awake, that's good. I wouldn't want you to miss all the fun. I was just getting started."

"Alec, please don't hit me again." I was terrified. He raised a hand holding a wine bottle in the air. He drank straight from the bottle. "Please Alec, please put down the bottle."

"DON'T TELL ME WHAT TO DO!"

He hit my head with the edge of the wine bottle and my head fell to the ground. I heard a loud thud and could feel a hot liquid running down the side of my face. I touched it and looked at my hand and this time the last color I saw before I passed out was red.

Cailin hated leaving Libba, especially when he knew she had too much to drink and it was probably his fault. He desperately wanted to go inside her house, tuck her into bed, and watch her sleep for the rest of the evening. He knew that would not be the way things would have transpired though.

He could still feel her hot sweet breath on his tongue after she parted her lips ever so slightly, inviting him to enter her. He still tasted her, and it teased his appetite even more. No, if he would have stayed, neither one of them would have slept.

Cailin took his time driving home, deciding to ride by the restaurant to make sure Libba's car was okay and then cutting through the mountain to go home. It was there, safe and sound, just like he knew it would be. Cailin shook his head and thought about what Mike said to him. Could he really be in love with Libba this soon? He knew he never felt this way about another woman in his life. He thought about Libba every second of every minute. The two weeks away from her had left him emptier than he ever imagined. But love? He knew he cared deeply for her and he wanted her. Oh, how he wanted her, every bump and curve of hers. But he wanted Libba to be completely sober when he took her to bed for their first time. He wanted them both to remember *that* adventure.

He turned around in the parking lot and started heading back when his cell rang.

"Hello."

"Help me!"

"Libba? Is everything okay?"

"Cailin! Help! He's here! He's back and he's drunk, and—"

"Libba? Libba!" Cailin could hear another voice, a man's voice. The sound was muffled, so he couldn't make out the words, but he could make out the tone and it was dangerously brutal. Libba was in trouble, and he knew her ex-husband was the cause. Cailin dialed Mike's number and conferenced him on the call.

"Come on Mike, answer."

"Cailin, why are you calling so late, what's going on?" Mike was still half asleep.

"Mike! Call 911. I've got Libba on the other line and she's in trouble."

"What?" Cailin spit out Libba's address and ordered Mike to call an ambulance and the police. "Cailin, are you sure you're not overreact—"

"Mike, she's still on the line. Listen." He stopped speaking so they could both hear what was happening.

They heard Libba's muffled voice: "Please, Alec put down the bottle." Then a man yelled, followed by a loud thud.

"She said he's there and he's drunk. I think her ex-husband is there. I can feel it. I'm on my way. Please Mike, call 911. I can't hang up my cell in case she comes back."

"Okay, okay. Be careful. I'll call 911. Call me back as soon as you can."

Cailin gunned the engine and sped towards Libba's house. He prayed time would be on his side and he would get there before it was too late. He didn't know what to expect when he arrived, but he knew he would do whatever it took to make sure Libba was safe. Cailin was not ready to lose Libba, especially when he had only just found her.

His truck hugged the curves of the road as he approached seventy miles per hour. The road was dark but Cailin knew them like the back of his hand. He had driven these roads since before he had his license and he guessed he could be at Libba's house in less than ten minutes. He was almost there when a white Ford Explorer came out from nowhere. The fool was driving recklessly and had his high beams on, virtually blinding Cailin, making him swerve and almost run off the shoulder. Cailin was able to correct the truck but not before swiping the guardrail and the other driver hitting the traffic sign.

Cailin slammed on his brakes.

At the speed he was going, the driver surely damaged his car. He was torn between helping the other driver and racing to

Libba's; but Libba was in danger and he had to get to her before it was too late. He turned and looked out his window, but the Ford was gone, leaving the traffic sign leaning in the wind.

Cailin arrived at Libba's house literally a few seconds before the EMS. Jared was one of the paramedics on duty; the other was a young-looking man, probably in his early twenties. He was short and stout with dark curly hair. Jared had not changed much throughout the years, except for a new tattoo that he sported on his left forearm. He was almost as tall as Cailin, heavyset, and wore his hair short, with a slight flip at the front. He was getting out of the ambulance as Cailin ran to the front door.

"Libba! Libba, open the door!" Cailin pounded both fists on the door and tried the handle. It was locked. He rammed his shoulder against the door.

"Cailin! What are you doing here? What's going—"

"She called me. She was afraid. She's hurt." He rammed the door a second time, then a third; it budged but did not open.

Jared told Cailin to stand aside. He leveled himself on the heels of his feet, and with his hands up like a boxer, he rocked back and forth. Suddenly he lifted his right leg and kicked as hard as he could. The door swung open.

"Libba!" Cailin raced through the house and stopped dead in his tracks. Libba was lying on the floor, her head surrounded by a pool of blood.

Jared followed Cailin inside the house. They saw the small figure lying on the floor at the same time and Cailin quickly went to her. He was about to pick her up when Jared stopped him.

"Don't touch her," he said as he surveyed the situation and put on medical gloves. His hands hovered slowly over her as he examined her motionless body.

"Is she—" Cailin couldn't get the word out of his mouth.

"No, no, she's just unconscious. Cailin … she's in bad shape." Caleb, the other paramedic appeared and moved Cailin carefully out of the way. Cailin felt so useless standing there, watching but not being able to help. If only he had come inside with her this would never have happened. He could have protected her. He could have saved her. It was all his fault.

Cailin couldn't watch as Jared and Caleb worked on Libba. He turned around and slowly scanned the room. He could follow the trail of her demise. He saw the empty Amstel beer bottles, the broken glass on the coffee table, the tipped over chair, vomit, an empty wine bottle, her purse …

Cailin walked to her purse and picked it up, underneath was her cell phone. It was still connected to his. He hung up the line and sat down on one of the chairs. Jared turned and looked at him.

"I'm sorry, Cailin. Looks like someone did a number on her." Jared's face was sincere. Cailin had to swallow to hold back the agony he was feeling. "How do you know her?"

"We met a few weeks ago. We just left Murray's. I dropped her off and a few minutes later she was calling me and—" He dropped his head to his hands and rubbed his forehead. "Jared, I should have been—will she be al—"

"She'll be okay." He placed a hand on Cailin's shoulder in comfort. "We need to get her to the hospital and call the police." He looked at Libba's purse and phone. "Don't touch anything else okay. You understand?" Jared did not look accusing and Cailin understood. Libba's house was now a crime scene.

"Is there someone you can call for her?" Jared asked.

Cailin thought for a moment. He still had her business card in his wallet from the time they had lunch together while waiting for her tire to be repaired. It had Trish's cell phone number on it.

"Yes. One of her friends that works with her."

"You should call her and tell her to meet you at the hospital. It's going to be a long night." They moved Libba to the ambulance and Cailin watched as they slowly drove away, then he jumped in his truck and followed. He would call Trish after he called Mike.

Mike said he would take Noah to the Stanleys and meet him at the hospital. Cailin was grateful. He was not sure if he could stand being at the hospital alone, or rather, alone with Trish, whom he didn't even know. He was afraid to call her, to explain to her that because of him, her friend was in the hospital, beaten to unconsciousness.

"H—hello?" Trish answered groggily.

"Is this Trish, Libba Spencer's friend? This is Cailin Wade."

"Huh? Yeah, this is Trish. Who did you say you were?" At the sound of Cailin's voice, Trish was starting to wake up.

"This is Cailin. Cailin Wade, um, I had a date with Libba tonight."

"Cailin? What are you doing calling me? What's going on?"

"Trish, don't panic but there's been an accident—"

"What! What the hell did you do to her? I swear I'll—"

"No, wait. Calm down. I took her back to her house, but her ex-husband was there, and I didn't know. She called me ... he beat her, Trish ... bad." Cailin could barely continue. "The ambulance is taking her to the hospital right now. Can you meet me there, as soon as possible? I called you because I don't know who else to call for her."

"Oh my gosh. What—How bad is she?"

"Pretty bad. Get to the hospital as soon as you can, and I'll fill you in." As he hung up the phone with Trish, a tear fell from his eye. He had to pull over. Cailin cried for the first time since losing his parents.

CHAPTER 7

THE SOUND OF SILENCE

Martha stood on the porch watching Mike gather Noah from the backseat of his Ford Escape hybrid. He had called her and said there was an emergency and she quickly volunteered to keep Noah; he was like a grandson to her. Mike was very brief on the phone, not giving out much information, but Martha knew she would have at least a couple of minutes to find out what was going on. She hoped there was nothing wrong with Cailin, but she had a feeling.

"I've got a bed ready for him. You know where to take him." Martha held the door open for Mike as he carried Noah into the house. She followed him to the spare room that was set up for guests.

"What kind of emergency has you hauling your son out in the middle of the night, Mike?"

"Cailin—but don't worry, he's okay. He's at the hospital with Libba, you know the girl whose tire he changed. They had a date. Apparently, her ex-husband came home, and they fought. Not Cailin and the ex; Libba and her ex. Cailin had left already." Mike laid Noah on the bed, tucked him in, and gave him a gentle kiss on the cheek. "She's at the hospital right now. Cailin called me, then Jared called me, too. You remember Jared?" He stood and faced Martha. "Jared said Libba was unconscious, most likely has a concussion and there were a lot of bruises, blood … But Martha, he said Cailin was pretty shaken up. He really cares for her, you know?"

"Yes, I do know. I suspected as much the first time he told me about her. He loves her." It was more a statement than a question.

"But he hasn't realized it yet," they both said it at the same time.

"Give him my love." Martha squeezed Mike's hand. "I'll say a prayer for everyone. Go now, don't worry about Noah. He'll be fine over here, and you call me if you need anything."

"Thanks Martha." Mike kissed the back of Martha's hand and took off for the hospital.

Trish jumped out of bed and ran to her closet. She threw on a pair of faded blue jeans with a hole in the left knee and a gray sweatshirt. She ran to the bathroom, brushed her teeth, and pulled up her stark red hair in a ponytail. She looked at herself in the mirror. Libba would never allow her to go out in public dressed like that much less meet Cailin looking so dreadful, even under these circumstances. She ran back to her closet and changed the sweatshirt for a periwinkle blue button up. The holey jeans would have to do. She grabbed a jacket and ran outside, dialing Mallory as she jumped into her candy apple red mustang.

"Hi, Trish."

How could she sound so happy at two o'clock in the morning? "Mallory, did I wake you?"

"Oh, no. I stayed up late watching the Hallmark channel and doing my nails, and now I'm having trouble going to bed. What's up? You sound rushed."

"Libba's in the hospital. I'm on my way to pick you up. Be ready in fifteen minutes."

"Libba's in the hospital—but I have Olivia."

"Damn! Is there someone who can watch her?" Trish had forgotten about Mallory's daughter.

"Trish! It's two in the morning. Who am I going to call at this time of night? I'll just bring her with us. She'll be good. We'll be ready."

"K, I'll fill you in when I get there."

When Trish arrived, Mallory was peeking out the window and began running toward the car with Olivia before Trish could even park. She buckled the car seat in, buckled Olivia in, then jumped in the front seat. Trish looked at the two of them.

Damn, really? Mallory looked perfect as if she were ready to go to work and Olivia as though she were going to a birthday party. *How did she do that, she always had her act together, even her daughter's act!* Trish thought. She looked down at the hole in her jeans; she was glad she had at least changed out of the sweatshirt.

Mallory turned to Trish, "Why are you staring at me? Do I not match?" Mallory looked at her outfit.

"Ugh Mallory! You always match! Even your nails match! Even your daughter matches!" Trish wished she could be as organized and prepared as Mallory.

"Never mind. Look, Cailin called me."

"Cailin? You mean, Libba's Cailin."

"Yeah, yeah. He called a few minutes ago. That jerk Alec, her husband, ex-husband, beat up Libba and they're taking her to the hospital."

"Alec. Are you serious, he's back? He *beat* her did you say? I never took him for the type. He's so ... nerdy, I mean, quiet, you know? How did Cailin say Libba is doing?"

"Bad, really bad. He sounded a mess too—really worried about her, ya know?"

"Hmm? That's because he ..." Mallory's dark brown eyes grew wide as she contemplated. Her eyes always said so much about her. Trish looked at Olivia. She had her mother's eyes.

"Because he what?"

"Never mind." She peered at Olivia in the back seat. She was sitting quietly, looking out the window, hugging her stuffed rabbit. "I hope Libba's okay."

"Me, too."

They sat in silence while Trish sped along the highway. Mallory kept still except for a soft nervous strumming of her fingers over her purse. Trish knew she was deep in thought. That was Mallory's personality. Mallory didn't bother much to argue or complain about things she couldn't control. Trish wondered what Mallory was thinking. *Trish* was thinking about the different ways she could torture Alec, but she was sure Mallory was thinking something totally different. Mallory did not like negative energy and she never spoke badly of someone unless, in her opinion, it was substantiated. She was so optimistic, no doubt because she did not want to expose those feelings to Olivia. She was such a great parent and Olivia was picture perfect, just like her mother. She was very disciplined for a four-year-old and smart, too. Yes, Mallory was an excellent single mother, but more so, she was just an all-around first-class person.

The hospital emergency room was slow for a Friday night. There were a few people waiting—one man appeared to have a stomach virus, there was a family with a sick child, and someone with a broken leg. The EMS squad was dispatching to pick up a couple after receiving a call about a car accident. Trish, Mallory, and Olivia walked into the hospital and approached the information desk. They found out that Libba was been taken to the lab for tests. The receptionist did not have any information about her condition but directed them to a waiting area around the corner that was less crowded than the one they had just walked through.

They were told that once Libba was assigned a room, Olivia would be allowed up to the floor but not in the room. When they arrived at the waiting area, two men were sitting quietly in the small room. A television was on, but neither was paying attention to it.

Mike looked up and noticed a little girl still clutching a stuffed rabbit with her left hand. She looked so pure and innocent and had big round dark eyes. He followed her other hand to the woman who held it. He saw where she got her eyes from; there was no denying the woman was the little girl's mother. They both looked elegant standing there together. He immediately stood up, remembering his manners.

Cailin raised his head at Mike's sudden movement. He looked up and saw three girls. He knew who they were by his conversations with Libba. Thank goodness the redhead looked more worried than angry. Libba had mentioned Trish's temper and he wasn't sure if he could handle a lashing from her tonight. He felt miserable for having to break the news to her about Libba, but he stood up and joined his brother's side.

"You must be Trish." Cailin extended his hand. He shook Trish's hand, then Mallory's. Trish had a very sturdy handshake. "I'm Cailin. This is my brother, Mike."

Mike stepped forward to shake hands with Trish. Mallory bent over and picked up Olivia.

"Hi. This is Mallory and her daughter, Olivia." Mallory smiled and said hello and Olivia gave a shy wave then buried her head in Mallory's neck. Mike smiled at the gesture.

"Nice to meet you both," Mallory said as she rubbed Olivia's back. "What happened? Do you have any news on Libba's condition? The receptionist wasn't much help."

They sat down and Cailin explained everything he knew, which wasn't much. He told them that Jared said the police would be coming and they would most likely be questioned about Libba's ex-husband. It was evident that Trish did not like Alec, but Cailin seemed to think that, so far, she approved of him. Cailin did not have many details on Libba's condition. She had a lot of bumps and bruises and was still unconscious when they rolled her to the lab for tests and x-rays.

"Mommy, can I lay down on the couch?" Olivia had quietly sat next to Mallory the whole time. Her small voice was barely audible. Mike noticed how tired the child looked. He felt sorry for her. She should be at home in bed.

Olivia adjusted herself on the couch resting her head on Mallory's lap.

"Is there someone you can call to pick her up?" Mike asked. "We may be here a while."

"Why, is she bothering you?" Mallory snapped at Mike. Mike leaned back defensively. Trish looked at Mallory in shock. Cailin's mouth popped open. The room was silent.

"I think my brother is just concerned for your daughter, Mallory." Cailin's voice was very sincere. "Noah, Mike's son, is with a family friend. If you've no one else to call at this hour, I'm sure we can make arrangements for you. We'd like to help ... so you can be here for Libba." Cailin looked down at Olivia. "She would be safe and well cared for. You have nothing to worry about."

Trish spoke now. "Olivia is a good girl. She won't be any trouble."

"I don't doubt that. I simply meant that she might be more comfortable in a bed and Mike's right, we're going to be here a while and I expect the police will be here soon, too."

Mallory looked at Mike. Her eyes seemed to grow as if in recognition of something. "I'm sorry. I don't know where that come from." She seemed embarrassed for the way she had responded to Mike. She turned to Cailin, "I appreciate the offer, but I'd rather wait. If she becomes restless then, maybe. Thank you for the offer though."

They sat quietly watching Mallory brush Olivia's hair. So many thoughts were running through each of their minds. Mallory was surprised at how she had overreacted to Mike's statement. He didn't mean any harm by it; he was only being polite. She was being rude; that was *so* unlike her. She peeked at Trish; she knew Trish would say something later.

Trish was nervously shaking one leg. She was thinking about what she would say to the police once they arrived. She would tell them everything she knew about Alec, everything. Libba knew she didn't like Alec and Trish knew Libba could do better than him. She had. Cailin seemed like a perfect match for her and his brother was nice too. She glanced at Mike; he was following the rhythm of Mallory's hand.

Mike was no longer worried about Olivia. The little girl seemed to be wholly content sitting next to her mother. Mallory began to hum a lullaby softly in the girl's ear. Olivia smiled and snuggled closer. Mike thought it was the most beautiful thing he'd ever witnessed—the natural bond of mother and child. He understood how Mallory felt. Especially when times are rough there's nothing like being sheltered in the comfort of your family. He noticed Mallory wasn't wearing a ring, perhaps Olivia was Mallory's shelter. He knew Noah and Cailin were his. He looked at his brother. Poor Cailin.

Cailin sat back in his chair with his hands clasped together over his head. He was tired. He was tired of being alone; tired of not having someone to share his world, his bed, his life. He did not want a life of solidarity; a life, he equated, without Libba. His heart tightened at the very thought of her. He wondered when they would bring her to her room. He merely needed to see her, to touch her hand, to be with her, to know she was okay. He pressed his eyes tightly together and prayed that she would forgive him. He promised himself he would not leave her alone until her ex was behind bars.

A sound drifted into the room. They all turned to see the elevator doors open and Libba lying on a hospital bed. A middle-aged nurse carefully pushed the gurney out. She spotted the group sitting in the waiting room and nodded her head. Everyone stood up but Cailin was the first to reach Libba. She looked so fragile laying there, an IV in one arm, the other covered with bruises. Her head was bandaged with heavy gauze and one eye was swollen shut. She was sleeping or unconscious, Cailin wasn't sure which.

"How is she?" he managed to ask.

"She'll survive, she's only sleeping. We gave her something for pain so when she wakes up it won't hurt as much. She may sleep for some time." The nurse sounded very sympathetic. "We had her up in the lab for tests and the doctor will be right down to fill you in. I need to get her into a room and get her vitals. I'm sorry, but I can only allow one visitor at a time."

Cailin looked at Trish with pleading eyes. Even though Trish wanted to be with Libba, she knew Cailin was in agony. She hoped Cailin knew what happened wasn't his fault.

"Go with her, Cailin. I'll go next." Trish nodded.

After the nurse had gotten Libba settled into the room, she took her blood pressure, oxygen levels, and temperature then left. Cailin pulled a chair next to the bed and sat. He looked at Libba and cautiously took her hand in his. She seemed so fragile lying there completely immobile except for the steady pattern of her breathing. The room was quiet. Cailin could hear the strumming of the equipment and the steady *drip … drip … drip* of the IV. He lifted her hand to his lips then rested them on his cheek. He stared at Libba willing her to wake up, but she did not. Cailin could not remember the last time he prayed. It must have been shortly after his parents were killed. He looked up at the ceiling, closed his eyes, and wished an unselfish prayer. He would do anything to have Libba wake up that instant, but he knew she would not. She could not. She did not.

Cailin remembered the first time he met Libba. It seemed so long ago and yet it was only a few shorts weeks. He had memorized every detail of his precious fairy. Even with the bumps and bruises, Libba still looked as beautiful as she did the first time he saw her. He wasn't sure what to say to Libba. What do you say to someone who can't hear you?

Libba, it's me, Cailin. I'm so sorry I didn't make it back in time but I'm here now. I'm with you. Hold on, Precious. Don't you let go, not now, not when I've just found you. I've waited too long for you to come into my life and now that you have, I don't know what I'll do without you. Please, please wake up Libba. I need you, I— Cailin's thoughts were interrupted when someone knocked. He turned towards the door.

"I'm sorry to disturb you." The elderly nurse was back. "The police are here and would like to talk to you."

Cailin could see Mike and Trish talking to the police officer in the hallway; Mallory was still sitting on the couch with Olivia. "I'll be right there." He gave Libba's hand another kiss and stroked the hair from her face. He leaned down and murmured the last of his thoughts into her ear. Then, he warily walked towards the others.

My whole body ached. My head pounded and my arms were sore and heavy as bricks. I had a rusty taste in my mouth and a sour stomach. I tried to open my eyes, but I could not. A light shown through my eyelids and I could hear the faint humming sound of florescent lighting. I had no idea how long I was unconscious or how I got here. I wasn't even positive where *here* was, although I was sure I was in a hospital. I knew why I was here; I could clearly recall every second before I passed out. I had never been that frightened in my life. What did I do to Alec to have him hate me so much? As if leaving me wasn't bad enough, he had to come back and try to kill me, too? How could I miss the signs that Alec was so unstable? Were there any signs to notice or did he just snap? I simply could not understand how someone you loved and lived with for so long could suddenly attack you. I shuddered at the thought, sending pain, both physical and mental, right through me. I lay there listening to the sound of silence around me. I was in too much pain to stay awake, so I allowed myself to drift back into the solace of lifeless wonder.

Cailin and I stood in the middle of the forest surrounded by tall trees that reached the heavens. In front of me, I could still see the dense haze of a full moon but Cailin was facing the sun, golden rays reflected in the depth of his eyes. I wondered how this could be possible, to be present in the dark and the light at the same time. Then I realized, we were not bound to the earth as we know it. We floated, drifting in the realm of another world. Here, my body did not hurt; my heart did not ache. I was alone except for the presence of one other. The one I would be with for the rest of my life. He placed his arm around my waist, and together we went further into the wood. It was quiet. Silent was the sound of our footsteps crushing the leaves on the ground beneath. Sparrows followed us through the woods and though they chirped, I could not hear them. For me, they sang a mute melody.

Cailin spoke to me in soft words. I watched his tender lips as they moved but made no sound. He smiled his wicked smile and though I knew I was dreaming, his smile still sent flutters through my stomach. I spoke to him, but he did not respond. I reached for him, but he simply smiled and let me go. He turned down a sodden trail, walking towards the sun and leaving me alone.

I looked in the other direction and the moon was no longer bright. Darkness surrounded a lone figure atop a huge rock. Alec stood there, looking down at me; a crow sat on his shoulder. It opened its mouth unleashing the unearthly sound of a muffled screech. I knew the crow signified that death was creeping closer, but of whose death I was not sure. I ran towards Cailin as fast as I could, seeking the tranquility that his presence surrounded me in. When I reached him, he held a green vase with a single rose inside. I looked up to the sky and was blinded by the light. His hand gently stroked the hair from my face as he leaned down and whispered in my ear, words I could not hear.

CHAPTER 8

THE LONGEST HOUR

L ieutenant LeBrecque grabbed his keys and walked out of the station. He was on his way to Blowing Rock Hospital, another domestic dispute. He did not like answering these types of calls. No matter how hard he tried, he could not understand how a man could abuse a woman he supposedly loved; more so, how could a woman keep going home to a husband that abused her. He knew what the Domestic Violence Statistics reported. Every nine seconds a woman in the U.S. is physically abused or assaulted; domestic violence is the leading cause of injury reported by women surpassing rapes, muggings, and vehicle accidents combined. He also knew that 42 percent of murdered women are killed by their partners or spouse. Lieutenant LeBrecque had five female siblings and because of them, he supported women's rights and he would never tolerate anything like that happening to his sisters. He was very defensive of them, of females in general, which is why he became a police officer. Lieutenant LeBrecque had a protective nature; he knew this, and it suited him fine.

When Lieutenant LeBrecque stepped out of the elevator, he spotted three adults and a child sitting in the waiting area. Two of the adults stood up and approached him. They had just finished introductions when Cailin appeared.

"I'm afraid I need to ask you all a few questions." Lieutenant LeBrecque pulled out a tiny notebook from his shirt pocket. "Which one of you called 911?"

"That would be me," Mike quickly answered.

"And how do you know Libba Spencer?"

"I don't. I was calling for my brother."

The officer looked at Cailin, "Why didn't you call 911?"

"I was on the other line with Libba. I conferenced Mike in so he could call the police."

"You were on the phone with her while she was being accosted?" He pointed at Cailin, then at Mike, "... but you're the one who called for help?" Mike nodded. "And what about you?" Lieutenant LeBrecque looked at Trish.

"Me?" Trish asked. "I called Mallory so she could ride with me here. We're Libba's friends," she said gesturing to Mallory. "Cailin called me on his way to the hospital."

"Okay. I think I'd like to talk to each of you one on one. Starting with you," he said, pointing at Mike. "Let's see if they have an empty room where I can interview you. I'll be right back." A moment later Lieutenant LeBrecque came back and asked Mike to follow him, leaving the others to wait behind.

Within a few minutes Mike returned to the waiting area. "He's ready for you," he said to Cailin, then turned to address Trish. "Why don't you go in the room and be with Libba? Cailin might be a while and at least you'll have a chance to visit with Libba in the meantime."

Mike sat down next to Mallory and looked at Olivia.

"That was quick" Mallory said. Olivia was still sleeping on her lap.

"Well, I really don't know anything," Mike replied. "I made

a phone call and then came here to support my brother. He really likes her, Libba, I mean." Mike looked at Mallory. He didn't want to tell her he thought Cailin was falling in love with Libba. She turned to him and their eyes caught for a quick second. Her eyes were growing again, and Mike was fascinated by them. "Your daughter ... she's an unbelievably beautiful child. Takes after her mother—her eyes, I mean. Um ... would you like a drink or something, there's a vending machine around the corner."

Mallory blushed.

Mike was embarrassed. He assumed she probably got a lot of compliments from men, but this was the first time he had complimented a woman—especially one this beautiful—in a long time, even if it was originally directed towards her daughter.

"That would be nice," Mallory replied. "Thank you."

"Anything in particular?"

"Surprise me." Mallory smiled and tucked a loose strand of hair behind her ear. Mike walked away, glancing back at Mallory before he rounded the corner.

Cailin walked into the room and sat in a chair across from Lieutenant LeBrecque. He wasn't sure how much help he could be, but he would do anything to help get Libba's ex-husband behind bars.

"I understand you were on a date with Ms. Spencer tonight."

"That's correct," Cailin said.

"And what time did you last see her ... before she was picked up by the EMS?"

"I dropped her off just after one o'clock. We had dinner at The Ridgeline, then went to Murray's Pub, and then I took her home."

"And you left right after? You didn't walk her in the house or anything?" Lieutenant LeBrecque wrote a few notes in his notebook.

"No sir. I thought about it—walking her inside, I mean—but

I didn't." Cailin didn't tell the officer that his thoughts at that time were less than gentlemanly and that was why he had left. "I watched her go inside her house and then I drove away."

"And you went straight home?"

"No. I rode by the restaurant where Libba left her car to make sure it was okay. After that, I got a call from her. She said, 'help me'." Cailin swallowed hard. "She said, 'he's back and he's drunk' and then there was a lot of muffled sounds, but I heard her say something like 'please don't hit me again.' I didn't want to hang up in case she came back, so I conferenced my brother on the line and he called 911."

"Who do you think she was talking about?" The officer looked at Cailin as he continued to write in his notebook.

"I think it was her ex-husband. She recently got a divorce."

Lieutenant LeBrecque stopped writing and looked Cailin square in the eyes. "Hmm? How long have you known Ms. Spencer?"

Cailin looked at the officer. For some reason he didn't like the officer's tone of voice. "I've known her for a couple of weeks. We met the night the jerk walked out on her with no explanation at all. Tonight, was our first date."

Cailin heard voices outside the door. The doctor had finally arrived and was talking to Trish in the hall. Cailin stood up. "Are we done for now? I'd like to talk to the doctor if you don't mind."

The officer scribbled in the notebook, then said, "One last thing. You say she called you on your cell?" Cailin nodded. "Mind if I see your phone a minute." Cailin handed him his cell phone. The officer pushed some buttons then gave the phone back to Cailin. "You can go now but send in the girl would you, the one with the red hair."

Cailin hurriedly joined Trish and the doctor in the hall, then introduced himself.

"I was telling Ms. Knight your friend is going to be all right.

Obviously, there are several bruises, but they'll heal in no time. There are no internal injuries, but her ribs and stomach took a good beating, so she'll be sore for a few days. She has a concussion and she's still unconscious. I think she's still in shock. There's really no reason why she hasn't come to yet. We're monitoring her condition. Even with the pain meds she should have woken up already, but she hasn't."

"There's no brain damage is there?" Cailin asked. He could tell Trish was nervous; she was fidgeting with her hands.

"No, none that I can tell. Like I said, she should be awake but she's not. Perhaps if you all take turns talking to her, she'll wake up sooner." He placed a clipboard under his arms. "I'll be back to check on her in another hour. I recommend only one at a time when visiting her."

"Certainly. Thanks, doc." Cailin shook the doctor's hand, and the doctor left to talk to the nurses on duty. "Trish, I'm sorry. I should have never left her alone tonight. I should have walked her in—"

"Cailin, don't. It's not your fault." Trish raised her hand to stop Cailin from speaking any further. "You didn't know he would be there. I don't blame you and I'm sure Libba wouldn't either. I'm grateful to you. If it weren't for you, who knows how long she would have been lying there. You got her here in the nick of time and that's what counts."

"I can't believe he could do this to her. What kind of man is he?" Cailin shook his head. "Speaking of which, Lieutenant LeBrecque wants to see you." Cailin turned to look at Lieutenant LeBrecque, who joined the doctor at the nurse's station. The elevator doors opened. Jared was helping another nurse push out a hospital bed carrying a young male who looked to be in his early twenties. The nurse rolled the gurney to a room a few doors down from Libba's. Jared stopped when he reached Cailin.

Cailin shook Jared's hand. "Busy night."

"Yeah, two pickups in less than an hour. This one's a car accident, hit and run. The other driver apparently was drinking; there was an empty Amstel light bottle in the front seat. He left his Explorer running. Must have jumped out and took off. The other car had OnStar, that's how we got the call."

Cailin turned his head sideways looking at Jared, then pressed his fingers to his temples.

"Oh man, I'm sorry, Cailin. I shouldn't have mentioned it was a hit and run. I didn't mean to bring back any bad memories." Jared was very apologetic. Trish looked at both of them obviously having no clue what Jared was talking about. She didn't know Cailin and Mike had lost their parents in a hit and run accident four years earlier.

"No, it's not that, something you said though … not the hit and run part." Cailin stood there trying to think. Something about what Jared had said sparked a memory. "OH SHIT!"

"What, what is it?" Jared was looking anxious now.

"There were empty Amstel light bottles in Libba's house. Remember?" Flashes of the night's memories charged through Cailin's mind. He could clearly see Libba's house as if he were back in her living room. There were five empty beer bottles. His mind backtracked. He was nearly run off the side of the road by a white Ford Explorer. "Jared, what color was the Explorer?"

"Huh, the color? Why do you want to know?"

"Jared, just tell me. What color was the Ford Explorer?"

"White. It was white!" Jared said.

Cailin knew the driver of the Ford was Alec. That was the only car he passed on the way back to Libba's house.

"I think it was *him*. On my way to Libba's, I was nearly hit by a white Ford Explorer. My truck swiped the guardrail and the Ford hit a road sign. I was going to get out but when I looked, the other car was gone so I sped to Libba's. I didn't pass another car on the way to her house."

Jared looked at Trish and Cailin. It was too coincidental. "I don't know Cailin."

"Jared, remember there were empty Amstel bottles in Libba's house. It can't be a coincidence; it has to be him. He hurt Libba, now he's hurt some complete stranger, too. We've got to tell Lieutenant LeBrecque."

"Wait," Jared had to think; he couldn't believe what he was hearing. This was the second time in the past hour that he had seen Cailin and if what Cailin was saying was correct, Libba's ex-husband had put two people in the hospital in less than an hour's time. If the same guy was responsible, they had to catch him, and quickly too, before someone else suffered.

After a few seconds, Jared spoke again. "Ok, maybe you're right. If nothing else, we should at least tell the police what you think and let them figure it out." At that, he walked with Cailin and Trish to talk to Lieutenant LeBrecque.

Mallory watched as the trio approached Lieutenant LeBrecque, who was still standing at the nurse's station. She strained her neck trying to find out what was going on. Mike returned from the vending machine holding two Sundrops and a pack of powdered donuts. He looked at the group who was now gathering at the nurse's station, then to Mallory. He knew she wanted to be a part of whatever was going on. "Mallory, go. I can keep an eye on Olivia. I have a six-year-old, I think I know how to parent." Mallory looked anxious but torn between her daughter and her friend. "Mallory, please. This is why I'm here, to help. She's your friend, you should be there."

"I don't want to be a burden," Mallory said.

"I don't think *you* could ever be a burden." Mike grabbed a pillow off the couch and gently lifted Olivia's head, accidently touching Mallory's thigh a little more than was necessary. Their eyes caught.

"Sorry, I didn't mean to …" Mike cleared his throat, he was so close to her that he could smell her scent. Just like her eyes, her scent fascinated him. He couldn't make out the sweet combination, but it fit her perfectly. Mallory scooted out from under Olivia's head and Mike placed the pillow there. He opened a Sundrop and handed it to Mallory. "Surprise."

Mallory gave a short giggle and took the drink from Mike. She drank deeply, not realizing how thirsty she was. "I'll be right back. Thank you, Mike." She set the drink on a magazine and quickly left to join the group.

Mike watched her as she drank admiring her long throat and her lips against the bottle. She was very alluring. He bet she wasn't even aware of the potency of her beauty. She spoke—bringing his mind back to focus—and then he watched her walk away towards the others. He sat on the floor in front of Olivia and lifted his knees to rest his arms. He checked the time. It was three o'clock in the morning now. Mike closed his eyes. It had been a long hour and he had a feeling it was going to be an even longer morning.

"Trish, what's going on?" Mallory approached the nurse's station. Everyone was talking at the same time and no one seemed to hear her. She touched Jared on his arm. "Excuse me. Could you tell me what's going on?"

As Jared turned to glance at Mallory, his mouth dropped. *Who is this voluptuous woman touching my arm?* He followed her face to her hand and she quickly let go.

"Oh, hi. I'm Jared, and you are …"

"Hi Jared." Mallory did not have the patience right now for niceties; she simply wanted to find out what was going on with Libba. "Do you know what all the fuss is about? Is it Libba? Is there something wrong?"

"Oh, sorry, is she one of your friends too?" Jared said, noticing her perfectly round plump breasts. He suddenly wanted to squeeze them but resisted the temptation. "Um ... Cailin thinks the ex-husband may be the cause of another accident."

"Trish!" Mallory had her attention now. She wanted to get the story from Trish, not Jared. He made her nervous. She didn't like the way he was looking her up and down like she was some piece of fruit he wanted to peel and take a bite out of. She moved out of his reach. "How's Libba and what's going on?"

Trish took Mallory aside and explained Libba's condition. Then she told her Cailin's theory about Alec. "Well, I think you need to talk to Lieutenant LeBrecque and tell him everything you know about Alec, and I do mean *everything*." Her eyes grew and she raised her eyebrows as if conveying a secret signal. "I'm going to see Libba."

Mallory turned to go to Libba's room. As she left, she could feel Jared's eyes following her. It gave her a bad sensation, a dangerously bad sensation. She shrugged her shoulders and walked through the door pausing to look at the clock on the wall. Only an hour had passed but she was getting tired. She looked down the hall into the waiting room. Mike was sitting on the floor in front of Olivia with his head tilted back, his mouth slightly opened. He was sleeping. They both looked so peaceful together. The sight of them immediately calmed her as she walked into Libba's room.

Trish couldn't believe they had been at the hospital for an hour. She was beginning to stress out. So much was happening, she wasn't sure how much more she could take. There was no change in Libba's condition, and she still had not awakened. Cailin was accusing Alec—who was also wanted for beating up her best friend—of a hit and run. To top that off, she was about to spill her guts to a police officer and tell him everything she didn't like about her friend's ex-husband. Ugh. She needed to unwind. She needed a glass of wine, a cigarette, and sex—and not necessarily in that order.

Trish wasn't sure of Cailin's theory about Alec. True, she didn't like Alec, but was he capable of such madness? She wondered what must have happened to him to make him snap so suddenly. She thought Alec had left town. When did he get back, or better yet, why had he come back to Libba? Why had he left her in the first place? She sat in the empty room waiting for Lieutenant LeBrecque, who was refilling his coffee. She wondered what he thought about Cailin's theory.

When Lieutenant LeBrecque walked into the room, Trish sat up straight and tall. She was ready to get this over with. "Ms. Knight, sorry to keep you waiting."

"Please, call me Trish."

"Tell me Trish, what do you make of everything that's happened tonight?" Lieutenant LeBrecque opened his notebook and grabbed a pen lying on the desk.

"What do you mean, Libba and Alec or Alec and the hit and run."

"Let's start with Libba and Alec. What can you tell me about them?"

"Well, I've known Libba for about three years. She was one of the first friends I made when I moved here and started working at *Nostalgia Remembered*. I don't really know too much about Alec, but I never really cared for him." Trish leaned back in her chair and crossed her legs.

"A few weeks ago, Alec called Libba at work," she said. "He said he was leaving her, and by the time she got home he had packed his stuff and had divorce papers waiting for her. Libba tried to get information from his attorneys but they only told her what was on the papers, nothing else. Libba signed the papers and I can't say that I blame her either."

Lieutenant LeBrecque seemed to think about what she was saying. "And she just started dating Cailin, is that right? She didn't want to wait to see if her husband would change his mind, come back to her? What about his family, do you know anything about them?"

"Ex-husband, and no, I guess not. He made his decision and he left. Why should she take him back? And I don't know anything about his family. By what I understand, Alec hasn't been in touch with his family in years. Libba never really talked much about his family. I assume because she didn't know much about them."

"Hmm, and what about Cailin? How long have they been going out?" Lieutenant LeBrecque turned the page in his notebook.

"Tonight, was their first date. They met the day Alec left Libba."

"You sure they didn't meet before that, maybe they were seeing each other before her ex left and maybe that's why he left her or maybe that's why he came back?"

"What? No! They *just* met. Besides, Libba's not the type to have an affair. Maybe Alec, but not Libba!" Trish was on the verge of anger. Lack of sleep was not helping her temper, but she tried to calm down as best she could.

"Hmm?"

"Hmm, what? What are you getting at?"

"Ms. Knight, Trish, I'm just trying to find out what his motive is. Alec has no record of violence that I can find in the system. Until your friend wakes up, we don't even know for sure if it was her ex that did this to her and not some random attack. There wasn't another witness—"

"But Cailin said—"

"Cailin said she called him and said, 'he's here,' NOT 'Alec's here.' I have to give him the benefit of the doubt. You know, innocent until proven guilty."

"What about guilty until proven innocent? I know he did this to her …"

"Why do you think that?

Trish crossed her arms over her chest. "I could never figure out what she saw in that man. He wasn't … nice. They never did anything together, never had people over to their house. They went to a couple of work Christmas parties, would have one drink and then Libba would make up some excuse to go home. Libba said he wasn't the social type, but after one drink, well let's just say he seemed pretty social to me."

"Go on." Lieutenant LeBrecque set down the pen and crossed his hands over the table.

"I think he has a drinking problem. I think that's why they didn't do much in public, and I *don't* think this is the first time he's hit her. Last year she took off work for two days because said she had food poisoning. She came into work that Wednesday with marks under her eyes that she tried to cover with makeup. She claimed she was dehydrated from puking. To me, it looked like she had the remnants of two black eyes. Another time, she claimed she got some bruises by falling from her attic. Libba is NOT the clumsy type and where the bruises were didn't make sense for the fall. I think he did this to her all right and he needs to pay. He needs to be arrested."

Lieutenant LeBrecque was silent while he thought about what Trish said. In his experience, when a married man had a woman that he abused and could get away with it, he didn't leave her unless he had another woman he could abuse. He needed to get back to the station and do more research. He needed to see if he could find Alec's whereabouts for the last few weeks. He feared Libba might not be the only woman in danger of Alec. He stood up, closing the notebook and putting it back in his pocket.

"Is that it? What about Cailin's theory about the hit and run?"

"I've already sent a crew to Libba's house to take fingerprints, understanding Alec's might still be there since he used to live there, but we're looking to see if there are any different ones in case someone else did this to her. They're also going to check out the vehicle from the hit and run. If there are any and they belong to Alec, I need to find this guy and quickly. Who knows where he may be heading … or who he may be heading to?" He walked towards the door and turned, "Trish, I'll be in touch with you soon. I'm sure I'll have a few more questions for you and Cailin, and I especially need to talk to Libba when she wakes up. Call me when that happens." He handed her his business card and walked out of the room, leaving Trish alone.

Trish closed her eyes. She was so tired. It had been the longest hour filled with more stress than she could handle. If she could only nap, she would be okay. She rested her head on the desk and within a few moments she was sound asleep.

CHAPTER 9

ONE FOR ALL AND
ALL FOR ONE

Two years ago, my mother took me to get my wisdom teeth pulled. I had all four of them extracted at the same time. I remember going to the dentist, inhaling the laughing gas, and waking up several hours later at home in bed. Whatever happened between the laughing gas and waking up, I really have no memory. I can only recall bits and pieces, like putting my seatbelt on in the car, reading grocery store advertisements while my mother picked up my medicine, and sitting on my couch with my mother telling me I should go to bed. To my mother, I was awake but not alert. To myself, I existed only partly in the form of a shadow and not my entire being.

I thought of this as I lay in the hospital bed because, once again, I was a shadow, and it was hard for me to distinguish what was a dream and what was the flicker of reality. I knew I had dreamt but what my dream meant I was not sure. The dream had occupied my mind and while I dreamt, time had passed over me—seconds that I could never get back, minutes that were spent, hours that were lost forever. I could see Cailin sitting next to me, but just as quickly as I saw him, the image faded and became Trish, and then Mallory. Now, Cailin was back. I concentrated as hard as I could to wake up, and this time, to stay awake, to stay alert. I didn't want *this* moment to escape me. I heard him say my name. It sounded so lovely rolling off his lips, like my name was meant for his lips alone. I wanted to hear him say it again.

"Libba, Libba, Precious, can you hear me? Wake up." He squeezed my hand.

"Cailin?" My throat was very dry. I could see Cailin now, but he was still very blurry. He held my hand in his and I wondered how long he had been sitting there. "What time is it?"

"It's 11:37 in the morning." He leaned over me and rubbed the hair out of my face, careful not to touch me too hard. "How are you feeling?"

"Thirsty. Can I have some water?" Cailin walked out of my view but within seconds he was back. He tilted my head so I could drink. My head pounded with the movement. I tried to open my eyes wider to see him, but that hurt, too.

"You've been unconscious all night." He looked at me sympathetically. "We were beginning to wonder if you would ever wake up."

"We? Who else is here?" I tried to sit up, but the pain was too great.

"Easy now. If you haven't noticed, you're not in the best of shape." Cailin looked at me. I stared deep into his eyes but all I could see was pain and a trace of … guilt?

I looked at my arms and saw the purple bruises. My stomach hurt, my head hurt, my eye hurt. "How bad am I?"

Cailin paused before answering. I wasn't sure if he would sugarcoat it or tell me the truth. No, I believed he would tell me the truth; he always said what was on his mind.

"The doctor was here about thirty minutes ago. He said you

should be back to normal in a few days. Nothing is seriously wrong with you, but you have a lot of bruises ... your eye." He pointed at my left eye, the one that hurt. "It's pretty swollen. I imagine it hurts." He grabbed my hand and rubbed his thumb across it. "They have you on an IV to give you pain medication. Libba, the doctor said you should have woken up hours ago, but you didn't ... you had me worried." He closed his eyes and held my hand to his lips. Softly he kissed my fingertips. The gesture was so caring. I knew he had genuinely been afraid for me.

"I tried—I tried to wake up, but I just couldn't. I can't explain it but, it was like I was awake, sometimes, but I wasn't here. Are Trish and Mallory here? I saw them, I think."

"Yeah, Trish, Mallory, and her daughter, Olivia, and my brother, Mike, they're all here." He shrugged. "I wasn't sure who to call so I called Mike, and then I called Trish, and well, Trish called Mallory."

"Wow, they all came."

"Of course, they did." He moved his lips and gave a half smile. "Do you need anything? Are you in much pain?"

He looked so sad. I could deal with the physical pain I was in, but Cailin ... the pain I saw on his face. The pity. I was so ashamed. I closed my eyes to hold back the tears, but I couldn't hide the shame I was feeling.

"Shh, it's okay, it's *okay*." Cailin stood up and leaned over me. He skimmed my cheeks softly with his lips. "I'm so sorry I wasn't there for you, Libba. If I would have come in with you this would have never happened. Can you ever forgive me?"

What was he talking about? Did Cailin blame himself for what happened to me? If he did, that would explain the traces of guilt I thought I recognized.

"Cailin, this is not your fault. Don't you dare blame yourself!" I took a deep breath. "I don't want you to see me like this. You shouldn't be here. None of you should be here. I'm so sorry."

I turned my head away from Cailin so he couldn't see the tears running down my face.

"Libba, what are saying? I'm not going anywhere, and I don't think your friends are either. We care about you. We're not going to leave you here alone, not after all this. In fact, I'm not leaving you alone at all until they catch this guy."

"You mean he's still out there?"

"Yes." Cailin pursed his lips and squinted his eyes. He stared at the IV.

Drip ... drip ... drip ...

"They haven't caught the bastard yet," Cailin replied.

I wasn't sure what to say. I didn't remember anything once Alec hit my head and knocked me out. I knew Cailin must have come back to the house but what happened once he got there I didn't know. I looked at Cailin who was still staring at the IV.

"Um, do you think Trish and Mallory could come in? I'd like to see them, if you don't mind?" I spoke very quietly. I could tell he was in deep thought, but I didn't ask what was going through his mind. I couldn't, not now.

"Sure. I'll go get them." He squeezed my hand and walked out the door.

A few moments later, Trish and Mallory walked into my room. The guys must have been watching Olivia.

"Hey, you. It's about time you woke you," Trish said as she sat in the chair Cailin had occupied while Mallory stood behind her.

"Hi, Libba. You okay?" Mallory looked at me like a mother caring for her sick child.

Seeing the two of them made me feel much better. Not that I didn't want Cailin around but Trish and Mallory, well ... they were fast becoming my best friends and seeing them gave me strength, gave me hope. They helped me through so much in the past weeks that I knew I could talk to either of them about anything. I had so many questions, some that concerned Cailin, and

I needed to find out what was going on with Alec, too. I wasn't ready to talk to Cailin about Alec, but I knew it would come to that sooner or later and I wanted to be prepared.

"I'm all right. A little sluggish and my vision is blurry," I said rubbing my eye. "How bad do I look, do either of you have a mirror?"

Mallory pulled a compact out of her purse and handed it to me. I frowned. I looked horrible. I didn't want Cailin to see me like this or his brother; this would be my first time meeting him.

"It's not too bad," Mallory said, walking around the bed and placing a comforting hand on my shoulder. "You still look beautiful."

"Yeah, don't worry about it, Libba. Besides, Cailin's crazy about you. I doubt he even noticed how bad you look."

"Gee, thanks." Trish had a way with words. "Tell me, how did I get here? Did Cailin bring me here, and where's Alec? Cailin didn't give me any details and I didn't want to ask. He said they hadn't caught him yet. Tell me, what's going on?"

Trish was on the edge of her seat eager to fill me in on the past few hours. She spoke very quickly. "Well, Cailin got to the house right when the EMS got there. Jared, the paramedic guy, I guess he's an old friend of Cailin and Mike's, he said you were unconscious when they arrived and Cailin was really torn up seeing you lying there in your own blood. They brought you here and ran tests, x-rays and stuff, and they cleaned you up a bit, but apparently not too well." Trish stood up and picked something out of my hair; Mallory slapped her hand.

"Anyway, while you were unconscious, the police came, and we all had to give statements. Alec's on the run. Lieutenant LeBrecque—he's the guy assigned to your case—went back to the station but he said he'd come back when you wake up. And the doctor should be back soon. He's been checking on you every few hours. And, oh yeah! Right after we got here, the EMS brought in a guy from a hit and run and Cailin thinks Alec was driving the other car! Now Alec's wanted not only for assaulting you but also for driving under the influence, reckless and dangerous driving, AND, if the guy next door doesn't make it," she pointed a finger to the room next to mine, "Alec could be wanted for manslaughter, too!"

"What? Are you serious? Why?"

Trish finally took a breath and sat back down. She was so excited. Her mouth was trying to spit out all sorts of information before her brain forgot what she wanted to say. My brain, on the other hand, was beginning to hurt again just trying to keep up with her. Mallory noticed and interjected.

"Trish, slow down. We don't want to traumatize the poor girl any more than she already is." Mallory shot Trish a dirty look. Trish pouted, but closed her mouth.

"First of all, the police are looking for Alec," Mallory said gingerly, explaining everything to me. "On the way to your house, Cailin was run off the road by a white Ford Explorer. He said it was the only car he passed on the way to your house. It just so happens that not too long after we arrived here, a white Ford Explorer hit another car, hit and run, and the guy that was driving the other car was brought here. Cailin talked to Lieutenant LeBrecque. They're going to check prints from your house and the scene of the accident and see if they can trace it back to Alec. Right now, there's an APB out for his arrest for what he's done to you."

I turned my head away. How had it come to this point? My friends, telling me that the police were looking for my ex-husband, who had abused me and may be the cause of another person's demise as well.

"Secondly." Mallory carefully turned my head back to face the two of them, framing my face with her palms. "Don't be ashamed Libba, we're your friends, and we love you and we're going to get through this, together. One for all and all for one, right?" She smiled and nodded to me then to Trish. Trish nodded back but still didn't speak a word.

"Lastly, we've gotten to know Cailin and Mike pretty well these last few hours. They're good guys. And Cailin, well, Trish is right, he's crazy about you. It's driving him mad that Lieutenant LeBrecque hasn't come back and that we haven't heard anything about Alec's whereabouts, but mostly … he's been worried about you. We've been taking turns sitting in here, although Cailin would prefer it better if he could stay in here the whole time, but he does let us rotate. He blames himself for what happened to you."

I started to protest when Mallory raised her hand to stop me. "We all know it's not his fault but none of us can figure out why. Why would Alec do this to you, Libba? Can you not think of any reason?"

I shook my head. I had no idea why Alec would do this to me. I had no idea why he left me in the first place. What I did know was that Alec was drunk and he must have come to the house that way, because I barely had any alcohol at home, only what was left over from our girl's night weeks ago. This was not the first time he hit me after drinking, but it was the first time he put me in the hospital.

"He's hit me before," I whispered.

Neither Trish nor Mallory said anything, but they did exchange a glance. I looked at Trish. "You knew, didn't you?"

"I suspected. No social life, remember? I watch a lot of crime TV and put together the clues." She looked at Mallory, then back at me. "I told Lieutenant LeBrecque."

"What did he say?"

"He said … oh my gosh, I just realized something!" Trish jumped out of her seat, nearly knocking over my IV.

"What?" Mallory and I were both on edge.

"Was Alec having an affair? Lieutenant LeBrecque wondered where Alec was heading to or *who* he was heading to. What if

Alec was having an affair and now, he's on his way to abuse the other lady."

"We can't let that happen," Mallory said. "Libba, do you think Alec was having an affair? Did you see any signs?"

"No. No, I don't know."

Trish turned to Mallory and said, "We have to find out where he's been all this time. Do you think Rowan could help?"

"I'll ask." Mallory looked at her watch. "I'll call him and see what he can do."

"I need my laptop or my cell. I kept all of Alec's appointments and whereabouts on our shared Google calendar. Maybe there's something on it that can help. When are they releasing me anyway?" I was starting to feel energized. If we could find some way to help catch Alec and stop him from hurting someone else, I wanted to do it. It was time I stopped letting Alec win.

Trish pulled out her cell and started for the door, "I need to call Lieutenant LeBrecque. He wanted to interview you when you woke up."

"I'll see if I can locate the doctor and find out how much longer they plan on keeping you, then I'll call Rowan." Mallory grabbed her purse. They were both leaving me.

"But I don't want to be alone."

Mallory looked at me and smiled. "Don't worry, you won't be. I think it's time to rotate." She motioned towards the window that led to the hallway. Cailin was there, standing next to a man who looked similar to him except that he was slightly shorter and had dark hair. The man was holding Olivia who was resting her head on his shoulder. Olivia spotted me and waved, and I waved back. Mallory made to leave but I grabbed her hand first.

"Is that Cailin's brother, Mike, holding Olivia?"

"Yes, they seem to hit if off quickly and he's been quite helpful with her. Cailin, too. They took her down for lunch so we could come in and visit." Mallory looked at Olivia and they made funny faces at each other and Mike and Cailin both started laughing. I looked at the five of them. They really did care for me. Thinking of that warmed my heart and I couldn't help but laugh, too.

Mallory gave me a comb and toothbrush and helped me to the restroom so I could freshen up. When I came back to my bed, Mallory had straightened and tightened the sheets, fluffed the pillows, and folded down the bed coverings like night service at a five-star hotel. Now, she was taking Olivia from Mike's arms.

"Hey, feeling better I see," Cailin said, helping me into bed. "Guess you just needed some girl time."

"Yes, I'm feeling a lot better, thanks." I looked up at Mike. They had the same chin.

"This is my brother, Mike. He already knows who you are."

"It's a pleasure to meet you, Libba." Mike's voice was a little more authoritative than Cailin's, but I could now see how much they favored each other. I could tell they were related; they both had the same cobalt blue eyes.

"Nice meeting you. I'm sorry it's not under better circumstances."

"Yes, well, don't worry about that." I noticed him peek at Mallory and Olivia as they walked away. "You have some good friends. You're lucky."

"Yeah, they are good friends. Thank you, by the way. Thanks to both of you for being here." I looked at Cailin. "Cailin, I don't know what to say."

He put his finger over my lips. "Don't say anything. We'll talk about it later but for now, are you hungry? Do you need anything?"

"Food would be good. And coffee."

"Why don't I go check on that for you?" Mike offered. "I'll leave you and Cailin alone for a while." He left and quietly closed the door behind him.

Cailin leaned back in the chair and crossed one leg. He looked so tired. I wondered if he had slept. He didn't say anything though, just sat, contentedly, watching me. He didn't make me feel uncomfortable; instead, I felt safe and peaceful. I adjusted, turning to lie on one side and I noticed him smile, ever so slightly.

"What are you smiling about?"

"Caught that did you? I was just admiring your curves."

There he goes again speaking exactly what was on his mind. I was beginning to get used to it. I don't think I blushed … that much.

"You look tired," I said. "Did you get any sleep?"

"I slept enough. We all kind of dozed in the waiting room. Your friends are nice. I like them. I can see us hanging out together. Olivia and Noah would get along well, too."

"Who's Noah?"

"Noah is Mike's son. I guess I never told you, did I? Mike is a widower. His wife Ellen died a few years after Noah was born. He's six." Cailin closed his eyes and stretched.

"How awful. I'm sorry to hear that."

"It's all right. It was a while ago and Mike's a survivor. It was hard for him at first, for a long time, but you know, you cope and adjust. He's a great dad." Cailin rearranged himself in his chair, then decided to scoot it closer to me so that our faces were only inches apart.

"Thank you for being there for me. Looks like you've rescued me twice now." I reached out my hand for his and he grabbed it.

He leaned in and tenderly stroked the hair from my face. This time I heard him clearly when he whispered in my ear, "No, Precious, don't you know? You're the one who rescued me."

"Rescued you from what?" I asked.

"From being alone."

A different nurse was now working the dayshift. She brought Libba her lunch, which consisted of dry turkey, dry mashed potatoes, cold corn, hard bread, and unsweetened tea. Cailin was disgusted. He offered to go to the cafeteria and get her something else, but she didn't want him to leave. She pretended to eat but he noticed all she did was move the food around her plate.

"The doctor should be here within the hour," the nurse said. "He's making his last rounds before leaving for the day so it shouldn't take long." She took the tray from Libba's bed. Cailin had charmed her into allowing all of them into Libba's room to visit. Olivia and Mallory sat on the floor coloring when Mike stood up.

"Here comes Lieutenant LeBrecque." Mike looked down at Mallory at the same time she looked up to him. "Olivia, do you want to go to the vending machine with me and get some more donuts."

Mike offered Mallory a hand as she stood up. Cailin noticed Mallory shyly look away as their hands touched.

"Can I, Mommy?"

"Of course, you can." She looked at Mike, "Thanks for doing this. I really don't want her hearing anything, if you know what I mean."

"It's my pleasure." Mike smiled at Mallory and picked up Olivia, then walked out the door as Lieutenant LeBrecque was walking in. Libba sat up in the bed.

"Hi everyone. Ms. Spencer," he added as he nodded at Libba. "I'm Lieutenant LeBrecque. I hope you're feeling better."

"Yes, thank you. It's nice to meet you." They shook hands and Lieutenant LeBrecque took out his notebook.

"I need to ask you a few questions about what happened last night." He looked at everyone in the room who had not budged a bit. "Do you mind if we have some privacy?"

"Sir, I don't mind if they stay. Please, I'd like for them to."

Cailin offered his chair to Mallory and stood next to the bed like Trish, each flanking a side of Libba's bed. "I have nothing to hide."

"Ma'am, I'll need you to give me details. Are you sure you can be explicit with your friends present?"

Cailin noticed the Lieutenant looked specifically at him. "Libba, if you want, I can go," he offered. "Or I can stay, whichever you prefer."

Libba looked at Trish and Mallory. "One for all and all for one, right?" They both nodded.

Cailin wasn't sure if Libba really wanted him there or not, but he assumed it would be easier for her if Trish and Mallory were by her side. She didn't ask him to leave, so he stayed, and put his hand on her shoulder.

Libba probably thought the gesture was for her moral support but Cailin knew it was more to brace himself for what he was about to hear. This was the moment he had been dreading. He was curious and wanted to know exactly what that bastard had done to her, but he wasn't sure how well he could handle hearing it, especially coming from Libba's own perspective. He knew it would be hard for her to relive the night's events and he wanted to be there for her. He wanted to hurt the son of a bitch who did this to her and make him pay, but Cailin thought of himself as a fair man, and before he came face to face with Alec, it was best he knew the whole story.

Lieutenant LeBrecque looked at the four of them. "Very well then. I'll have to ask that no one interrupts Ms. Spencer while she gives her statement."

Lieutenant LeBrecque asked Libba a series of questions and Libba answered everything as truthfully as she could. It was hard for her, Cailin could tell, but she didn't falter, and he never removed his hand from her side. Libba told Lieutenant LeBrecque about the previous times Alec had abused her and how he would drink and drive when they were younger and in high school. He asked about the type of work Alec did and the places he traveled on business trips, family history, and regular behaviors and routines. Lieutenant LeBrecque was very thorough with his interview and Cailin noticed he seemed to take more notes than when Cailin had spoken with him. Cailin was relieved when Lieutenant LeBrecque closed his notebook and stood up. The questioning was finally over.

"I only have one suggestion, if you don't mind." At that, Lieutenant LeBrecque looked at all four of them. "Ms. Spencer, I think it would be a good idea if you could stay with one of your friends for a few days, give us some time to find your ex-husband. I've got your information and will call you as soon as I have a lead, but if you think of anything, if any of you do, please call me immediately."

"We will." Cailin shook his hand and walked him to the door. When he turned back around, Mallory was handing Libba a tissue to wipe her eyes. Cailin had stood behind her and could not see her face while she spoke, but now that he could, oh how hard that must have been for her. Even Trish's eyes were a little puffy. Cailin felt sorry for all three of them, but as he looked at them, he witnessed a bond that he knew was rare. Even in the midst of this entire calamity, he could see their friendship shine through all the darkness that surrounded them. Theirs was truly a strong friendship and they were right—one for all and all for one.

CHAPTER 10

LETTING GO

My eyelids were getting heavy. I was starting to feel the effects of the pain medication I received before checking out of the hospital. I watched Noah and Olivia playing in Trish's backyard; Noah was showing Olivia the new soccer skills he had learned. Cailin was right; the kids hit it off quickly and were having such fun playing together.

Trish was inside cleaning her condo before the others returned. The police had taken photos and fingerprints and were now analyzing the information, so they agreed to let Cailin, Mike, and Mallory go into my house. Cailin and Mike were cleaning up and repairing the back door, while Mallory was grabbing my laptop and packing my bag. I would be staying with Trish until the police found Alec, which hopefully wouldn't take too long. I wanted to stay at my own home but at the insistence of everyone, especially Cailin, I finally caved in and agreed to stay with Trish. Trish was excited to have a temporary roommate.

It didn't take long for the trio to return. On their way back, they stopped and picked up pizza, hot wings, and a few sodas. Trish's little condo was crowded with all seven of us inside, but no one seemed to mind or complain. I looked around and couldn't believe how well everyone was getting along. To think, a few months ago I barely had any friends and would never have been amid such a friendly gathering. Today, right after the most tragic thing to ever happen to me, I was surrounded by a whole group of loved ones. I hated the misfortune that fate seemed to drop on me so abruptly, but then again, I was grateful for it, for fate had also brought me two best friends and equally as important, it had brought Cailin into my life.

Cailin sat down on the couch and motioned for me to join him.

"You okay? You look a little tired?" he asked.

"I'm fine." I sat down next to Cailin and he wrapped his arms around me, turning me slightly so he could get a better look at my face. My left eye was slowly starting to look a little better, I thought.

"Well, Libba," Mallory said, walking up to us. "I'm going to call an Uber so Olivia and I can go home. She needs a good night's rest, and we have mass in the morning."

"Ok thanks for coming out and staying so long," I turned to Cailin, "Oh! Do you think Mike could—"

"Hey Mike! Do you think you could give Mallory and Olivia a ride home?" Calin called to Mike.

"Oh no, I couldn't ask that! He's already done so much today," Mallory said. "We can take an Uber, really."

"That's nonsense, I don't mind." Mike grabbed Olivia's bunny rabbit and Noah's soccer ball. "Noah! Time to go," he called.

Mallory looked at me, her eyes growing wider and wider. I smirked and snuggled into Cailin's arms. He tried to conceal his delight but couldn't help but grin. He turned his head and buried himself in my hair trying to hide from Mallory's view. Trish snorted and turned her back, quickly pretending to cough. Mike didn't seem to notice a thing. He was too busy collecting the kids.

"Ladies, it was a pleasure meeting you." Mike tipped his head to me and Trish and handed Olivia her bunny rabbit. "Despite the circumstances, I had a good time. We need to do this again."

"Mommy, can we watch Noah's soccer game tomorrow?" Olivia was holding her bunny and flashing her big dark eyes at Mallory. I doubt Mallory could ever refuse when her daughter looked at her that way.

"Please Ms. MacDonald" Noah begged. "The only ones to ever watch my games are Dad, Uncle Cailin, and the Stanleys."

Mallory seemed stunned. She looked around the room no doubt putting two and two together; even the children were ganging up on her. She looked at Mike and held his gaze, staring into his eyes. They were as deep as a blue ocean and gave off a sense of tranquility. Mallory shook her head and then turned away.

"We'll talk about it in the car. Come on kids. Let's go." She politely smiled at me and Cailin and grabbed Olivia's hand, then started for the door. *Playing matchmaker, are they? Well, they'll just have to wait until tomorrow to see what I decide. That will show them,* she thought.

Trish could no longer hold in her laughter. As soon as the door closed, she burst out laughing.

"HA! Did you see her face? Oh, you guys are in for it! You know she knows what you're up to."

"What, I'm not up to anything?" Cailin said coolly. "I just figured why get an Uber when Mike could take her home. I'm sure he didn't mind, he probably needed to get Noah home too."

"Are you going to watch Noah's game?" I asked sleepily.

"I normally do. I can pick you up if you want to go," he said, now twirling my hair in his fingers.

"Hey if everyone else is going, then I am, too!" Trish said.

"We don't know if Mallory and Olivia are going or not, but I'm sure if you call and tell her we'll all be there, then they'll go, too." Cailin looked at the two of us. "Mike will be pleased. I think he's developing a thing for your friend, Mallory."

"Really," said Trish, obviously not having noticed a thing between the two of them over the past fifteen hours.

"And why do you say that?" I didn't want to tell him that I saw Mike watching Mallory at the hospital.

"I just have a feeling, that's all," he said.

Cailin was now preoccupied, playing with my hair, and inhaling my scent. I had showered while he was gone and now, relaxing in his arms, I was ready to fall asleep at any moment.

Trish looked at the two of them. They made a handsome couple. She thought about Mike and Mallory. They could be a perfect couple, too, instant family. She, on the other hand, didn't have anyone. There was no one that she was interested in or anyone who was interested in her. She *had* been fine with being single, but now that one of her best friends was dating and soon her other best friend would be dating, too, where did that leave her? She sulked.

"I'll call Mallory and tell her we're all going to Noah's game, then I think I'm going to bed. Cailin, would you mind locking up when you leave?"

"Um, I will," he said. He looked at Libba; she had closed her eyes and her body was settling into his. He wasn't leaving just yet. He liked the way her body fit next to his. Plus, his heart wasn't ready for the absence of her. Two nights earlier, he had turned down his chance to watch her sleep only to have her get hurt. Tonight, he would stay awhile to make sure she was safe, and to make sure his heart was safe.

I woke the next day feeling much better. Trish had allowed me to sleep in and it was already nearing noon. I knew Cailin must have tucked me in, because I didn't remember how I had gotten to bed. I wish I could have been awake for that, when Cailin carried me to bed. The next time, I would make sure I was awake, wide awake. I smiled to myself at the thought.

I walked into the kitchen. Trish was making coffee. "Sleep okay?" she asked.

"Yeah, thanks. What time did Cailin leave, do you know?"

"No, but he left you a note." Trish pointed to a piece of paper on the table. "Mallory didn't answer last night but I left her a message and sent her a text that we would be at Noah's game. I bet she'll be there."

I picked up the note and read: *Miss you already. I'll pick you two up at 12:30.*

"Libba, can I ask you something?" Trish handed me a cup of coffee and sat down. She didn't wait for a reply. "I think you and Cailin make a great couple and I think he really, *really* likes you."

"Yeah," I sighed. "I think I really, *really* like him, too."

"Yeah! Sooo, tell me, how was it last night?" Trish seemed eager to hear all the juicy details.

"What do you mean?" I caught a glimpse of Trish's fiendish smile. "Trish!" I gasped.

"You mean you didn't sleep with him?"

"No! … No! I guess he carried me to bed but that's all, and I don't even remember that. Trish, I just got out of the hospital. I don't think Cailin is the type to take advantage of a woman right out of the hospital."

"Ok, ok. I just wondered. Gee. But when he was playing with your hair last night, I swear he looked like he was willing."

"You think?" I crinkled my nose. It flattered me to hear that someone thought Cailin wanted to have sex with me. Shoot, I was flattered to hear that anyone wanted to have sex with me. I have always been self-conscious and to think that someone saw me in *that* way, and that it was noticed by one of my best friends, well …

"Duh! I give it a week."

"Trish! You're unbearable." I looked at the time. "I'm going to shower. He'll be here soon."

Libba was still drying her hair when Cailin arrived.

He stood at the door watching his precious fairy. He liked the way her fingers ran through her golden locks; how she lifted her hair and it fell down her back like rays of sunlight. The air from the blow dryer shot her scent toward him arousing him more than it should. He imaged himself taking her to bed right then and there, but he knew he couldn't. He shouldn't.

Libba saw him watching her in the mirror and turned to face him. Cailin didn't immediately move; at the moment he had untamed thoughts on his mind. He raised an eyebrow at Libba and gave a half smile, then crossed his arms in front of his chest.

For seconds, Libba stood there, waiting for his next move.

Slowly, Cailin began to walk, stopping directly in front of her. He leaned down and skimmed her cheek softly with his lips. Her face was warm, *so warm*, he thought, and he noticed she had closed her eyes and was shaking ever so slightly.

"Why are you trembling? I haven't even kissed you yet," he whispered into her ear.

Cailin kissed Libba slowly and gently as if committing the moment to memory. She parted her lips slightly and his tongue entered, smooth and warm. For now, he only wanted to give Libba a small taste, which was more than enough to tempt and leave her wanting more. He stopped and tucked a piece of hair behind her ear. Her eyes were still closed, and he saw her sway just a little, before stepping away from her.

"I'll let you finish getting ready now," again he whispered, and then turned and walked out of the room.

Libba stood frozen on the spot. Finally, she managed to breathe and open her eyes.

When they arrived at Noah's game, the others were already there talking to the Stanleys while Noah was warming up on the field.

Martha and Mallory were in the middle of a conversation when Martha looked up and saw Cailin walking toward them. He was carrying a bunch of lawn chairs and was flanked on both sides by two beautiful women, one blond, the other a redhead. Martha knew Libba was the blond, and she beamed at the sight of them. She was finally going to meet the girl who had stolen Cailin's heart.

"Hi Martha," Cailin dropped the chairs on the ground and kissed Martha's cheek.

"Two beautiful women, Cailin? What, one wasn't enough for you?" Louis joked and shook hands with Cailin.

Cailin could only grin.

"I see Mike must have already introduced you to Mallory and Olivia. Martha, Louis, this is Trish Knight," he gestured to Trish, who was on his left, and they all shook hands. "And this is Libba Spencer," he said as he lightly rubbed the small of Libba's back.

"So, *you're* the girl who's ruffled Cailin's feathers," said Louis. Libba blushed.

Martha reached over and gave Libba a careful hug. "It's so nice to finally meet you, darling." She looked at the three ladies standing in front of her. "It's nice to meet all of you. I see why my boys were running all over town in the middle of the night." She turned to Libba. "I'm so sorry for what happened to you, dear. I hope you're feeling a little better."

"Yes, a little better thank you," said Libba, who didn't seem at all embarrassed that the Stanleys were aware of what happened to her. In fact, if Martha had to guess, Libba was probably relieved that she didn't have to explain the black eye—though barely noticeable under her makeup—that she was still trying to hide with her sunglasses.

Cailin arranged the chairs on the lawn so the ladies could sit down. Instantly, they fell into conversation. Martha watched Cailin as he stood behind Libba's chair talking to Louis. Mike and Olivia were running up and down the sidelines. Every time Noah ran by the gang, he would wave, and Martha was afraid he might lose sight of the ball several times, but she knew he was excited because this was the largest group that had ever came to one of his games to watch him play.

"Go, Noah!" Olivia yelled, jumping up and down.

Noah played a hard game. The first half, he played striker, outrunning all the other kids on the field. He scored four goals for his team while the other team only scored twice. During the second half, Noah played goalie, or keeper, as Louis called it, and not a single ball passed him. His teammates scored another three goals winning the game, seven to two. After both teams shook hands and were released to their parents, Martha watched as Noah ran straight up to Mallory.

"Ms. MacDonald, Ms. MacDonald! Did you see? We won, we won!" He gave her a big hug. Olivia joined in. Mallory wrapped her arms around the two of them and they all started jumping up and down, cheering and laughing. Mallory kissed Noah on the top of his head then looked up. Mike was watching her.

Within seconds, everyone was joining in on the celebration, but Olivia seemed most excited; this was the first soccer game she had ever gone to and it was obvious that she thought Noah was the best player from either team. Martha could tell Olivia was in awe of Noah, so she took her with Noah to get an after-game snack while the others packed to get ready to leave.

As they were returning, Martha saw Mallory approaching

Mike, who was now helping Cailin pack all the chairs. Mike stopped what he was doing and faced Mallory and Martha couldn't quite read the confused expression on Mike's face, but she did hear what they were saying.

"Thank you for coming to the game today, Mallory. It means a lot to Noah ... and to me."

"It was a lot of fun," Mallory replied. "Thanks for inviting us. Noah is a very good player. You must be proud."

Suddenly Martha had an idea. "How about everyone comes back to our house for burgers?" she suggested, eyeing both Cailin and Mike.

"Fine with me," Cailin said. "Libba, Trish, sound good?"

They nodded.

Mallory turned to Mike.

"I'd love to Martha," Mike said as he gathered his things, "but we need to get home. I have some work to do."

"Dad, *please*," Noah begged. "Everyone else is going. You're going, too, right, Ms. MacDonald?"

Mike looked at Mallory.

Martha could tell Mallory wasn't sure what to say. For some odd reason, Martha had the feeling that Mike did not want to go if Mallory was going to be there. Martha knew without a doubt that Olivia wanted to go, and she hoped Mallory wanted to also. Martha liked seeing everyone hanging out together and if Mike weren't there, how could anyone play matchmaker.

Mallory looked at Noah. "Mike, if you have things to do, Noah can ride with us and I can drop him off later. After all, I do owe you a favor?"

"Fine then," Mike mumbled. "Yes ... I think that will be fine, thank you."

Martha noticed Cailin looking at Mike, no doubt questioning his sudden odd behavior just as she was.

They walked in groups to the parking lot. Martha walked

with Louis and Mike, Mallory with the kids, and Cailin, Libba, and Trish made another group. When Mallory turned toward her car, Mike slowed his pace, watching as Noah helped Olivia into her car seat, and then Mallory checked both children before getting into the driver's seat. They waved as they left.

Martha noticed Mike as he tried to fake a smile, then he shoved his thumbs into his front pockets and walked, head down, toward his car. Martha wasn't sure what to make of that.

"Come on, slow poke," Louis said as he opened the door for Martha. "We've got burgers to make."

"Yes, dear," she said as she glanced one more time at Mike, who was already in his car, backing out of the lot.

Everyone was sitting on the back deck laughing. Louis was telling stories of Cailin, Mike, and Ginny when they were younger. Ginny had stopped by to drop off some new books and magazines for Martha.

Martha stood up. "Cailin, do you mind giving me a hand in the kitchen? I think Louis can entertain all these beautiful women by himself for a while."

Cailin knew Martha was going to question him about Mike. He walked into the kitchen and started piling up plates and utensils.

"Before you ask, I should tell you, I don't know, Martha."

"What are you talking about, Cailin?"

"You're going to ask me why Mike really didn't want to come, and I don't know. I thought he would enjoy being here. He had such a good time with everyone yesterday at Trish's house, so I don't know why he didn't come today."

"Huh. I'm surprised you don't see it." Martha pulled the ketchup and mustard from the refrigerator. "You're his brother after all."

"Oh, I *saw* it Martha. I'm a little sharper than that, you know,"

Cailin joked as he grabbed some napkins from the cabinet. "I'm quite sure Mike likes Mallory and that's why I'm confused as to why he's not here. Maybe she said something to him on the way home last night when he gave her a ride or, I don't know, maybe he really had things to do."

"Or he's just as confused as you are." Martha took the French fries out of the oven and tossed them into a basket, shaking salt on top of them. "To think, one Wade brother is afraid to let go of the past, while the other is afraid to accept his future. Well, the one thing I hope you boys are mindful of is the here and the now, Cailin. Don't be afraid to accept the gifts God gives you. He knows what's right for you, when it's right for you, and *who* is right for you."

"Oh, Martha, I think you may be the one confused now."

Martha looked at Cailin with chagrin. "And what do you mean by that?"

"You may be right, maybe Mike is afraid of letting go of Ellen. Mallory would be the first woman he's even been slightly interested in since Ellen died and I'm sure he's battling himself over whether Ellen would approve or not. But you're wrong about *this* Wade brother." Cailin piled everything they collected onto a big tray and picked it up. "I've seen my future, she's right outside that door, and I'm more ready for it than you think."

Martha opened her mouth, but before she could even comment, Cailin winked at her and walked out onto the deck.

When Mallory pulled into Mike's driveway, she had the weirdest sensation of déjà vu. It was like she was driving home after having been away for a long time. It was a comforting feeling that felt natural and instinctive. She parked the car and shut down the engine, and for a few seconds she sat there enjoying the feeling. When she realized Noah had taken off his seatbelt, she got out of the car and opened the door for him. Olivia had fallen asleep within five minutes of driving, so Mallory left her locked in the car seat and was careful not to awaken her.

Mike was waiting at the door as she walked up with Noah.

"Thank you, Ms. MacDonald," Noah said wrapping his arms around Mallory's waist and giving her a big hug. Mallory bent down and kissed the top of his head.

"It was my pleasure, Noah. And thank you for playing with Olivia all day. I know she had a lot of fun."

Noah ran into the house grinning and giving Mike a high five as he passed.

Mike leaned against the doorway staring at Mallory, one hand in his pocket, the other holding a bottled water. Mallory returned his stare. She wasn't sure but he looked … mournful?

"Is everything all right?" she asked, cocking her head to one side.

"Yes. Thanks for taking Noah today. I would have hated it if he couldn't have fun with everyone on my occasion."

"It wasn't a problem at all. Did you get a lot of work done?" Mallory noticed a lot of boxes strewn on the living room floor. Mike adjusted his stance, blocking her view any further but getting a better view of her car.

"Yes, I did, thanks. I'd ask you to come in, but my guess is that Olivia is sleeping," he said with a tone of finality to it.

"Yes, she is. Well, goodnight then. See you later." Mallory started for her car.

"Sure, see you later."

From her car, Mallory could see Mike turn around and go inside.

Mike listened as Mallory drove away, then he packed all the photos back into the many boxes scattered on the floor. When he got to his favorite picture of Ellen he stopped and stared at it for a long while. Finally, he smiled and kissed the picture.

"Ellen, I'll always love you." He carefully placed the photo

back in the box and secured the lid, saying goodbye to his first
love and closing the door to his past.

Throughout the following weeks, Trish and I carpooled to work
every day. She was careful not to let me out of her sight. I think
she must have been under Cailin's strict rules, but I didn't ask. I
didn't want to seem ungrateful even though it was a bit unnerv-
ing. Cailin was busy mobilizing a new project and was only able
to call, not visit, for days. Jared told him the victim from the hit
and run suffered one broken rib from the air bag and a shoulder
burn from the seat belt, not much damage considering the extent
of the accident.

Lieutenant LeBrecque called and said the prints at my house
and those at the scene of the hit and run matched. Now, Alec was
wanted on both charges. I spent the time going through Alec's calendar and even our bank statements trying to find anything that
might help Lieutenant LeBrecque determine his whereabouts but
to no avail. Of course, he would never leave a paper trail. Alec was
thorough and I was sure he would not leave any sign of his plot.

Mallory talked to Rowan who was starting a side investigation
of his own. He had called in favors from some of his friends but so
far, he too had not found anything to help.

The end of the week had finally arrived, and Trish and I decided to take advantage of our half day Friday to go shopping.
Later, we met up with Mallory at the coffee shop. Olivia was
spending the weekend with a friend who was having a birthday
party sleepover.

"What are we doing tonight? I'm childfree until five o'clock on
Sunday and I don't want to waste any time," Mallory said sipping
on her Caramel Macchiato.

"I was thinking of going by my house and checking up on

things," I said, "maybe even staying there tonight. I'm sorry, Trish, but I'm beginning to feel like I've overstayed my welcome and I think it will be all right if I stayed at my house from now on."

"But we don't know where Alec is, Libba." Trish popped a chocolate covered coffee bean into her mouth. "We agreed, you're not staying there alone until we do. We'll go with you so you can pick up some more of your things."

Mallory yelped and I noticed she slightly jumped out of her seat.

What kind of noise was that, I thought? "Was that a hiccup?"

"Sorry," said Mallory. "Sometimes I do that. I think it means that something either really great or really terrible is about to happen. I just never know which."

"Or maybe it means you just have gas!"

"That was a good one Trish," I laughed. "Come on let's go into that shop there. I'd like some new lingerie." We all laughed and got up to cross the street.

As we left the coffee shop Mallory leaned against a brown Chevy Astro with a Grateful Dead sticker on it, so she could tighten the lace on her boot. She yelped again and this time I noticed goose bumps on her arms.

We finished shopping and headed back to my place. I bought more lingerie than I planned. I wanted all of *that* type of clothing to be new for when Cailin and I became intimate. I had a feeling the time was drawing nearer and nearer, and I knew I was ready for it. I was ready to let go of the past and accept my future. A future I knew would include Cailin.

Jennifer took her time packing her bags. A plane ticket to Las Vegas sat on the dresser next to her purse. By lunchtime the next day, she would be out of this town and on her way to having the time of her life. Tonight, she would stay in a hotel and then, in the morning, she would stop by the nursing home to say goodbye to her grandmother; after all, she was the woman who had raised her. That was the least she could do.

Her grandmother enjoyed their visits and Jennifer did, too. She hoped her grandmother would be okay with not seeing her for a while, but she knew there was no need to worry. Her grandmother would be fine; she was a survivor and so was Jennifer. Her grandmother understood that Jennifer wasn't the type to stay in one city for long. By now her grandmother was used to her comings and goings, and probably even expected that it was time for Jennifer to move on. Like always, Jennifer would say goodbye before she left and, like always, she would cry and promise to come back as soon as she could.

There was a knock at the door; the taxi driver was early.

"I'll be right there," she called. Jennifer took one last look around the house, grabbed her bag and opened the door.

"Where do you think you're going?" Before Jennifer could say anything, she was hit on the head with a hard object. She fell to the ground and was able to manage a dim look at the man standing in front of her before she blacked out.

CHAPTER 11

PATIENCE

I stayed at Trish's for over a month and it was time for fresh clothing. Of course, Trish and Mallory did not let me go home by myself. When I walked into the house a terrible dread came over me. My house seemed very empty and deserted. I felt no warmth or connection to it. It was neither a place filled with joy nor grief. It was simply there—a dwelling, a house but not a home.

I thought about the Stanleys' house. That was a home. A home filled with love and laughter and many good memories that floated in the air. Trish's condo was full of energy and excitement, and even Mallory's apartment spoke of a child's love and fun times.

My house had no stories to tell except for one that I was trying my best to forget.

"I think I'm going to put my house up for sale," I said out of the blue.

"You are? Why do you want to do that?" asked Mallory.

"Well, I won't be getting back with Alec—not that I want to—and I think I need to start over, start everything over. I want everything to be new: a new house, a new car, a new wardrobe, everything. I want a clean fresh start."

"Do it," Trish said grabbing the remote control and turning on the television.

"Don't you think you should think about this for a while first, Libba?" Mallory asked. "I mean, you don't need any added stress in your life right now and selling a house can be quite stressful."

"Oh Mallory, don't be such a sour puss. If she wants to sell the damn house, then let her put it up for sell." Trish surfed through the channels. One news channel covered some sort of peaceful protest while the local news covered a missing woman. Trish finally settled for the food channel.

"I'm not a sour puss! I'm just trying to be reasonable. If Libba thinks through all this and still decides to sell the house, then I'm all for it. I'll even help her pack. But for her to sell it on a whim is not sensible."

"Come on, ladies," I said, "I was just thinking out loud. And Trish, Mallory is not a sour puss. She's probably right … I don't need any more stress right now." I sighed.

No, I didn't need any more stress than what I was already going through. Alec was still out there somewhere. For all I knew he could be watching us right now, but I felt safe with Trish and Mallory. Surely, Alec wouldn't be stupid enough to try anything with witnesses around. I wished the police or Rowan could find something but so far neither one had.

We hung out at my house for a while, raiding the cabinet for any snacks that might soon be expiring. I tossed around several outfits trying to figure out what to pack for my next week at Trish's house. It was more like cleaning out my closet than packing. The idea of a new wardrobe was still on my mind. I finally finished packing my bag, then I grabbed my mail and we all headed out the door.

My cell rang. It was Lieutenant LeBrecque. He agreed to meet us over at Trish's house. I called Cailin to let him know and he said he was already on his way to pick me up for our date.

Cailin was at Trish's for a few minutes when Lieutenant LeBrecque arrived. He only had a little bit of information but wanted to share it with us. The car from the hit and run belonged to a woman by the name of Regina Smith, who had reported her car missing after she'd gotten off work that evening. Apparently, Alec had rented a post office box in Raleigh, a city about three hours away, so he most likely was living in that area. The post office was located only a few blocks away from where the car had been stolen. Lieutenant LeBrecque was working closely with the Raleigh police, who were also on the lookout for Alec. He was still investigating but he wanted us to know what he had found out. In the meantime, he suggested that I continue to stay with someone since Alec was still on the run.

"Thank you for coming, Robert." Trish stood up to walk Lieutenant LeBrecque to the door. Mallory and I exchanged a glance at each other.

When Trish returned, Mallory spoke first.

"Well, that was awfully nice of *Robert* to come by and tell us the news." She looked at me and we both giggled.

"Very funny," said Trish. We continued to laugh. "Hey now! He said I could call him Robert. Is that a crime?"

"You tell us, has he handcuffed you yet!" Mallory was really laughing now. She was working on her second glass of wine and getting a little tipsy.

"I'm lost. Is there something going on that I should be aware of?" Cailin must not have noticed Trish's informality with Lieutenant LeBrecque.

"NO, THERE'S NOT" Trish barked. "And you guys better get going before I make you take Mallory with you!"

Mallory made to lock her mouth and throw away the key, but she managed one last laugh before she did. I jumped up and grabbed my jacket. I knew Trish and if she got mad enough, she would definitely send Mallory with us.

"Come on, Cailin," I said, grabbing his hand and inching out of the room. "See you ladies later. Don't wait up for me!" I grinned as Cailin and I backed out the door.

"What are we doing tonight?" I asked as we got into his truck.

"Oh, I thought I would stick to the traditional dinner and a movie, if that's all right with you."

"Sure. As long as I get to pick the movie." Cailin looked apprehensive, no doubt wondering what movie I would want to watch. I smiled cunningly. He would have to be patient to find out.

Cailin was craving pasta so we decided to eat at a little Italian restaurant not too far from Trish's condo. Cailin requested a table tucked away in the back of the restaurant. It was refreshing to get away from the chaos of the past few weeks. I was working on a new initiative at work and it was taking up much of my time. Cailin had been traveling two to three days out of the week for a project he was working on and we both needed a break. Tonight, I only wanted to concentrate on Cailin and me, and it seemed like Cailin wanted the same thing, too. He talked a lot but in a relaxed, laid-back sort of way, and every now and then, when I looked at him, it seemed as though he had other things on his mind, like he was scheming. I hoped he was thinking of the two of us and how our night might progress. I know that's what I was thinking about.

"Have you thought about what movie we should watch," he asked lazily.

"Uh-huh. Tell me, what do you prefer, comedy or a chick flick?" I purposely was trying to make him panic.

"Neither! Is that what you're really in the mood for?" Oh, if he only knew what I was really in the mood for.

I chuckled. "Don't worry I was thinking about that new Wonder Woman movie. I think I'd like some action tonight."

"Oh, I'm fairly certain they'll be some action tonight." Cailin put on a devilish smile.

This time, I reciprocated.

"I hope so," I said, looking him in the eyes and holding his gaze.

They'd been going out for well over a month, but it would be the first time that Cailin brought her back to his place. Perhaps it might be a first time for something else, too. He couldn't believe he had waited this long to be with Libba. With other girls, he would have bedded them a long time ago. In fact, it wasn't unlike him to sleep with someone on their first, and only, date. But Libba was different. Not only because of when they met and the things that happened between them, but because he wanted to make sure their first time was special, because Libba was special.

Cailin had called Merry Maids to clean his house. Having traveled so much lately, he had not spent much time cleaning after himself and it was beginning to look like a bachelor's pad with clothes strewn on the floor and dishes piling up on the counter. Cailin loved his house. It was always a favorite of his growing up and when he noticed the 'For Sale' sign while driving by one day, he stopped and knocked on the door. He told the owner he was going to buy the house; Cailin had not even looked at the inside.

After Mike's wife died, Cailin and Mike lived in their parent's house raising Noah together but when Noah turned four and started preschool, Mike suggested that perhaps one of them move out. Mike wanted Cailin to have a normal life, as he called it, one that included his older brother dating and not babysitting. Cailin knew Mike felt guilty about the two of them living together. Mike always seemed to feel like he was taking advantage of Cailin. What Mike didn't understand was that Cailin liked helping to raise Noah. He wasn't sure when or if he would ever have a child, and Noah was his only nephew. He loved him like a son and wanted him to grow up in the house that he and Mike had made so many fond memories.

Cailin's house sat high up on the mountain. The back of the house had a deck that covered the entire rear and from the back deck that overlooked the valley, you could see the tops of the buildings of Blowing Rock Village. A glass sliding door led from the living room to the deck and from the deck there was another set of doors leading to the master bedroom. A wide two-way, built-in fireplace separated a small sitting area just outside the master bedroom from the rest of the long expansive deck.

Sometimes, he imaged himself married with kids running around the house, playing hide and seek or flashlight tag in the middle of the night. Other times, he saw himself sitting alone on the back deck, drinking a beer, and listening to music. He never knew which dream would hold his future, but he was quite content with either outcome. That was, until he met Libba. Now, he wasn't so sure if he could stand the latter. He was itching for change, for a new adventure as Mike had called it, but he would have to be patient to get there.

Libba walked in and seemed amazed at the beautiful interior. The house was a single-story ranch. It boasted hardwood floors throughout and a huge immaculate kitchen displayed granite counters and ceramic tile flooring. Warm colors donned the entire space creating a wonderful feeling of home comfort. There was even a huge fire crackling in the fireplace.

"Wow … this is beautiful," she said, quietly walking around and noticing all the horse brass, large antique keys, and antique ginger bottles. He had not overdone one collection and all the pieces were perfectly placed in just the right spot. Libba stopped in front of the fireplace admiring the painting showcased over the mantel.

"Is this *Crossing the Breaks* by G. Harvey?"

"Yes, it is. You know his work?" Cailin didn't walk with Libba but his eyes followed her.

"Only a little. I like how you have it displayed with the musket." Libba's hand hovered over the mid-eighteen-hundred Turkish musket, being careful not to touch it.

"Thank you. And in case you're wondering, no I didn't decorate the place. I mean, I found all the antiques and trinkets, but Ginny and Martha put it together for me to make it work. I knew what I wanted, but I didn't know how to show it and they have a knack for that sort of thing."

"I'll say. They did a wonderful job." Libba stopped in front of a horse that stood about eighteen inches tall. It was decorated in bright colors of blue, pink, green, and yellow. Cailin noticed how her eyes sparkled; she appreciated antiques as much as he did.

"Lovely, absolutely lovely. Where did you find this one?"

"Actually, I bought that piece at Hanna's in town when my parents were still alive. It's one of my earliest acquisitions, I guess you could say."

"Cloisonné."

"Pardon?"

"This is cloisonné. Your horse, the way it's decorated is called cloisonné. You see, the makers take these little filaments and attach it to the surface exactly how they want the design to look. Then it's filled with colored paste enamel and heated. The enamel, or cloisons, is so closely joined, so smooth, that it seems like a paintbrush changed colors in mid stroke. If you close your eyes it would all feel as if it were one pattern but in reality, its many patterns put together."

Libba closed her eyes and ran her hand across the horse's back. As Libba touched the horse, Cailin realized he could no longer watch her from across the room. He wanted to be near her to feel her touch, too. He walked toward her, but she didn't notice him approaching and she turned to step into the kitchen.

"Do you actually like to cook, or do you just have a gourmet kitchen for the heck of it."

"Believe it or not, I love to cook. I'm no chef or anything but I'm rather good at throwing things together that somehow end up tasting pretty decent. At least to me, anyway. I'm especially good at breakfast." Cailin moved closer to Libba. He rubbed her cheek with the back of his hand and stared deep into her hazel eyes. He thought he could feel the blood pumping in her veins. *Patience, Cailin*, he thought. *Not yet … let the desire run through her.* He took her hand and guided her to another room.

He walked around showing her most of the house, being careful not to take her to his bedroom; he didn't want to seduce her too soon. Back in the kitchen, Cailin opened a bottle of wine then they returned to the living room. They moved in front of the glass door and Cailin pulled the curtains revealing a soft glow of lights from down in the valley.

Libba stood in front of Cailin and stared out the window. The view was breathtaking. She sipped her wine and sat the glass on a table, rubbing the back of her neck.

"Here, let me. Just relax." With one hand Cailin massaged the nape of Libba's neck.

"Um, that feels good," she shrugged her shoulders in a most seductive way.

"And how does this feel?" Cailin bent his head and gently brushed his lips to her temples.

"That feels even better."

Libba's breathing quickened, tempting him even more. With both hands Cailin gently rubbed her skin, sliding her bra straps down her shoulders. Libba did not object; she tilted her neck encouraging him to do more. His nose skimmed the line of her collarbone as he smelled her sweet scent, tasting her with his tongue. He moved slowly, ever so slowly, taking his time to caress and tease, tease and caress. *Patience, Cailin, let her enjoy ... pleasure her first.*

Libba moaned and her chest rose. That did not go unnoticed by Cailin.

His hands moved forward finding what he so desired. Her nipples hardened beneath his hands, arousing him as she leaned her body into him. Their bodies molded together, him leaning into her, her back into him. They fit together like a perfect puzzle connecting at just the right notch.

Cailin moved his hands lower, Libba's body adjusted slightly and she moved her hand to his thigh, squeezing lightly. Slowly, he lifted the hem of her dress and ran his hands along her legs then to the small of her waist, thumbing the top of her panties. Libba touched one of his hands and Cailin paused, waiting to see if he should stop. Libba moved his hand inside her panties and he found the wet spot between her legs. She panted as she breathed in time with every stroke of his fingers. Their bodies danced to the rhythm of an unheard song; their hearts in harmony with one another.

Cailin looked up and saw their reflection in the glass. Libba looked so beautiful, her body so perfect. He nuzzled her head and directed her to look at their reflection, too.

"Do you see?"

Libba looked and then closed her eyes.

"Precious," he sucked at her neck. "Open your eyes." He plunged his fingers deeper inside her, driving them in and out, in and out.

Libba opened her eyes.

"That's it, Precious. Relax. Watch."

Cailin pressed Libba closer so she could feel the strength of his erection through his pants. She reached back and grabbed his hips, forcing him to thrust harder and harder. He watched as her breasts bounced with every thrust of his hips. Cailin loved the shape of her breast; he wanted to see them, he needed to taste them. With his free hand he cupped her breast. It was so firm, just like he imagined. He squeezed her breast a little harder, holding her body to his, pressing tighter and tighter, thrusting harder and harder, until he felt her body quake around his fingers inside her. Libba reached down and found the bottom of her dress. Cailin paused so she could pull it over her head and take off her bra. Now he could see the beauty of her breasts and feel the soft skin around her hard nipples. She turned to face him. Her nipples ached for the heat of his hot breath. He leaned down and grabbed them between his teeth, sucking and tasting with his tongue, with his lips, while his fingers found its way back to her warmth.

He wanted to scoop her up and take her to bed right then but not yet, he would wait. *Patience, Cailin*, he told himself again. He would pleasure her in several different ways before allowing his own release. He wanted to find out what she enjoyed and how she enjoyed doing it.

Libba couldn't help but run her hands through Cailin's hair. She held on as if letting go of him would stop him from completing his task. Cailin felt her soul come to life with every flick of his tongue as if her soul were buried deep inside her and only he could suck it out.

Libba ran her hands down Cailin's back. He pulled her close and grabbed one of her legs, sliding his hand under her thigh and lifting her leg off the ground. Cailin held her tight and rocked with her until her hips bucked and he knew she was about to reach her point. Libba's soul swelled with delight and encompassed her entire being and as her soul crept to life, she arched her back in anticipation of what was to come. Cailin drove his fingers faster and faster, deeper and deeper, until he felt her body tremble in utter satisfaction. Cailin could have sworn he saw her soul lift right out of her body and settle on top of her heart. He felt her entire body erupt, and she then fell limp against his chest.

Cailin wrapped his arms around her waist and stared at their reflection. He could hold her like this forever he thought. He leaned down, softly kissed her cheek, and rested his chin on her shoulder. Together they watched the moonlight over the lake. It was the first time, and the second, that Cailin pleasured Libba but he was definitely still aroused, and the night was still young. His adventure was only beginning …

The next morning Libba awoke to the sun shining on her back. She listened. She could hear Cailin fumbling around in the kitchen and smell the freshly brewed coffee wafting in the air.

She grabbed the shirt Cailin had worn the night before and put it on, smiling and taking a deep breath as she did so. Being with Cailin was the best sexual experience she had ever had. She couldn't remember how many times she had shuddered under his touch; she lost count after the third time, and at that point, they had still not even had actual intercourse. She was amazed at the amount of self-control he had; to satisfy her needs, over and over, before thinking of himself. Cailin had taken his time with Libba and in turn, she had surrendered herself to him. When they finally did join, she felt complete, as if it were meant to be, as if they shared one heartbeat, one soul.

Cailin stood in the kitchen wearing only his flannel pajama bottoms. Libba walked into the kitchen to find him cooking bacon, eggs, and homemade blueberry pancakes. He poured her a cup of coffee and handed her the cream and sugar.

"Good morning, Precious. Sleep well?"

"Um, I did," she said, fixing her coffee and smelling the plate of pancakes. "Smells good."

"Yes, you do," Cailin said wrapping his arms around Libba's

waist and kissing the tip of her nose. Libba pulled him closer and lifted her head, nipping at his chin.

"Ooh, the pancakes!" Cailin exclaimed and quickly grabbed the spatula to flip them.

Libba chuckled, "Sorry."

She sat at the bar watching Cailin as he finished preparing breakfast. Suddenly she was no longer hungry for pancakes but had a craving for something else.

"Did you want to go to Muirfield Manor today?" Cailin asked. "I haven't had a chance to take you there yet."

"Yes, but there's one thing I'd like to do first, if you don't mind." Libba moved the griddle and shut off the stove. Slowly, she started to unbutton the shirt she was wearing. Walking backwards, she motioned with one finger for Cailin to follow her.

"No … I certainly don't mind," he said, wiping his hands on a towel, then tossing it on the floor as he followed Libba back to bed.

Muirfield Manor was located on a huge parcel of land off Main Street. Even though the two-acre property was located inside the city limits and easily within walking distance to the many shops and restaurants of the village, it was a rather private dwelling. The long driveway, which was expanded to accommodate at least a dozen cars, was slightly hidden from the road and one had to look for a white picket fence to know they were nearing the entrance.

Getting out of Cailin's truck I was greeted by the sounds of water and, looking around, I noticed a small walking bridge built over a small pond with water falling from decorative stones that formed a miniature manmade waterfall. A fairy that sat on a stone lily blowing butterfly kisses appeared to float in the middle of the pond.

A sidewalk that was about six feet wide and made of stone

pavers, twisted through the yard and led to the front of the house. Steps led up to a huge porch that wrapped around both sides of the house and ceiling fans were spread throughout.

Cailin purchased the house the previous summer and had finished landscaping the east side. From what I could see, the yard was beautiful. I admired the scenery noticing two trails on either end that presumably led to gardens tucked away for privacy. A huge rock blocked a portion of the path to the right. A hazy premonition flashed through my mind as I stared down the trail, but it left as quickly as it arrived. Something moved in the brush and two sparrows flew out of a tree, flying right over Cailin's head.

"It's beautiful," I said. Cailin took my hand and led us down the path to the left.

"Come, before we go inside, I want to show you something."

Evergreens, daylilies, and hydrangea surrounded the trail leading to a quaint small open field. There was a swinging bench, a gazebo, and other lawn chairs and tables tucked away in different parts of the yard. Toward the back, a huge maple tree that was perfect for climbing provided shade for almost the entire field.

"You did this?" I asked.

"Yeah … you like it?"

I nodded my head.

"When Mike and Noah come over, we hang out on this side a lot. Noah normally practices his soccer and Mike and I sit over there." He pointed to a set of chairs that sat low to the ground.

I could picture him and Mike, sitting in the chairs, drinking their beers while Noah ran around the open space. The area was perfect for that kind of family fun, but I could also imagine it being used for intimate gatherings, small social events, and even simple moments of solitude. From where we stood, I could still hear the sounds of the waterfall and looking to the North, I could see the beautiful hills that surround Blowing Rock Village.

Cailin stood next to me with his hands now tucked into

his back pockets. He was staring at the tree as if remembering something.

"You must be so proud. You've made remarkable changes, Cailin. I remember what it used to look like. I rode by about two years ago and it was so rundown. You'd never know it was the same place. It's so beautiful and peaceful. What's the other side look like?"

"I haven't really worked on that side yet except for cutting the grass once. It's rather overgrown. For some reason it didn't appeal to me like this side did. I've spent a lot of time here and in the very back." He pointed to an area directly behind the house. "I know I need to finish the other side, but right now I'm really anxious to see the interior completed. I would like to have the whole place done by the end of the year, although that might be pushing it." Cailin shrugged. "We'll see."

"You said you were thinking about making it into a bed and breakfast, right?"

"Yes. Sometimes I change my mind though. I initially bought it as an investment but I'm growing quite fond of it, or maybe I'm growing fond of the work. I don't know." He chuckled. "Anyway, enough of that, let's go inside and I'll show you around."

The interior of Muirfield Manor was as beautiful as the garden Cailin had showed me and I could tell he had already done so much work in the house. As I walked inside, I could smell a faint scent of new paint on the walls and the odor of freshly sanded hardwood floors. Even though he was in the middle of restoring the place, it still possessed old world charm boasting the turn of the century and of times long past. As I stood there taking in the site in front of me, I was struck with a false wave of nostalgia, as though the house was trying to show me all that once was, or perhaps all that could be.

The three-story home contained twelve bedrooms—a master suite and three smaller bedrooms on the top floor, another large suite and two individual bedrooms on the second floor, and only two bedrooms on the first floor. Tucked away in the back of the first floor were three other bedrooms, situated such that they formed their own private wing. This area was smaller and Cailin assumed they may have once been servant's quarters, but I felt they had their own special charm. The manor also had a living room, parlor, screened-in sunroom, kitchen with an eat-in dining area, a large dining room, butler's pantry, a library, and too many bathrooms to count. Once restored and decorated, I knew it would be as breathtaking as it probably was when originally built, perhaps even better.

"I still have a long way to go but I'm getting there," Cailin said.

"I don't think this house is in any rush," I replied, gazing from the floor to the ceiling.

"You're right about that. But sometimes I'm so eager to see the finished product that I just want to hurry things along and be done with it. Other times, I want to take it slow. I know I'll find out so much more about this old house if I take the time to explore every little nook and cranny."

"Well, personally, I think I like the patient Cailin better." I placed my arms around Cailin's waist and drew him close. "If I remember correctly, last night you were the most patient person I've ever met." I kissed his chin and stuck my hands in his back pockets to pull him closer. "And you did a lot of exploring …" *Kiss.* "Every …" *Kiss.* "Nook …" *Kiss.* "And cranny."

Cailin leaned his head down to kiss me back. "Well, you know what they say. Patience is a virtue."

CHAPTER 12

THE ESCAPE

J ennifer opened her eyes but could not see for the darkness that surrounded her. The last thing she remembered was getting ready to leave for Vegas, then she opened the door and Alec was there holding her garden gnome. How long ago was that? Bastard. How dare he show up out of nowhere and hit her over the head with the gnome from her front porch, only to wake up, bound, and on the cold hard floor of a beat-up smelly van. He must have drugged her because she never slept too soundly, and it felt as though she had slept for hours. She thought she remembered waking up once. They must have gone over a bad patch of road and the rough terrain had wakened her. She was so groggy that she fell back to sleep without even having the energy to get a good look at her surroundings. Now, here she lay trying to grasp her situation.

Jennifer's eyes were starting to adjust to the darkness. She figured she was still in the same smelly van she had been in since Alec grabbed her from her home. A wall with a screened window separated the cargo area from the front seats and it appeared that something was placed over the front windshield to block the light from coming inside. The damn thing smelled awful, like stale alcohol, mulch, and body odor. Though no light shined through any windows, there was a tiny square of sunshine coming from one spot near her feet. She could feel a cold breeze blowing in from the hole.

She couldn't believe Alec knocked her out and dragged her to who knows where. Her hands and feet might have been bound but she wasn't scared; she was pissed, and her temper was flaring. Whatever drug he used had quickly worn off and now she was wide-awake and very alert.

Jennifer swore when she got out of this holy mess, she would kill him. She wasn't a woman who held a grudge; on the contrary, she got even and then could walk away as if she never met you. She already left two men after getting what she wanted from them. Alec was no different, except that he was the first one to kidnap her! Son of a bitch. Yes, he would pay, Jennifer would make sure of that.

She inched her way to the small hole and positioned her body as flat as she could. First, she took a deep breath. The air was crisp and clean. She could smell the fresh scent of pine trees and evergreens. She peeked out the hole with one eye. By what she could tell, the van was parked in a rock clearing or perhaps a stone driveway and they must have been near a river because she could hear the soft sound of rushing water.

She debated. For sure the van was locked from the outside; Alec would not leave her alone where she could simply open the door and walk away. Should she kick and scream, make noise, and try to get someone's attention or should she wait for him to come back, pretend she was still sleeping, and then kick his ass when he returned? If she made noise and Alec arrived, she would have to defend herself. Either way, she needed to find a way to free her hands and feet if she were planning on running or fighting.

Her eyes scanned the van for anything she might use to untie herself with or use as a weapon. Nothing. Not even a rusty old nail. She looked at the screened window and stood up as much as she could, advancing toward it. She turned her back to the screen and felt around it. That's what she was looking for! A screw was sticking out just enough that she could rub the tape that was binding her hands against it.

She worked quickly; there was no telling how long Alec had been gone or when he was returning. How long had she been awake? Five minutes, maybe ten? She rubbed and rubbed. There! Finally, her hands were free. She dropped to the floor and began working on the tape around her ankles. She dug her fingernails into the tape trying to rip the edge, pulling, and struggling until her legs were free, too. Her hands skimmed the back door, but it was locked. She needed to figure out what to do next.

Alec rolled over in his sleeping bag and peeked out of the tent, looking at the van he had stolen the day before. Jennifer must still be sleeping inside, there was no noise coming from that direction. He gave her enough drugs to keep her asleep for a whole day. He doubted she would wake anytime soon, and he still needed to figure out what to do with her. He was working on that, but he was having problems keeping his thoughts straight and he knew he was getting things mixed up. Why was that so difficult these days? He needed to concentrate. No, he needed a drink, then he would be able to think clearly and figure out his next move. He grabbed the bottle he left next to his sleeping bag the night before and drank deeply. The beer was stale, but it quenched his thirst.

He thought about Jennifer. He would talk to her and explain why he knocked her out. She would understand or he could make her understand; he had his ways of getting his message across to women. But he didn't think it would come to that. He didn't want to hurt Jennifer; after all, she wasn't Libba. Libba got what she deserved, but Jennifer, she only made one mistake. Her first mistake. Her last mistake. Alec knew she would not falter again.

He thought about the last couple of months. He planned everything so perfectly—his divorce paperwork with Libba, getting a job in Raleigh, moving in with Jennifer. He started a new job when he moved in with her. He didn't like working there as much as he liked his other job, but he quit that one when he left Libba. That way she couldn't find him unless she searched very hard.

He walked out of work one evening after Jennifer kicked him out and never returned. His co-workers called him on his cell, but he didn't answer. He didn't want to talk to anyone. His boss called him so much that he finally ditched his phone in the sewer. It was a shit job, anyway. Now, they had no way of finding him and he liked it that way.

What had gone wrong with his perfect plan and why had Jennifer started acting strangely? At first, he took it out on Libba but seeing her lying unconscious had brought back memories, bad memories. Memories he did not want to think about right now. At present, all he wanted to think about was how to get Jennifer back. He came back for her after all, and when she woke up and they talked, he knew she would agree with him. They were meant for each other. She belonged to him and no one else.

He wondered if Libba thought about him often. She probably did, probably sat around most nights pining for his return. She should be so lucky. He didn't need her, and he didn't want her, but for some reason, he didn't want anyone else to have her either, especially that trucker guy. How could she go out with someone like that? Country boy, driving his big truck like he was some cowboy on a black stallion. Oh, please. The thought made Alec sick and angry.

Why was his temper such a problem these days? He wasn't sure what was happening to himself. One day he was fine and thinking rationally, and the next day he was sitting around contemplating things that should never cross a sane man's mind.

Maybe that was the problem. Alec was no longer sane, at least not like he used to be.

He thought about his father and the changes he noticed in his father before they had sent him away. Alec was young but he remembered …

His father had come home late again. His mother had helped him with his homework. Alec and his mother had dinner together and were on the couch watching television when his father walked in the house. Alec could tell his father was drunk and so could his mother. He hated when his father drank. He would come home and send Alec to his room and then the screaming would start. He would hear his father yelling, hear his mother crying, and hear the loud thumps of fist against flesh, fist against bone. The night of his twelfth birthday was the last time he saw his mother. His father had beaten his mother and Alec fell asleep to the sound of her crying. The next morning when he awoke, his mother was gone. His father was passed out on the couch still in his clothes from the night before. Alec had run to his mother's room to find that all her clothes and belongings were gone. That day, Alec's father was arrested, and Alec was taken into foster care. He never heard from his mother again.

From then on, Alec hated his father but even more, he hated his mother for abandoning him. Why she had not taken Alec with her he would never know. She left him without a worry for his well-being, without a worry for his soul, without knowing what his father would do to him, without so much as a last goodbye. He had never forgiven her for that.

No one knew his story, not even Libba. They met during high school. Alec had told her about living in foster care and he introduced her to the last family he lived with toward the end of high school but after they were married, he no longer kept in touch with them. For the first two years of their marriage, they exchanged Christmas cards and Libba had included a letter with each card but all they got in return was a card with a simple signature, *The Newsome Family.* Their third year of marriage, the Christmas card they sent to the Newsomes was returned. Alec told Libba to forget about them and he scratched their name off their card list. Every time Libba tried to bring up his foster parents, he and Libba would argue and eventually, Libba learned not to talk about them.

Alec shook his head trying to clear his thoughts. These were things he vowed not to think about, yet he was doing so more and more. He took another drink from the bottle. It was empty. He needed a fresh beer, then he supposed he would check on Jennifer.

Alec rolled out of his sleeping bag and grabbed his toiletry tote. He walked to the van and listened. Jennifer must still be asleep. He would go to the bathhouse, then walk down to the general store, come back, and fix breakfast. She would like that. She would be hungry when she awoke. He would feed her while they talked. Yes, she would like that, he thought.

The general store was stocked with basic camping provisions including fishing bait and canned foods. He nodded at the old man sitting behind the counter watching Jeopardy. Alec purchased his things and stood there for a minute watching television with the old man.

"The temperature is supposed to be dropping this weekend, so you better make sure you bundle up," said the old man.

"Oh, I think I'll be leaving this afternoon, but thanks anyway." Alec grabbed his bag and was heading out the door when the show was interrupted with Breaking News.

Police are still searching for suspect Alec Spencer, who is wanted for questioning in the brutal attack of his ex-wife, Libba Spencer and for the hit and run of Everett McPherson, a local Appalachian State University student. A picture of Alec appeared on the screen. *Alec Spencer was last seen in the Blowing Rock vicinity. Anyone with news of his whereabouts should call 911 or the local sheriff's department.*

Alec pulled his baseball cap lower down his forehead and raised the collar of his jacket. His pace quickened until he was a short distance away from the store and then he took off running toward his camp. He had not watched television in days and had no idea the police were looking for him, nor was he aware that he was suspected in the hit and run of the McPherson boy. How could they know it was him? He decided he had to get out of there, and quick. The old man grabbed a set of keys from the counter, got out of his chair, and walked to the door. His hearing might be failing, and he had plenty of pain in most places of his body, but his vision was perfect, the one thing that had never given him any problems in his sixty-two years. He looked at the man rounding the corner and knew without a doubt that he was Alec Spencer, the man on the news. He walked over to his phone and called his cousin Robert.

Robert answered his cell on the second ring.

"Hey, Tom."

"Hey, Robert, how's it going?"

"It's going. What's up? I've only got a few minutes. I'm sort of in the middle of something right now."

"Sorry, don't mean to bother you," Tom said. "I know you've probably got a lot going on but that's why I called. I think Alec Spencer just left my store."

Jennifer pressed her ear against the side of the van. She could hear someone rummaging around outside and knew it must be Alec. She heard the sizzle of water dousing out a fire and then smelled the strong scent of smoke. She listened carefully. Yes, it was Alec;

she could hear him talking to himself and cursing about some boy and a car. He sounded worried and panicked. What was going on?

She knew she would not have much time when Alec opened the door. She would have to act quickly.

Alec took down the tent as fast as he could and rolled everything up in one parcel. He shoved his sleeping bag into its case and stacked the rest of his camping gear next to the side of the van. He stuck his hand in his pocket for the keys, but they were gone. Where were his keys, he knew he had them with him at the general store? Damn it! Could he have left them in the store? He traced his steps in his mind and then he remembered setting the keys on the counter when he paid for his things. Now what was he going to do? There weren't a lot of people camping on this area of Grandfather Mountain. It would be easy to steal another car but getting back here and then off the mountain without getting caught could be risky. His best bet would be to get his keys from the store, but he wasn't sure how he could do that either. Surely, the old man had recognized him and for all Alec knew, the police were on their way right now. He opened a beer and took a big gulp. He could do this, he thought, he just needed to finish his drink and then he would head back down the mountain and somehow sneak into the store to retrieve his keys.

Back at the general store, Alec peeked in the window and scanned each of the narrow aisles. He didn't see anyone shopping and the old man wasn't behind the counter either. If he opened the door slowly, that should be enough to stop the bell from ringing, at least he hoped.

He looked around to make sure no one was in sight.

Slowly, Alec opened the door. The bell shifted but did not ring.

He moved the door another inch and then another. The door opened with barely a sound. Alec walked in and checked the counter, but his keys were gone. He crept behind the cash register. For the store to be so clean, the area behind the counter was a mess. He moved stacks of paper, checked inside shoeboxes and canisters, moved rags, opened bottles, and even rummaged through the trash but could not find his keys. He pulled open every drawer and finally there they were in the last drawer he opened. He pocketed his keys and walked towards the door, pulling it quickly in his hurry to get out and forgetting about the bell at the top of the door. Just then, the old man from before appeared from the back room. Their eyes met and Alec flashed an evil grin then burst out the door.

Tom ran behind the counter and grabbed his shotgun and pellets. He loaded the gun and ran outside, aimed, and fired, but he was too late. Alec rounded the corner as a flock of birds scattered from the trees.

Tom went back inside and picked up his phone. As he dialed Robert's cell, he checked his cash register and then noticed the drawer under the counter was open and the keys that he had placed in there earlier were missing.

"Robert LeBrecque here."

"Robert, it's Tom. He was just here again. I came from the back room and he was sneaking out the door."

"I'm three minutes away. You okay?"

"Yeah, I took a shot at him but missed."

"What! Tom, you can't do that! *Don't* do that. And I want him alive. I'm almost there."

Robert rounded the last corner and parked haphazardly in front of the store. Tom ran out of the store before Robert could get out of the police car. He filled Robert in on everything he knew, then pointed him in the right direction. He told Robert that as far as he knew, no one was camping on that part of the mountain. Robert said he would drive part of the way and then when he spotted anything out of the ordinary, he would stop and continue on foot.

Jennifer lay on the floor of the van pretending to be asleep. It wasn't the best of plans, but she figured when Alec opened the door, if he got close enough, she would kick him as hard as she could and grab whatever he was holding and shove it into his face. That might give her a little bit of time to jump out of the van and run.

Alec made it back to camp without the old man following. In his haste to get into the van and escape, he clicked the button on the keys and unknowingly unlocked all the doors. Grabbing his belongings, he opened the back door and was greeted with Jennifer's foot knocking him square in the face.

He stumbled backwards falling and dropping his things on the ground. When Jennifer saw him, she was so angry she jumped on top of him screaming, yelling, and swinging her fists.

"What the HELL do you think you're doing ALEC SPENCER? How dare you knock me out and tie me up like an animal! I should kill you, you son of a bitch. What the HELL?!"

Jennifer kicked Alec in the crotch and slapped his face.

Now, the alcohol was pumping in Alec's veins. With the anxiety of knowing he was wanted by the police, being caught in the general store by the old man, and now Jennifer pounding on him in a wild frenzy, he snapped, and his temper was out of control … something Jennifer had yet to witness. He turned on her with a fire in his eyes that she had never seen in a sane man before. She could smell the alcohol on his breath, and she knew she was in danger— real danger, the kind of danger that made you fear for your life.

In one movement, Alec wheeled on his feet, picked her up, and threw her against the van. She screamed and swung her hands at his face, gouging both of his eyes with her long, fake nails.

Robert had rolled down his window and was driving very slowly in search of any signs for Alec. He took a deep breath and could smell the faint scent of smoke. He got out of his police car, steadied his gun in his hands, and listened very carefully. From a distance he heard a woman screaming and took off in the direction of her scream.

He heard someone running through the woods and as he ran in that direction, the woman's screaming and crying became louder and louder. He spun around a huge pine tree and nearly collided with Jennifer. She let out a loud wail and started swinging her fists.

"Shh, shh. I'm a cop. It's okay, it's okay. I'm a cop."

Jennifer was so frantic she barely noticed who was standing in front of her. Robert could tell she was terrified. He tried to speak as calmly as he could.

"Ma'am, are you all right? Who did this to you? Was it Alec, Alec Spencer?"

Jennifer nodded frantically and pointed behind her. "Yes, yes, he's ... drunk and mad and dangerous!"

Robert looked over Jennifer's shoulder. He positioned her behind the pine tree to shield her as he stepped to the side to get a better view of where she had pointed. In the distance he could see a man lying on the ground near a brown van. The backdoor to the van was still open. The man seemed to be in pain as he was holding his stomach and cursing very loudly.

"Is he armed?"

Jennifer shook her head. "I don't know. I don't think so."

"Stay here," he whispered to Jennifer.

Robert positioned his gun and started walking toward Alec. Alec looked up and saw Robert coming. He stood, faced the Lieutenant, and flashed his teeth in an evil grin. In the flicker of an instant he jumped in the back of the van, closing the doors behind him. Robert burst off running after him, but Alec was too quick. He started the van and sped off down the mountain, leaving the Lieutenant standing alone in the clearing.

Cailin and I left Muirfield Manor and walked down Main Street wandering through the antique shops in the village. We stopped by Hanna's—the place Cailin had purchased his cloisonné horse—and Cailin spent quite some time admiring a bronze statue of another horse and equestrian rider sculpted by Edgar Bertram in 1878. He was still undecided as to whether to purchase it or not so we decided he should think on it over lunch. We left the Storie Street Grille and were heading back to Hanna's—Cailin decided he would purchase the bronze statue after all—when my cell phone rang. I pulled the phone from my purse and looked at the number. It was Lieutenant LeBrecque.

"Hello?"

"Ms. Spencer? It's Lieutenant LeBrecque. Have you got a minute to talk?"

"Yes, what's going on? Is everything all right?"

Automatically I squeezed Cailin's hand. He stopped walking and looked down at me and I knew he could tell something was wrong. He wrapped his arm around my shoulder and gently led me to a bench away from the crowds. Cailin sat patiently while I talked to the Lieutenant. I knew he could tell by our conversation that Alec was causing more trouble and the Lieutenant was worried about me.

"How long ago … no, no I'll be okay … yes, of course, I will … thank you."

I hung up the phone and put my head down in my hands. Cailin brushed my hair with his hand.

"Did they find him?"

"Kind of … oh Cailin, I just don't understand what's wrong with him. It's like he's a totally different person from when we were married. He said Alec was up on the mountain holding some lady named Jennifer hostage. Hostage! Can you believe that! She said he knocked her out and kidnapped her. Alec was drunk and they got into a huge fight, but she managed to escape in the woods. She bumped into the

Lieutenant when she was trying to get away. He was searching the woods. Thanks to Jennifer he found Alec but not in time. Alec escaped. He was driving a brown Chevy Astro van, but he's probably ditched it by now. I don't get it; I just don't get it! How could I have been married to someone like that and not even know it!"

"Libba," Cailin whispered my name soothingly as he continued to rub my hair. "Maybe there's something more to what's going on with him than we think. I mean, maybe he *did* just wake up one day and snap, or perhaps he has a chemical imbalance that is triggered with alcohol. It affects people differently and every time we turn around and hear his name, alcohol seems to come into play. Did he drink that much around you?"

"Not really. I never kept that much in the house. I guess it's a good thing, huh?"

"Yeah."

We sat in silence and I thought about what Lieutenant LeBrecque told me. Cailin was doing a good job being calm and patient but I could tell what he really wanted to do was to find the bastard and hurt him like he had hurt me, Jennifer, and the McPherson boy. So what if his thoughts were less than amiable? To sit there and watch someone you care about suffer surely would prompt a certain level of hatred in anyone.

I leaned my head against Cailin's chest and felt that familiar electric surge pass between us. His warmth calmed my soul.

Cailin wrapped his arm around Libba's shoulder and they walked back to Hanna's. He purchased the Bertram statue and they returned to Muirfield Manor. Later, as they drove to Trish's house Cailin couldn't help but scan the roads in search of a brown van. He would do everything in his power to keep Libba and her friends safe.

He thought about the first conversation he had with Martha about Libba. Fate dealt him his hand all right and it was his turn to place his bet. Cailin was tired of Alec holding all the aces but not anymore. What Alec didn't know was that when Cailin played, he played to win, and for this hand in particular, the stakes were too high to lose. He told Martha he saw his future and every time Libba was right there with him. No, he was not about to lose this hand.

CHAPTER 13

DÉJÀ VU

Noah's team won the last game of the season. After the game, they celebrated with ice cream and cupcakes and then the coach handed out trophies to all the players. He was so excited as he approached the coach to get his trophy. Everyone was there—his dad, Cailin and Libba, Mallory and Olivia, Trish, Ginny, and Martha and Louis—and Noah had the biggest group of fans there. Even Jared and Caleb managed to show up during the last few minutes of the game and Caleb brought his nephew, Tyler, who went to school with Noah.

Noah grabbed his trophy and ran into the cheering crowd.

"Dad! Ms. MacDonald! Come, look!"

Noah gave his dad a very quick hug and then ran straight to Mallory wrapping his arms tight around her waist.

Mike had taken a step forward but then stopped dead in his tracks when Noah gave Mallory a hug, though it wasn't that long, or affectionate. He looked around to see that everyone was staring at them with wide grins on their faces; everyone that is, except Jared. Mike wasn't sure but it looked as though Jared was jealous ... envious ... mad? He wondered why Jared would have these feelings towards a little boy. If anyone had reason to be jealous it was him. Mike was used to getting all of Noah's attention and now that they had met Mallory, it seemed like Noah always wanted her attention more. Mike didn't much mind, what bothered him the most wasn't that Noah wanted Mallory's attention, but that he wanted her attention, too.

Jared caught Mike looking at him and immediately turned away. That simple movement, for some reason, gave Mike an uneasy feeling and instantly he felt as though he should be defending Mallory's honor. Mike wasn't sure why he felt this way because he had known Jared for years and, for the most part, thought Jared was a good guy. But still, he couldn't help but feel strange about the way Jared was looking at Mallory and Noah.

Noah ran back to Mike to show him his trophy and Mike picked him up and gave him another big hug.

"Wow, Noah! That's a big trophy you have there!"

"I know, isn't it great! Ms. MacDonald said I should put it on a shelf next to the team pictures. Can I Dad?"

"Of course, you can. We'll do that this evening before you go to bed. How about that?"

"Great! I got to go show Olivia and Tyler."

Noah ran away as quickly as he had appeared.

Everyone started cleaning up, picking up trash and packing up their chairs and coolers. Mike turned around and saw Jared walk up to Mallory. He noticed Jared place his hand on top of hers when she reached for her cooler. He was just close enough to overhear their conversation.

"Looks like Mike's kid has a bit of a crush on you. I can see why though."

"I beg your pardon? Noah does not have a crush on me. How dare you even think that of a boy his age?" Mallory asked with a touch of annoyance in her tone.

"All I'm saying is the boy has good taste." Jared ran his hand over Mallory's and took the cooler away from her setting it back down on the ground. He looked her up and down, his eyes stopping at her breasts.

"And what is that supposed to mean?" Mike noticed Mallory take a step backward, crossing her arms around her waist.

"Oh, come on, I'm trying to pay you a compliment. You know you look good. I'm just letting you know I think you look good, too." Jared took a step toward Mallory reaching to touch her arm.

Mike could no longer tolerate listening to the conversation and by how Mallory was reacting, she was done with Jared too. He stood up and walked toward them, standing a little closer to Mallory's side than usual, but being careful not to touch her.

"Mallory, why don't I finish up here while you get the children?" Mike stared directly into Jared's eyes as he spoke.

Mallory didn't say a word as she turned and abruptly walked away, seeming grateful to Mike that she no longer had to deal with Jared and his wayward eyes. Mike could tell Mallory didn't like Jared and wondered if it started when she met him in the hospital. Mike knew Jared was a player and wanted him to have nothing to do Mallory.

Mike and Jared stood face to face, neither of them speaking to the other. Mike was trying to decide how he should handle Jared. They were friends, though not close friends, but they had always gotten along very well, and Mike knew Jared didn't mean any harm. Finally, Mike spoke.

"Jared, I think you need to leave Mallory alone. I think you make her uncomfortable."

"What do you mean? We were just talking, that's all."

"Jared, you might have been talking but your eyes were saying more than your mouth. Don't you think she noticed you staring at her breasts?"

"Well, they are nice. You can't tell me you haven't noticed."

Mike huffed and shook his head. He hadn't noticed, not

really. What appealed to him most about Mallory were her eyes, the way she smelled, her smile, and the bond between her and Olivia.

"Mallory is a lady, a genuinely nice lady and a single mom, Jared. She deserves more respect than that."

Jared looked at Mike, examining his expression.

"You want her don't you," he asked.

"That's none of your business, Jared."

"It is my business because I want her too. Guess we'll just have to see who gets her first," Jared said and turned to walk away.

"Jared!" Mike grabbed his arm turning him back around to face him. "This isn't a game. Stay away from her."

"Or what?"

Mike didn't say a word.

"That's what I thought. Mallory's a big girl. Oh, I'm sorry what did you say, she's a 'lady'. She can make up her own mind. By the way, thanks for the heads up or rather, for telling me to keep my eyes up. I'll remember that. I'll be seeing you around."

Cailin came up to Mike who was still watching Jared as he walked towards his car. Surely, he picked up on what had happened and could read the look in Mike's eyes.

"Hey, everything okay?"

Mike didn't speak.

"Mike, I said is everything okay? What's up with Jared?"

"Jared is a jerk, that's what's up with Jared." Mike looked around. "Where's Mallory?"

Cailin and Mike turned to see Mallory coming in their direction with Noah and Olivia in tow. The three were laughing and smiling and Olivia was singing a song that evidently, she was making up the lyrics to as she was singing. An overwhelming feeling of joy came over him as he looked at the three of them. He took off running toward them, high-fiving Noah's hand, then scooping up Olivia and swinging her in the air.

Olivia smiled and laughed and as Mike set her back down, she gave him a big hug.

Martha came and stood by Cailin and together they stared at the four of them, looking like the perfect happy family. Surely, if Ellen was looking down from Heaven, she would be happy for them too.

"Looks like he might finally be ready to move on. What do you think?" asked Martha.

"Yeah, I think he might be ready to try," said Cailin.

Libba walked up and held Cailin's hand. She looked around to see what had caught their attention and began to smile as she watched the foursome.

"Martha, we're going by Muirfield Manor to show the place to Trish and Mallory. Do you want to join us?"

"No, I think I'll let you kids have fun on your own today. Louis and I have some yard work to finish." Cailin kissed her on her cheek and she walked away to join Louis.

Mallory yelped for the third time since arriving at Muirfield Manor. Her motherly instincts told her that something was wrong.

"Olivia, stay where I can see you okay."

"Mallory, chill out," said Trish. "There's not much she can get into around here. Besides she's with Noah and he knows this place like the back of his hand."

I wondered what was wrong with Mallory; I never saw her so uptight before. Mallory told Trish and me about the conversation she had with Jared at the soccer field and how Jared rubbed her the wrong way ... literally. Maybe what happened between them was still on her mind. Jared left the field before everyone else and was nowhere around. Mallory simply needed to relax and enjoy the day.

"I know I'm edgy," said Mallory. "But I just can't shake this feeling I have. I think the children need to stay on this side of the house where we can keep an eye on them."

I looked at Trish, shrugged my shoulders, and took a drink. "I'll go get them if it will make you feel better."

I set my drink down and headed toward the back yard, making my way to the backside of the west lawn. As I walked under the brush, goose bumps ran down my arms and the hair on the back of my neck stood up. Again, I had the strangest feeling of déjà vu but decided to ignore the sensation.

"Olivia! Noah!" I called out. "Come out, come out wherever you are!"

I heard a noise coming from the gazebo but didn't see anyone there, so I walked further into the garden.

"Olivia! Noah! Where are you? Come out, come out wherever you are!" I said in a playful voice. I saw Olivia peek from around the side of the house. Olivia tried to giggle quietly but was not doing such a good job at it. I crouched down and slowly approached the side of the building. Olivia and Noah let out a loud scream, laughed, and took off running as I chased the two of them around the house.

As they approached the front entrance of the lawn, I thought I heard someone behind me. I stopped chasing Olivia and Noah but the two of them continued running and laughing.

A cold dread ran down my spine. I stopped and slowly turned around, eyeing a dark figure standing atop the huge rock that sat to the side of the path.

It was Alec.

I froze. In the distance I heard an owl screech. This time it was no dream.

I wanted to run. I desperately wanted to run, but I was so frightened that all I could do was stand there and stare. I couldn't even manage to let out a scream. I thought about what Alec did to me only a few weeks earlier. I thought about Everett McPherson, the boy hurt in the hit and run. I thought about Jennifer, a woman I didn't even know except for the fact that my ex-husband had left me for her, kidnapped her, drugged her, and then tied her up in a van.

Alec hurt too many people and so far, no one was able to stop him. I heard Olivia and Noah laughing in the distance and knew there was no way I could let Alec get anywhere near them. There might be a lot of people in the other garden but would that matter to Alec. What if he had a weapon?

I mustered all the strength I could find to stand my ground and stared Alec directly into his eyes.

He stared back at me then bared his teeth in an evil grin. He jumped off the rock heading through the bushes toward the road and like that, he was gone.

Libba ran as fast as she could back to the east lawn, tripping as she entered the open field where everyone was waiting. Cailin turned to see her as she entered and immediately knew she was terrified and in danger. He ran to her, Mike following closely behind.

"Libba, what's wrong, what happened?"

"He's here. Alec. I just saw him on the big rock. He took off through the bushes, heading back toward the road."

"Stay here with Mike," Cailin ordered and took off towards the west lawn.

"Mike, he can't go by himself. What if he's armed? What if he has a gun! You have to go with him."

Mike hugged Libba trying to calm her down when Mallory and Trish ran up.

"What the hell?" Trish yelled. "Cailin took off running like a bat out of hell! What's going on?"

Mike looked at Mallory. Somehow, he knew she understood what he feared would happen if he didn't follow Cailin. He looked past her at Olivia and Noah, who had stopped playing and were standing frozen in the middle of the field.

Mike was torn between helping his brother and protecting Noah and the others.

"Mike ..." Libba pleaded.

"Mike, you should go help Cailin find Alec," Mallory said with as much reassurance as she could muster. "We can handle it over here,"

"Hell yeah, we can handle it here! I brought my mace," said Trish.

Noah and Olivia somehow managed to squeeze in between Mallory and Trish. Mike looked at Noah and put his hand on his son's shoulder. He looked at Noah but before he could say anything, Noah spoke first.

"Dad," he whispered. "Go help Uncle Cailin. I can take care of Ms. MacDonald and the girls."

Mallory placed a hand on Noah's other shoulder and stared deep into Mike's eyes. As she looked at him her dark eyes widened, speaking to him alone. In return, he looked longingly into Mallory's eyes as realization set in. Jared was right. He did want Mallory. He wanted her heart because she already had a piece of his.

"Get the mace and go inside the house. Lock yourselves in the downstairs bathroom until either Cailin or I come and get you. Understand?"

They all nodded. "And call LeBrecque. Tell him what's going on."

Mike was about to take off when Mallory grabbed his hand.

"Mike be careful," she said and kissed his cheek.

Mike ran to the front and jumped into his car. When he spotted Cailin, he was standing at the edge of Main Street pacing back and forth and scanning the crowds of people walking about. Mike pulled over and rolled down the window.

"Do you know where he went?"

"Mike, what are you doing here? I told you to stay with the others!"

"They're fine. They're going to hide in the house and call LeBrecque. They'll be okay."

Cailin was worried about Libba but when he looked at Mike, he knew Mike was worried about his brother. He was glad Mike didn't listen to him; it felt better having his brother next to him. Besides, one of them had to be rational if they caught up to Alec and Cailin knew it wouldn't be him. Plus, with Mike beside him, Alec was outnumbered.

"Do you know what Alec looks likes?" Mike was looking around for anything out of the ordinary.

"I've only seen a picture of him when we went to Libba's to pick up her things that one time, but I remember. Just look for anything suspicious or especially an old brown van." Just then, Cailin looked down the hill and saw a man climbing into a brown van.

"Over there!" he yelled.

Mike's head turned automatically in the direction Cailin was pointing.

"Get in the car!"

Cailin jumped in, Mike taking off before the door was even shut. They sped down the hill following the van and dodging in and out of traffic. Mike ran a light and started blowing his horn warning people to get out of the way. Alec nearly hit a man crossing the street and another man yelled at Mike as he sped through a red light. Alec made a left turn and Mike was right on his trail. Alec made another quick right, but Mike continued straight missing the turn.

"Mike, back up, back up, he turned!" Cailin barked at Mike.

"I know what I'm doing!" yelled Mike.

He drove another few yards and made a sharp right heading straight into the course of the brown van.

"HOLD ON!"

Mike gunned the engine and Alec swerved, running off the road. Cailin jumped out of the car and ran towards the van but Alec was already out and running up the side of the mountain. Cailin chased Alec on foot running up the mountain and catching up to him. When he was just feet away, Cailin dove at Alec's feet, tackling him to the ground. They struggled but Cailin was too strong for Alec to get away.

Cailin was about to punch Alec right in the face when he stopped suddenly, staring at the man beneath him.

"STOP! STOP! WAIT!" The man lying on the ground begged Cailin.

"Who the HELL are you! WHERE'S ALEC, WHERE IS HE?" Cailin looked at the guy with fury in his eyes. This was not Alec; they had been tricked.

"I'm sorry man, I'm sorry. He paid me, the guy, he paid me one hundred bucks and asked me to park it down the road. Said he was just playing a trick on a friend. I got scared when I saw you following me, so I sped. Dude ... please ..."

Cailin couldn't believe it. He fell to his knees in defeat. Now what? Once again Alec had escaped and Cailin felt as though he had failed Libba. Mike walked up and looked at the two men on the ground.

"Cailin. Cailin, let him go. We have to get back to the house. What if Alec went back after he saw us leave?"

Cailin looked up at Mike who was trying to rush Cailin to his feet. It took him a second to register what Mike said to him.

"Oh SHIT! Libba, Noah! Let's go!" He turned and looked at the guy lying on the ground and offered him a hand to help him up. "I'm sorry dude, I thought you were someone else. You okay?"

"Yeah, yeah. Hey, what should I do with this van?" the guy

yelled at Cailin and Mike, but they were already heading back to Mike's car.

Mike looked over his shoulder and yelled back at the guy.

"Call the police."

Cailin buckled up and grabbed his cell. He needed to call Libba to warn her and the others. He stayed on the phone with her all the way back to the house, and she told him that Trish had called Lieutenant LeBrecque, who was now on his way over.

When they arrived at Muirfield Manor Libba came rushing out of the house straight into Cailin's arms. Noah and Olivia were right behind her running towards Mike, who looked as relieved as they were to see him. Trish and Mallory hung back at the door watching the whole scene from a distance.

Libba wrapped her arms around Cailin and held him tightly obviously glad to see him return safely.

"I'm sorry he got away," Cailin said. "We'll get him the next time."

"I'm just so glad you're safe. I was so worried. You didn't see him in the garden Cailin, he looked evil. I've never seen him look like that before. I was so scared."

"I know, but he's gone and you're safe now." Cailin ran his hand through Libba's hair and kissed her forehead. "You know I'm not letting you out of my sight, not until he's behind bars. You're staying with me for a few days. If anything happened to you Libba, I don't know what I would do."

Libba nodded and held Cailin close. That was a request she would never refuse.

Trish leaned against the porch railing and looked at Mallory who was watching Mike with the kids. Trish suspected that Mallory was beginning to like Mike, but she wondered why Mallory had snapped at him that first night back at the hospital.

"Do you remember when we first met Mike," Trish asked.

Mallory knew what was coming. She wondered why it had taken Trish so long to finally ask her.

"You want to know why I was rude to Mike, don't you?" Trish nodded. "I wondered when you would ask."

"Well, you're not going to make me beg, are you?"

Mallory smiled.

"No Trish." She waited a second to gather her thoughts. "I snapped because of the way Mike looked at Olivia."

"But he didn't look at her like she was annoying him. He just asked if she could go somewhere else to be nice, to give you a break so you wouldn't have to worry about Olivia while we were waiting at the hospital."

"I know."

"But then ... I don't get it Mallory."

Mallory took a deep breath before answering.

"Mike looked at Olivia like her father *should,* but never has," Mallory said. "He looked at Olivia with genuine care and compassion and I thought ... this is the kind of father figure she needs in her life. This man is a decent guy—a genuine, down to earth, good and decent guy." She shrugged, "I guess it just took me by surprise and made me think, that's all."

"Hmm? And the kiss earlier?"

"Oh Trish, that was just a kiss on the cheek for good luck, nothing more."

"Yeah right." Trish didn't say anything more since everyone was starting towards the door where they stood.

Mallory thought about what she said to Trish. Was it simply a good luck kiss or could she be falling for Mike? It was obvious that he had won over Olivia's heart and Noah certainly had a piece of her own. But her and Mike, she wasn't sure about that. Could he even be interested in dating her? He had rescued her from Jared earlier, but she attributed that to pure chivalry. Mike was like that, she thought.

She wanted to date; she missed dating. It had been a long time since she went out with a man and an even longer time since she was intimate with one. But finding someone who accepted her as a single mom was harder than she thought. Inevitably, she devoted her life to Olivia; her happiness was all she cared about these days. Was it the same for Mike?

She looked up and saw Lieutenant LeBrecque parking in the driveway.

Olivia and Noah approached the Lieutenant's car.

"Hi Occifer," said Olivia.

"Officer, Olivia. It's Off-i-sir," Noah corrected.

"Actually, it's Lieutenant," said Lieutenant LeBrecque as he stepped out of the car. Olivia stuck her tongue out at Noah then took off running past Trish and Mallory into the house, Noah following right on her heels. Apparently, they he forgot about the danger they were in a few minutes earlier.

Lieutenant LeBrecque spoke to Mike, Cailin, and Libba. They filled him in on what happened, and Mike told him where they could find the abandoned van. Cailin and the Lieutenant decided to walk the grounds one more time to make sure Alec wasn't still hanging around, although Lieutenant LeBrecque said he was sure Alec was probably long gone. Libba, Trish, and Mallory were on their way inside to check on the kids when Mike stopped Mallory with a gentle touch at her sleeve.

"Mallory, do you mind?" Mike gestured for her to stay a minute longer.

"Yes Mike, what is it?"

"I just wanted to say thanks. Noah seems to have grown quite attached to you and I know with you around, he felt safe while I was with Cailin, so … thanks, for being there with him."

"We were all together, Mike. It wasn't just me keeping him safe. We were all comforting each other." Mallory shrugged her shoulders elegantly and took a few steps away from Mike, heading back to the house.

"Mallory." Mike matched her steps and grabbed her hand stopping her once more. She froze, his touch sparking something inside her and catching her off guard.

"*I* wanted to be there to comfort you," he whispered. "I was scared for you and Olivia, too but ..." He looked unsure of what else to say.

Mallory wanted to speak but she couldn't remember what she was going to say to him. It was hard for her to make conversation when he was taking her breath away. They stood there staring at each other.

"Well, we better get inside and check on the monsters," joked Mike, as he turned and walked into the house.

CHAPTER 14

MARTHA'S PRESENT

Talking to my mother on the phone was exhausting. My mother was coming for an early Mother's Day visit and already I was dreading the weekend. This would be the first time she and Cailin would meet. It was the first Friday in May and Cailin promised the Stanleys we would be over for dinner, even though it was Mike's turn. Mike had to take Noah to a school play so how could Cailin say no. Now, not only was my mother coming to visit for the weekend, but she was also arriving early enough to go with us to dinner at the Stanleys'.

Cailin, of course, was calm about the whole situation. I, on the other hand, was not exactly thrilled because now I would not be able to spend the night with Cailin at his house on the mountain. After the incident with Alec at Muirfield Manor, I spent the following two weeks—a very romantic two weeks I might add—at Cailin's house but then I had to return to Trish's because Cailin was needed out of town again for work. I talked to him on the phone most nights while he was away, but I desperately missed him.

If I had it my way, Cailin would pick me up and we would drive to his house and spend the whole weekend in bed together.

However, with my mother coming into town that was definitely out of the question.

I supposed I shouldn't complain about my mother coming. After all, she was excited about meeting Cailin and deep down, I knew the Stanleys and my mom would get along well with each other. When Alec and I were married, my mother met the Newsomes but after the first couple of years of marriage she too fell out of contact with them. With no communication between Alec's foster parents, I thought my mother and Alec's relationship would improve, but that never happened.

I had a feeling Alec would be a topic of discussion and I was not looking forward to that conversation but wasn't sure how I would be able to avoid it. How my mother felt about Alec was a touchy story and I really did not want to talk about him with my mother, especially in front of Cailin or the Stanleys.

I hated discussing Alec in front of Cailin. It made me uncomfortable and I knew it was a sore subject with him, too. And why not? What Alec did to me disgusted Cailin and I completely understood that. What Cailin seemed to forget though, was that this Alec was far different from the Alec I married, and I couldn't help but feel sorry for him. No, I didn't love Alec anymore, not like I did when we were first married. I wasn't *in love* with him, but I still cared for him and his well-being and mental stability, which lately he seemed to be losing. I also feared for Alec because I had no idea what Cailin would do when their paths crossed again. Alec was digging his own grave and there was really no way for anyone to help him out of it.

My mother never liked Alec and never bothered to hide her feelings about him. In her opinion, he got what he deserved. I talked to her quite frequently the last few weeks, both about Alec and Cailin, but I had not told her about how much I cared for Cailin until the past week. Of course, that's why she suddenly wanted to come see me. She was curious about whether I had finally found the right person. In other words, she was coming to snoop.

"If you want, I can open a bottle of Stella Rosa and you can get drunk before your mother gets here," Trish joked. "I think I might even have a few of those small on-the-go bottles if you just want to calm your nerves."

That might not be such a bad idea, I thought. I grabbed the air pump and began filling the blow-up mattress. I was setting up quarters in Trish's little office nook, giving my regular bed to my mother who would be sleeping in 'my room'.

"Oh, come on Libba, it's not that big a deal. Besides, your mother is cool. She and Cailin will get along fine and you know she'll like Martha and Louis. She'll probably spend so much time talking to them that she barely pays any attention to you and Cailin."

"I know, I know, you're probably right, but I'm still nervous. I haven't had to introduce Cailin to anyone yet. He introduced himself to you and Mallory when I was in the hospital remember? Now, the first person I get to introduce him to is my mother! I feel like I'm back in high school going on my first date, except that Cailin will be picking up me *and* my chaperone who just happens to be my MOTHER! Don't you want to come with us Trish? You could be my cushion. I *need* a cushion, *please, please, please.*"

"Nope, I already have plans. Rowan and I are meeting for drinks and then we might go to a movie." She swung the sheets toward Libba who caught the other side and tucked it under the mattress.

"Rowan? Rowan Collier, my attorney? When did you hook up with Rowan?"

"Hook up? I haven't *hooked up* with Rowan. We're just going out for drinks, that's all." Trish smiled.

"That's all huh? Trish, I know you, and that smile on your

face tells me that drinks isn't the only thing on the menu. I didn't even know you knew him, when did you meet?"

"I haven't met him yet, tonight will be the first time so YES, one drink, maybe two, is all I have planned for tonight. It's sort of like a blind date. He's called a few times at work to see how you were doing and we started talking. Yesterday he called and for the first time he didn't use you as an excuse to talk to me. He asked me out and I said yes. I wasn't going to say anything to you because it's really nothing at all but now that you know, well … what do you think?"

"I think it's great!" I grinned and threw a blanket on the bed smoothing it out. "It's about time, no offense "

"None taken."

"I've seen you surfing on the internet looking for guys and I've always thought you should just go out there and meet someone on your own. Plus, Rowan is a good catch. I think you'll like what you see." I said wiggling my eyebrows at Trish. "He's a hottie, that's for sure."

"Libba!"

"Well, it's true. Of course, he's not as hot as Cailin, but very handsome." I grabbed a pillow and jumped on the bed testing it out. Trish grabbed the other pillow and hit me on the head with it.

"Uh huh," hummed Trish thoughtfully as if comparing the two in her mind.

"Did you hear that? I think my mom's here. Can you please get the door?" I begged.

Trish snapped out of her daydream and looked at me. Then she ran laughing through the living room to answer the door. My mom was finally here.

"Hi, Mrs. Daughtry!" Trish said giving my mom a huge hug. "Come on in. I'll get that for you." She picked up the suitcase and held the door open allowing my mom to enter.

"Hi Trish, it's so good to see you again. Didn't I tell you to call me Liza?" She touched Trish's hair in a motherly gesture. "You look beautiful as usual. Your hair is getting longer."

"Thank you, and yes, it's grown a bit since the last time I saw you."

"Hi, Mom!" I rounded the corner and gave my mom a big hug too. "How was the drive?"

"Not bad but you know how I hate the rain. It's starting to get a little misty out there," she said as I helped her take off her jacket.

"Yes, Mom, it's supposed to rain tonight but it doesn't look so bad out right now."

"Well, I don't plan on driving until I leave on Sunday and it's supposed to be a beautiful day. Are you driving us tonight?"

"No, Cailin is driving tonight, and he grew up around here, so he knows the roads pretty well. He should be here soon."

My mom turned her head and eyed me as if she were studying a painting.

"What, Mom? Why are you looking at me like that?" I groaned.

"Hmm? You look different."

"What do you mean, different?"

"I mean, simply the mention of his name seems to lighten you up. I can't wait to meet this Cailin."

Trish had taken my mother's suitcase to the bedroom and was just re-entering the living room.

"You don't have to wait long. I think he just pulled up." Trish peeked out the window. "Yep, he's here. Oh! He has presents!" she said, grinning at me mischievously.

"Presents? What do you mean presents?" I ran to open the door. Cailin stood there holding three beautiful arrangements of flowers.

"Whoa, you opened the door a little faster than I expected." Cailin flashed his wicked smile at me then looked up to see Trish and my mother standing behind me.

"Wow, greeted by three beautiful women."

"Oh, sorry. Come on in." I stepped back to allow Cailin to enter the house. He handed me one set of the flowers and kissed my cheek. After a quick second, he turned to face my mother.

"Cailin, may I introduce my mother, Elizabeth Daughtry. Mom, this is Cailin, Cailin Wade."

"It's a pleasure to meet you Ms. Daughtry. I see where Libba gets her beauty from." He smiled at my mom and handed her a set of flowers, too.

"These are for me? Libba was right, you are a gentleman." She craned her neck trying to look at Cailin then decided to take a step back so she could see all of him. "It's nice to meet you, Cailin. I've heard so much about you but Libba didn't tell me you were such a giant! I feel so short next to you."

"Mom, you feel short next to everybody," I joked, then looked back at Cailin. "She's the only person I know that's shorter than I am."

"Well, they say good things come in small packages, right?" Cailin turned to Trish and smiled. "These are for you."

"Ahh! For me!" Trish jumped up in the air clapping her hands like a child. Suddenly, she stopped and eyed him. "Wait a minute. What's the catch?"

"Trish, why do you always think there's a catch to every-thing?" He winked mischievously at her as he handed her the flowers and made a slight nod towards the kitchen. I don't think my mother noticed the gesture.

"Oh … oh!" Trish realized what Cailin meant by his nod. "Liza let's go to the kitchen and see if we can find a vase for your flowers. I think I have several, but you can choose what you like." She grabbed my mother's hand and led her to the kitchen, winking back at Cailin as he held up three fingers and mouthed the words *three minutes*.

As soon as they were out of the room Cailin wrapped his

arms around my waist and pulled me to him, bending his knees just enough so that our faces met. He leaned close to my ear and breathed my name, "Libba."

Softly he kissed my neck, then trailed his lips toward my mouth. He kissed me slowly parting my lips with his tongue. Between his kisses, he continued, "I dreamt about you last night." His mouth trailed to my other ear. "But in my dream, you didn't taste this good." His tongue ran down my neck, licking and tasting.

"Cailin stop, my mother and Trish are in the next room. What if they come out here?" I leaned my head back, placed my hands on his waist, and pulled him closer. I could feel him getting aroused.

"You might be saying no but your actions aren't telling me to stop." Cailin slipped his cold hands under my shirt. "Don't worry, we have a few minutes."

"How can you be sure? Oh ..." Cailin's hands were now caressing my breast, his thumbs tracing over my nipples.

"I have ... about sixty ... seconds ... trust me," he said nibbling at my ears again.

"What—"

Cailin didn't allow me to finish my sentence. Again, his mouth found mine as he plunged his tongue inside. I couldn't help but to succumb to his embrace. I pulled him tighter so that I could feel how hard he was beneath his jeans; but as suddenly as he began, he stopped kissing me and let go. He turned me around to face the kitchen and took the flowers that somehow, I was still holding. Strategically, he placed the flowers in front of him as Trish and my mom re-appeared in the living room.

"Did you find a vase?" he asked.

"Yes, we did," my mom said. "Trish has a nice collection. Libba, let's go find one for your flowers too."

"I'll help." Cailin nudged me with the flowers from behind and we began walking toward the kitchen. "Thanks," he mouthed at Trish and winked to show his gratitude for his three minutes alone with me.

Trish excused herself so she could get ready for her date. My mom, Cailin, and I walked into the kitchen and started rummaging through the cabinets.

"How about this one?"

I turned around as Cailin took a rose out of the arrangement. He placed it in the green vase he picked out and held it out to me.

I froze, my face turning stone cold.

"Libba, what's wrong?" My mother asked rushing to my side. "Darling, you look as if you've seen a ghost."

Cailin followed my glare. I didn't realize I was staring out the window.

He turned to see what I was looking at just in time to see someone, who looked like Alec, round the corner of the building across the street.

"Was that—"

"No. No, it can't be. It can't be. He doesn't know where I'm staying." I closed my eyes and buried my head in my hands. Cailin wrapped his arms around me, resting his chin on my head. This time he did not run after Alec but stayed with me instead. I think he knew it was just my imagination playing games with me.

"It's all right. It'll be all right," he cooed. Under his touch I was already starting to relax in his arms.

I know my mom suspected that I saw Alec. She rubbed my back and watched as Cailin comforted me.

Cailin went outside to check the neighborhood before we left for the evening. He made sure every window and door were securely locked. He even made sure Trish's outdoor motion sensor light was working properly before we left and insisted that if his truck was not in the parking lot when she returned that she should go to a neighbor's or call us and wait in the car until we arrived.

"I'll be fine Cailin, geez. You're acting like my dad! Give me a break." I could tell that Trish was becoming annoyed with Cailin and feeling like he was being overly protective.

"He does that," I said. "Ginny warned me on our first date together that he has a tendency to overreact."

"I'm not overreacting. I'm simply making sure she's safe," Cailin insisted.

"Well, I agree with Cailin," My mom said. "Who knows where that man is or what he's up to?"

"Oh, Mom."

"Don't you 'oh, Mom' me. There's nothing wrong with taking precautions especially when that man is still on the loose."

All I could do was hang my head in defeat. Cailin could tell I did not want to have this conversation now.

"Trish just be careful okay," said Cailin. "We'll probably be home before you anyway so there's no need to worry."

Cailin closed the door behind us, checking one last time to make sure it was locked. He waited until Trish left the parking lot and then he backed out, his eyes roaming as we left. Everything seemed to be in order as we drove away, heading for the Stanleys' house.

It was a short drive from Trish's condo. When they arrived, Louis was putting the steaks on the grill and Martha was busy in the kitchen. Cailin knocked on the door and walked in, not waiting for Martha to answer.

"Martha," he yelled.

"In here, Cailin." Libba and Liza followed Cailin into the kitchen.

Martha was taking a pound cake out of the oven and placing yeast rolls inside. The smell of the pound cake lingered in the air.

"Whatever you're cooking sure smells good," said Cailin.

Martha turned around to see Cailin grinning from ear to ear.

He bent down and gave her a big hug picking her up slightly from the floor.

"What has you in such a good mood tonight?" Martha laughed.

"I don't know, maybe because I'm surrounded by three beautiful women, twice in one night!"

"You really are a big flirt," said Martha. She slapped his leg gently with a dish cloth. "Hello Libba, how are you tonight?"

Martha stepped toward Libba and gave her a hug, too.

"I'm doing well Martha, thanks. It's good to see you again." Libba placed an arm around her mother drawing Martha's attention to her. "Martha, this is my mother, Liza. Mom, this is Martha and that's Louis over there." Libba pointed to Louis, who was out on the deck, saluting them with a bottle of beer. Everyone looked at Louis and waved at the same time.

"Well, if you ladies will excuse me, I'm going to give Louis a hand. Martha, these are for you" Cailin smiled and handed Martha an arrangement of flowers like the ones he brought to Trish's house. He also brought a bottle of Stella Rosa, which he knew was quickly becoming Libba's favorite wine.

Cailin placed a hand on Libba's cheek, rubbing it with his thumb. They didn't speak but the way they looked into each other's eyes said a million unspoken words. Cailin gave a half smile and then walked out onto the deck, grabbing a beer from the refrigerator on his way out.

"Well, Liza," Martha said, "I think those two are smitten. What do you think?"

"Oh, I agree Martha, did you see how they looked at each other just now?"

"Hello!" Libba complained. "I'm right here. You gals are talking about me like I'm not even here."

"Don't worry, dear. We're just stating the obvious. That's all." Liza looked at Martha and they both started to laugh.

"Liza, can I offer you a glass of wine?" asked Martha.

"Thank you, then we can really talk about the two lovebirds!"

"Well I'm certainly glad you two ladies are getting along so well and so quickly," Libba said sarcastically.

Martha poured them each a glass of wine, and they sat down in the living room while the men grilled the steaks. Conversation flowed easily between Liza and Martha as they realized they had more in common than they thought. They were around the same age too.

"Martha, Libba tells me you've been like a mother to Cailin since his parents passed. He seems like a very respectable young man." Liza turned to face Libba. "I really like him."

"He's a good man, Liza. Him and his brother. We were always close, even when his parents were alive. But about a year and half ago I got sick, pneumonia, and the boys came over to help Louis take care of me. Right when I got better, Louis fell one weekend when he was out skiing with some friends and broke his hip, so then the boys were coming over helping me to take care of Louis. They helped do the yard and take care of the house, and now I think it's just habit that they come over here. It's either that or the home cooked meals!"

They were all laughing at that when Cailin and Louis entered the house.

"Steaks are ready!" yelled Louis.

Louis walked in the kitchen and went to the sink to wash his hands, then he turned around to meet Liza.

"Hi Liza, I'm Louis," he said. "Sorry I didn't come in earlier to introduce myself."

"It's nice to meet you, Louis. Thank you for having Libba and me over for dinner. I'm sorry for the last-minute notice."

"No problem at all. Cailin knows he can always invite his friends over. The more the merrier."

Martha had already set the dinner table so Cailin and Libba

helped take the rest of the meal to the table. Louis said the dinner grace and they all began to eat.

"Liza," said Louis, "is that short for Elizabeth?"

"Yes, it is. So is Libba's name, didn't she tell you?" She looked around the table to see three heads shaking. She sighed and turned to Libba who looked innocently down at her food. "My grandmother was named Elizabeth and she went by Beth, Bethie actually. My mother was named Elizabeth and she went by the nickname Elli. I go by Liza and then of course there's Libba." She turned to look at Cailin and said, "I hope whenever Libba has a daughter that she'll keep the tradition and name her Elizabeth too."

Cailin did not falter one bit. "I think Elizabeth is a pretty name. You never told me Libba was short for Elizabeth," he said as he gently squeezed her hand. "And what nickname would you give your daughter?"

Libba started to feel a little flushed. She could not believe she was sitting at the Stanleys' dinner table with her mother and Cailin and talking about baby names. She had prepared herself for all types of conversations, but not once did she imagine this as a topic. Her mouth was getting a little dry. She reached for her glass of wine, took a sip, then answered.

"Um, I probably would call her Elizabeth, no nickname, then whenever she has a daughter, she can start the chain all over again."

"You hear about boys being named after their fathers all the time but never do you hear about a mother's name. I think that's a nice tradition ... unique," said Martha. She looked at Cailin. He was mesmerized with Libba, and Martha could imagine the two of them with a daughter.

All throughout dinner Martha watched Cailin. It was interesting watching the young man, whom she thought of as her own child, fall in love before her very eyes. She noticed how Cailin's eyes followed Libba everywhere she went, he listened intently to every comment she made, and most importantly, he couldn't keep his hands off her. He didn't touch her in a sexual manner; his touch was more intimate, close, caring. And she noticed that every time he touched Libba it seemed as though he transferred a part of himself to her. He gave her a part of his soul and with every part that Libba received, she too, gave back a part of hers in return.

When dinner was over, they returned to the living room where Martha served everyone a piece of her homemade pound cake. She served it with vanilla bean ice cream and drizzled with a bit of chocolate raspberry syrup. It was the perfect ending for a perfect dinner.

"Cailin, can you give me a hand with something before you go?" Martha stood up and walked down the hall. Cailin gave Libba a quick kiss and got up to follow Martha to the back of the house. When Cailin walked in, Martha was standing in the middle of the room holding a small box in her hand.

"I have something for you," Martha said, handing Cailin a little gray velvet box. He opened it and stared at its contents.

"I don't understand."

"You know your mother and I were best friends," Martha stared at the spot on the carpet where Cailin and Ginny had once played with fire and the carpet, after all these years, still wore a small burnt circle. "She gave this to me two weeks before she died. We were cleaning out our drawers and closets for a yard sale and she came across it. She didn't want to sell it. She told me ... for some reason she had a feeling that she was supposed to give this to me, but she didn't know why." Martha smiled and chuckled as if remembering a time from long ago.

"I thought she intended for *me* to sell it. Louis and I were having such a hard time back then and I thought your mother was trying to help us without actually giving us any money because she knew I would have never accepted that from her. Anyway, I didn't sell it. I told myself I would give it back to her someday and then, well of course, they were in the car accident. After that, I decided to keep it for sentimental reasons. I told myself I would know when it was time to give it up and so it seems, now is the right time."

Cailin couldn't believe what he was hearing. Did Martha really expect him to give this to Libba? He knew he loved her, but he wasn't ready for this type of commitment. Was he? He stared at the box.

"My father gave this to my mother, didn't he?"

"Yes, back then we called it a promise ring. Your mother told me that your father gave it to her the first time he told her that he loved her. It was a symbol that they were soulmates and he promised her that no matter what happened between them she would always be a part of his spirit. When he proposed to her, he gave her another ring as a symbol of his love and fidelity, but she always held onto this one."

"And you're giving it to me so that I can give it to Libba?"

"Yes. I don't expect you'll give it to her anytime soon, but I think she's the one. You even said so yourself Cailin, remember. You said you've seen your future and—"

"I'm not disagreeing with you Martha, I'm just a little shocked at the moment." Now Cailin stared at the spot on the carpet. "Is it that obvious?"

"If you're talking about how much you two already seem to be in love with each other, then yes."

"You see it in her, too? I thought I was imagining it because ... because I want her to be in love with me, too," he whispered.

"Oh no Cailin, it's not your imagination. I think after your parents died, you locked your soul away for fear that it would escape and never come back. Now it has some place to go and it has another soul to keep it company. You and Libba, you're survivors. Both your souls have been through a lot, yours locked away for so long and hers ripped apart in the matter of a day. But the two of you, you are survivors of the soul. You've each given the other a piece of your essence and that's what will make your love survive.

"You two click Cailin. I saw it the first time I met her. I never thought two people could fall in love as quickly as you two have but it happened. I'm sure of it Cailin, and I'm sure Libba is in love with you, too."

Martha knew she had given Cailin a lot to think about and she was right. Cailin thought, *what is she talking about? Survivors of the soul, my spirit, Libba's essence. It all sounds so magical. And love at first sight? Who am I fooling? She's right. Magic is real. Love at first sight does happen. And fairies,* Cailin smiled to himself, *they do exist.*

"Thanks, Martha. And thanks for giving me my mother's ring. You're right. Libba is my soulmate. No matter what happens to either of us, she'll always be a part of my spirit too."

Cailin tucked the little box in his pocket and turned to walk out of the room.

"Oh Cailin, one more thing."

"Yes, Martha."

Martha handed him a light bulb.

"Can you replace the light before you go? The others might ask why I called you back here, and the bulb really does need to be replaced."

Cailin laughed and grabbed the bulb, reaching up to replace the blown one. He was so tall he didn't need a step ladder. After changing the light, he gave Martha a big hug and kissed her cheek. Together, they walked out of the room.

When he walked back into the living room Libba looked at him with her beautiful hazel eyes. He touched the box in his pocket and went to sit next to the woman he was in love with—his magical, precious fairy. His soulmate.

CHAPTER 15

MATCHMAKER

Trish's date with Rowan had, or so I thought, turned out to be a success and she went out with him twice more since their initial drink-and-a-movie-night together. Trish wasn't quite sure how much she liked him; Rowan on the other hand, seemed very interested in Trish. After their third date, he sent to her at work a teddy bear holding a balloon, but Trish gave them to the receptionist claiming that it was entirely too early for him to be sending her gifts and, in her opinion, it made him seem needy and possessive.

"Oh Trish, it's only a balloon. It's not like he sent you a dozen red roses. Now *that* might be a little presumptuous. He's only trying to impress you for goodness sake!" I squeezed the last of my personal items into an old office supply box and looked around the room to make sure I had everything. I was moving into a different office two doors down the hall and Trish was moving into mine. We had secured the Claussen account together and Trish was promoted to Marketing Manager, a promotion I thought was far past due.

"Yeah, well I think it's a bit much. I mean we've only been out three times and he's already giving me stuff, like he wants to make sure I'm thinking about him all day long," she said as she dropped a huge stack of files on her new desk.

"I guess you certainly made a good impression. Trish you didn't …?"

"Didn't what?"

I looked at Trish to see if I could read any tell-tell signs. "You slept with him, didn't you?"

"No, I swear I didn't!"

I eyed Trish. It had been months since Trish was with a man and she was no longer hounding me about every detail between Cailin and me. The only explanation was that she had slept with Rowan and therefore was no longer in need of living 'vicariously through others' as she liked to put it.

"Trish!" I scolded. "Cailin and I were dating over a month before we had sex."

"Libba, one, that's your problem, and two, I promise you, I haven't slept with him okay? We've come close to doing it, but I didn't go through with it."

I crossed my arms and raised an eyebrow at her.

She scowled at me again. "I swear you better not tell this to Mallory, or I'll deny it and then I'll kill you but … I keep thinking about Robert."

"Robert?"

"Yes, Robert."

"Robert LeBrecque?"

"Yes."

"As in Lieutenant LeBrecque?"

"Yes."

"You mean the police officer—"

"Oh my gosh, Libba, yes, yes, yes! Lieutenant Robert LeBrecque, the police officer that took our statements at the hospital, the police officer in charge of your case, the police officer that's a bit older—not old, mind you, just older—and yes, the police officer that I keep envisioning putting me in handcuffs thanks to that stupid little remark Mallory made that one time." She crossed her arms to mock me, and then leaned against the desk. "I think he's sexy ... in a Kevin Costner kind of way."

I just stared at Trish without saying a word. When I could no longer hold it in any further, I burst out laughing.

"Oooh, Libba! I swear you PISS me off!" Trish had a quick temper. When she got mad her faced turned almost as red as her hair.

"I'm sorry," I laughed.

Trish stood up and started to walk away.

"Trish, really, I'm sorry! Don't go!" I yelled. Trying my best to hold in the laughter, I cried, "Please, Trish don't go. Come on, let's go get an early lunch, my treat, then we can come back, and I'll help you set up your new office."

We walked to the sandwich shop around the corner. Rowan had called Trish as soon as we walked out of the building and she had answered her cell, not realizing it was him. I listened to her as she politely—well, as politely as was in her nature—told Rowan she couldn't go out with him for a while, at least not until she had sorted a few things out. I could tell he was pressuring her to tell him what was going on and continuing to ask her out, so I moved closer to her side and spoke very loudly.

"TRISH, THE WAITRESS IS WAITING FOR YOUR ORDER. DO YOU WANT ME TO HAVE HER COME BACK?"

Trish placed a hand over her cell and mouthed, *thank you.*

"I'm sorry, Rowan," she said almost girlishly, "but I really have to go. I'm having lunch with Libba and we need to order ... okay, yes maybe later ... okay ... bye." She hung up her phone and lifted her hand to her head pretending to wipe her brow.

The hostess allowed us to choose our table since the lunch rush had not come in yet. It was already June, but the weather remained in the seventies making me anxious for the warmer weather to arrive. I couldn't believe I had met Cailin in February and we had been going out for four months now.

Trish chose a table near a window because she knew I would want to people watch while we had our lunch. The wind was beginning to pick up and I could tell that by the time five o'clock rolled around it would be wet and cold. In other words, a night Trish and I would most likely spend indoors and probably watching a new Netflix original. Cailin would not be home until late since he was working out of town again, but I would get to see him the next day at Muirfield Manor where we all planned to celebrate Mike's birthday.

"So, about those handcuffs," I teased.

"Oh, I knew I shouldn't have said anything to you!" Trish snatched a menu and suddenly, out of nowhere, she slapped my arm with it!

"What'd you do that for!" I yelled.

"Come on Libba, I was *really* hoping you would understand and maybe even offer to help, you know, slip him a hint that I'm available."

"I suppose I could mention your name the next time I talk to him. But mind you, it's not like I've talked to him recently. Things have sort of calmed down. I mean, I haven't seen Alec since that time I thought I saw him when my mom was visiting. Maybe he's given up and has decided to leave me alone after all."

"Hmm?"

"You don't think he's given up yet, do you?"

"I don't know," Trish replied, "but I was talking to Mallory about things yesterday and she doesn't seem to think so. For some reason, she said it feels like this is the calm before the storm, and you know Mallory, that girl has a sixth sense and can always tell when something is about to happen."

"Yeah, you're right … those damn hiccups of hers." I thought about the incident at Muirfield Manor and how Mallory was worried for the kids just before I spotted Alec on the big rock. If Mallory was worried, I probably should be too.

"I'm going to wash my hands." Trish stood up, but her boot caught the hem of her pants causing her to slip and lose her balance. As she did so, she reached out, threw her arms up to stop herself from falling and landed square into Lieutenant LeBrecque, slapping his backside with the palm of her hands.

"Trish!"

"SHIT!"

"What tha—!"

A chorus of expletives came from Trish, Robert, and me, all within a millisecond of the other.

Speak of the devil, I thought.

Shit, shit, oh grr-eat, thought Trish.

Well, well, Trish Knight, thought Robert turning around to see who had rammed into him. *I wanted to bump into her, but I didn't think it would be literal.* He raised an eyebrow and grabbed Trish's arm to help steady her. Trish automatically grabbed him back to get her balance, then let go to press her pants with her hands as if to iron out any wrinkles.

"Robert, I'm so, so sorry about that. I lost my balance, please forgive me," she said as she ran her fingers through her hair.

"No worries, no harm done. You all right?" Robert said to Trish as he fixed her chair to give her more room.

"Oh, I'm perfect now. Why don't you grab a chair and join us?" Trish asked, checking out Robert from head to toe. He was out of his usual business attire and was dressed casually wearing a pair of faded jeans and a blue plaid collar shirt with a white t-shirt underneath. He did sort of remind me of Kevin Costner come to think of it.

"Hi, Ms. Spencer," he said looking at me.

"Hello, please call me Libba, I think we've known each other long enough to toss out the prefixes."

"All right then, but you'll need to call me Robert if that's the case."

"Deal. Won't you join us? Trish was just going to the restroom, but we'd love for you to join us for lunch, if you have the time that is."

"Oh! Yeah … bathroom, that's where I was going." Trish nodded her head at Robert and gestured to me that I should mention her availability while she was away. "Excuse me, I'll be right back."

Robert sat down. Our conversation started with small talk about the weather and then turned to the food on the menu. By the time Trish returned I still had not found the opportunity to squeeze in a hint about the two of them going out. I wasn't really sure how to approach that subject anyway, but then Robert asked if we had any plans for the weekend and out of nowhere my mouth was speaking before I could tell myself to shut up.

"Actually … Trish just asked me to go with her to the wine tasting at the chateau on Saturday, but I can't because Cailin and I have plans. Hey, I know! Why don't you go with her or did you already have something planned for yourself?"

Trish looked at me with wide eyes, then looked at Robert.

Robert looked at me, then at Trish, then down at his menu.

"I'm sorry, Robert. Libba shouldn't have put you on the spot like that." Trish glared at me with harsh eyes. "It's just that I asked her to—"

"No, it's okay. I'd be happy to accompany you, Trish." Robert slowly looked up and smiled at Trish and in return, she smiled back with a look of utter happiness.

Trish removed the black baby doll shirt she was modeling and tried on one of her favorites that had three quarter length sleeves and made her look like a hippy. She was on her third outfit trying to decide what to wear for her date with Robert. They decided to attend the afternoon wine tasting, follow it with an early lite supper, and then a horseback riding tour before the sun went down. Then, unfortunately, Robert would have to excuse himself so that he could meet his cousin, Tom.

Trish told me that Robert and Tom were going night fishing in the swamps and, although she sulked about not being able to spend more time with him, she felt much better after I reminded her how mosquitoes loved her red-headed blood. Besides, we were going to Muirfield Manor for Mike's birthday party.

"You know what this reminds me of?" I asked as I sat on the edge of Trish's bed, which was still unmade and not only was a wet towel draped across it, but also the previous outfits she had tried on as well. "My first date with Cailin. I probably went through a dozen outfits before settling on the first one I had tried on."

"Not me," Trish said as she turned around to face me. "How do I look?"

She had settled on a pair of tan skinny jeans that she tucked inside brown leather boots. She paired it with a mustard brown scoop-neck blouse that was fitted at the bottom but flowed loose around her torso. A long gold chain with three beads and a tassel hung around her neck, and gold angel wing earrings dangled off her ears, softly swinging between her long red locks of loose, wavy curls.

"Perfect," I said. "Not too underdressed for the wine tasting and not too dressy for the ride. By the way, don't forget to be at Muirfield Manor by seven pm. We're having dinner then cake and presents. You did remember to get Mike a present, didn't you?"

"Don't worry, I'll be there, and I'm getting him a bottle of wine for his birthday." She grabbed her wristlet and we walked into the living room together. Within minutes Robert picked her up and they were heading out the door. I peeked out the window and watched as Robert opened the door for Trish and they took off on their first date.

I still had to wrap Mike's gift before Mallory and Olivia picked me up. Mallory was giving me a lift so I could go home with Cailin and not worry about leaving my car at Muirfield Manor. I had no idea what to get Mike for his birthday but had finally settled on a soccer ball picture frame. Inside it was a picture of the whole gang that was taken at Noah's soccer game the first time Mallory, Trish, and I had gone to watch him play. This was right after I was released from the hospital and I was the only one wearing sunglasses to cover up my black eyes. Noah and Olivia were in the center of the photo, Mike stood behind Noah, and Mallory stood behind Olivia. The four of them looked like the perfect family standing together in the middle of the picture frame.

I thought about the times I saw Mallory and Mike together. In my opinion they made a great couple. Noah and Olivia certainly played well together and already acted like brother and sister. Noah seemed very drawn to Mallory, often seeking her approval, and Olivia had wrapped herself around Mike since the first time they met in the hospital. The only thing stopping the two sets from becoming a foursome were the two adults.

Cailin noted that his brother appeared to be interested in Mallory, but I couldn't glimmer a single clue in Mallory's behavior that indicated she was interested in Mike. Trish said she had seen it though. Since the incident with Alec at Muirfield Manor, it seemed as though Mallory distanced herself from Mike. I never mentioned that quick kiss Mallory gave Mike that day, nor did Mallory bring up the subject. It was as if it had never happened. Perhaps that was the way Mallory wanted it to be, but I hoped not. They would make a great-looking couple, I thought.

Mike was a businessman and there was a very distinguished air about him, and Mallory was a very classy lady herself. She always had her act together and even when she was casually dressed, I thought she still looked better than anyone else. They were both very stylish and sophisticated in their own way and to top that off, both of their children were well-behaved, polite, and had great manners. They could make the perfect family, if only they opened their hearts and gave it a chance. I knew Mallory didn't like matchmaking and especially didn't like for people to get into her own affairs, but I thought maybe, just this once, I might have to do something my friend wasn't too keen about.

I heard a car pull into the driveway and checked the time. Mallory was early.

I walked toward the door, peeking out of the window before answering it, and saw Cailin getting out of his truck. *What is he doing here,* I wondered? I unlocked the bolt and opened the door watching Cailin as he checked the mailbox, grabbed its contents, then walked towards me.

"Hey, handsome, I thought Mallory was picking me up."

"She was supposed to, but she called yesterday to see if I needed help with the decorations. When I asked, 'what decorations?' she huffed and said *'really Cailin, you're such a man',*" he said in his best Mallory impersonation. "Anyway," Cailin stepped inside the house, threw the mail on the corner table, and grabbed my hips pulling me closer to him. "I thought I would work it to my advantage, so I played dumb and dumber, and finally got my wish. She's doing the decorations and I get to pick you up and sneak in a few undisclosed minutes with you before we leave."

Cailin leaned down and skimmed my neck with his nose, his breath heating my skin and sending chills down my spine. He wrapped his arms around me and lifted me quickly off the floor. My legs automatically wrapped around his waist and for a moment we stood like that, tasting and enjoying, enjoying and tasting.

"Well, I hate to deny you of your wish, Cailin, but—oh." Slowly, he snuck his hands under my blouse and rubbed my bare back. "Cailin … I still have to shower and get ready to go."

"Uh huh." He continued caressing my bare back with his

hands. "Shower … that definitely sounds like something I wouldn't mind right now." Still holding me in his arms, he started walking towards the bathroom, his hand now roaming over my bare breast. "Ooh, you feel so good," he muttered, his lips still covering mine.

He stopped just inside the bathroom and lifted my shirt over my head. He leaned me against the wall so that he could take off his shirt too. I started to lower my legs, but he grabbed them, instructing me to clinch him even tighter. With one hand Cailin reached into the shower and turned on the water. The room began to fill with steam radiating from the hot water flowing from the faucet. As the steam escaped the shower, the mirror began to fog, and I turned to look at our reflection. I could see Cailin's back, strong and muscular, flexing as he rocked me against the wall. The water wasn't the only thing heating the room.

When we arrived at Muirfield Manor, Mallory was emptying her trunk of what looked like half the contents of a party store. There were two loads of balloons on the front porch and she was now carrying a third, along with a bag full of fabrics all in coordinating colors of mocha brown, winter blue, and sea green. Of course, her color combination was perfect for Mike's party.

"Where's Olivia?" I asked as I grabbed a bag from the car. Cailin took the bag Mallory was currently holding and took the last two from the back seat.

Mallory grabbed a card and birthday present, closed both passenger doors, and locked the car. "Oh, she's with my mom," Mallory said. "She picked her up earlier and took her to a matinee so I could come and decorate before the party. She'll be dropping her off afterwards though," Mallory said as we all walked into the house.

Mallory stopped dead in her tracks and slowly looked around. Cailin and I had worked hard over the last month to get the house ready for today. Cailin wanted it to be a surprise for everyone and also wanted it to be the first of many happy memories at Muirfield Manor.

Ginny, Martha, and I had gone out one day and picked out colors for most of the rooms. Well, mainly Ginny and Martha had made the choices, but I went along for moral support. Their style and eye for interior decorating was far better than anything I could imagine, and I had no problem admitting to that fact. After we purchased the paint, we placed each bucket in their respective rooms and Martha used post-it notes so Cailin and I would know what color to paint and where.

The rooms on the bottom floor were painted but still empty of most furniture except for the kitchen, formal dining room, and parlor. These we had decorated, and Mallory now stood amazed at how good they looked. Cailin brought two long tables from his office and centered them in the middle of the living room, making one wide rectangular makeshift dining table. He placed folding chairs around the table for all of us to sit. There was a total of eight chairs, even though Cailin wasn't sure if Ginny would be able to make it. The Stanleys had chosen to stay at home since they had seen Mike the week before.

The parlor was painted in pale yellow and rich navy blue, and striped curtains flanked the ceiling-high windows. Centered at each window were Queen Anne storage benches and an old up-right piano sat in the corner closest to the entryway. A fifty-three-inch flat screen television hung over the fireplace, which Cailin framed with mosaic tiles. A rug just big enough for comfort but not too large to hide the hard wood floors, lay in the middle of the room. Cailin had yet to buy the rest of the furniture, and in order for everyone to hang out for the evening, he brought in lawn chairs and a couple of bean bags for the kids.

"Wow! You guys have done so much. It's beautiful," Mallory said in sheer awe.

"Glad you like it." Cailin said looking quite proud of himself. "I still have a lot of work to do but I'm getting there, slowly but surely."

Cailin decorated for the party according to Mallory's strict instructions while I started two large pot roasts with potatoes, carrots, onions, and celery—a meal Cailin said was Mike's favorite growing up. Mallory haphazardly placed all the balloons in the parlor and foyer, then decorated the makeshift dining table and chairs with the fabric I saw in the bags. She also laid a round mirror in the middle of the table where she placed a short bouquet of blue carnations surrounded by blue and green votive candles. She set the table with dinner plates that were blue with a mocha brown trim and topped the plates with green salad dishes. She even picked up matching water goblets.

"Can you believe I got all of this at the Dollar Tree! It doesn't look cheap does it? I mean, it's glass not plastic," she asked as she stepped back to admire her work.

"It's beautiful, Mallory. Then again, I'd expect nothing less from you." We both smiled and continued working. I still had the cake to decorate, Mallory wanted to decorate the powder room—just a few candles and flowers she insisted—and Cailin was making a playlist, trying to decide which songs to play that would be appropriate for kids, yet also not too boring for the adults, when we heard a knock on the door. Seconds later, Noah came flying around the corner followed closely by Olivia and trailing behind them were Mike and Mallory's mother. What seemed like a quiet decorating party was quickly about to change.

As Mallory's mother tried to explain why she was there, Olivia and Noah were also trying to explain their stories while mixing in parts of the movie at the same time. Mike was even trying to explain why they had arrived early and apologized for not calling on his way over. Everyone was vying for Mallory's attention. Cailin and I stood arm in arm watching from a distance.

"Those two need to throw in the towel and hook up already," Cailin whispered in my ear. "Look at them. She falls right into place with Noah, and Olivia clearly does the same with Mike. They're perfect for each other, almost as perfect as the two of us," he said kissing the top of my head.

"Yeah, somehow, we've got to get them together, but something tells me we won't have much work to do playing matchmaker. I think the kids have that department under control." *And they don't even know it,* I thought.

After all the raucous was finally over, Mallory's mother had no choice but to stay for dinner. As we imagined, the four ran into each other at the movies and as everyone was heading to Muirfield Manor anyway, Mike invited Mallory's mother to join the party too.

Ginny called to inform us that she couldn't get off work and she sent her love and birthday wishes to Mike. Trish was actually on time for a change and though I was dying to get the details of her date, I promised not to tell everyone that she and Robert had gone out. I decided to wait until we were back at her place to bring it up.

Dinner was a success. Mike thought the pot roast was exceptional and he was especially impressed with the simple yet elegant decorations that Mallory put together. By the time everyone was almost finished eating, the kids apparently had enough of the adult conversation and started throwing hints that we hurry with the cake and ice cream so we could go into the parlor for Mike to open his presents.

Mike opened Cailin's gift first. It was a Jimmie Johnson model race car; however, attached to the box was his real gift. Cailin made reservations for the two of them at the racetrack for the following weekend. They would have their own NASCAR experience and get to race one another at the Charlotte Motor Speedway.

"This is so cool, Cailin!" Mike exclaimed. "You know I'm gonna take you down!"

"In your dreams, my boy! I'm gonna drive circles around you and—" Cailin started but was quickly interrupted by Trish.

"Enough boys! Here, I got you some wine." Trish said as she handed Mike a gift bag from the chateau. Inside were two bottles of wine. The first bottle was a red wine called Marechal Foch, which Trish explained, was 'grapy' and paired well with pasta. The other bottle was a High Country Rose, which she said won a bronze medal at the North Carolina State Fair in 2007.

"Thanks Trish. Since when did you become a wine connoisseur? I thought you only drank the cheap stuff?" Mike smiled jokingly.

"Well, you thought wrong. My taste has become a bit mature lately," Trish replied back. She passed me a look that Mallory was quick to notice and in turn, Mallory squinted her brows together then raised one, knowing we were keeping a secret from her.

Noah and Olivia shoved a big box at Mike, both of them yelling, "open this one, open this one!" at the same time while jumping up and down in excitement. Written on the outside of the box in dark blue crayon were the words: To DAD, From Noah, With Love.

"Uncle Cailin helped me, but it was Ms. MacDonald's idea," said Noah, looking sheepishly at Mallory.

"Then I should hurry and open it, right!" Mike ripped off the wrapping throwing the paper to the floor. "A new mailbox?" he asked with confusion.

"It's not just any old mailbox," said Cailin, "open the box."

Mike opened the box to reveal a shiny black oversized mailbox. Noah had dipped his hands in yellow paint and decorated his handprints perfectly on one side. Cailin had neatly written the date underneath the prints.

"This is awesome Noah!" Mike said giving him a giant bear

hug. "The mailbox at home has surely seen its day. This is great, really. Tomorrow we'll put it up together, okay?"

"Okay," Noah said as he grinned at Mallory and was looking incredibly pleased with himself for giving his dad such a special gift.

"My turn, my turn!" yelled Olivia shoving herself between Noah and Mike and handing Mike a very thick envelope. "Mr. Wade, I paid for it with my pig food!"

"With your pig food? What is pig food?" Mike asked looking very puzzled, although I was sure he knew what she meant and only wanted to hear her explanation.

"Well, pig food is the qua ... the quart ... the quart doors, did I say that right, Mommy?" She turned to ask Mallory who was standing in the doorway.

"It's quarters, dear. Quarters," Mallory responded with a nodding approval.

"Right! Pig food is the quart-ters that my piggy eats. I put them in his belly and get to spend them, but only on special 'casions."

"Oh, I see," said Mike, "and you consider this a special occasion?"

"Course I do silly. It's your birfday."

"Well, I hope it didn't cost you a lot of pig food to purchase this."

"Only eighteen, and Mommy made me count all of them," she pouted, "and it took forever 'cause I kept messing up."

"Wow, eighteen quarters is a lot of pig food to count. Where did you get all these quarters from anyway?"

"Well, Nana gives me some when I get to stay with her, but Mommy gives me four," she said, holding up four fingers, "every Sunday for keeping my room clean. I get to put two in the money basket at church and I get to feed two to my pig." Olivia then lowered her head in embarrassment. "But sometimes when I get in trouble, I have to put three in the basket at church."

"But I'm sure that's never happened right?"

Olivia tried to cover one hand with the other as she showed Mike three little fingers and whispered in his ear how many times she had gotten in trouble.

"Three times but don't tell Noah."

"Don't worry, your secret is safe with me," Mike whispered as he kissed Olivia on the cheek.

Mike opened the envelope and inside was a talking birthday card. Mallory and Olivia had recorded themselves singing happy birthday to Mike. They sounded so cheerful singing together that Mike closed it and opened it again so that everyone could sing along.

The next gift was Mallory's. She walked toward Mike and handed him a rectangular shaped box about the size of a piece of paper but about three inches thick. Mike opened the package being careful not to ruin the wrapping, which of course matched the brown, blue, and green as the rest of the party decorations.

"I hope you like it," Mallory said as Mike opened the box. "I carved the design myself, then stained it."

Mike didn't say a word.

"My hand isn't as steady as it used to be, but I think I did an all-right job," she continued, sounding a little worried that Mike didn't like her gift.

"Mallory, this is beautiful." Mike showed everyone the keepsake box that Mallory had given him. It was made of mahogany wood and she had carved his initials on the bottom right corner. On the top left was the silhouette of a buck's head, about two inches tall and bordered with hearts of different sizes.

"Mommy says you put things in it that are dear to your heart,"

Olivia said to Mike. "That's why she drew the deer and the hearts in the corner. See." She pointed to the corner of the box.

Mike looked up at Mallory as he spoke, "Then I shall make sure I'm very particular about what I put inside it. Thank you, Mallory."

"Looks like it's my turn," I said, handing Mike my gift. After he opened it and showed everyone the photo, it seemed to pass from one hand to the next, everyone making comments about the day we watched Noah play his game. When Mallory's mom looked at the photo, she couldn't help but comment on Mallory and Mike with the kids in the center of the frame.

"You guys make such a lovely couple," she said loudly. "Don't you think so, Trish?"

Trish stood behind Mallory's mother and the two of them began to discuss Mallory and Mike as if neither one of them were in the room.

"Guys, please, not in front of the children." Mallory tried to interject. "Mother, have you no couth? You don't even know Mike and we're not a couple. Oh, Trish come on now!"

It was no use. Trish and Mallory's mother wouldn't stop talking and to top that off, Noah was even making remarks, although all Olivia could do was laugh and make kissy faces. Cailin nudged me but didn't say a word, and I knew better than to say anything. I wanted to play matchmaker and assumed the kids would handle things for me, but never had I imagined everyone would gang up on her.

"NOW, NOW," Mike stood up and spoke loudly over everyone, quieting the kids and causing all the adults to look in his direction. He walked next to Mallory and placed a hand on her arm.

Mallory slowly turned in his direction.

"If you would please … I think you are making Mallory a bit uncomfortable trying to match the two of us like that. However," he said turning to Mallory, "there might be some stock in what they are saying. How about it, Mallory?" He stared straight into those wide dark eyes. "Will you go out with me? It would be the best birthday present I could ask for."

The room was so quiet, I think even the kids were holding their breath.

Mallory scanned the room, looking at everyone and stopping to look at Mike directly into his eyes. As she did so her eyes grew in that way they seemed to do when she had just realized what should have been so obvious.

Her shoulders relaxed and then she sighed, "Yes, Mike. I'd love to go out with you."

CHAPTER 16

A VISITOR FROM
THE PAST

C ailin didn't like it. He absolutely did-not-like-it! But it was no use. There was nothing he could say or do to make me change my mind.

Even Trish and Mallory were on my side.

He could not win.

I insisted on moving back into my old house, but Cailin insisted I stay with him or Trish until Alec was locked up and he knew that I would be free from his fury.

No deal.

"You know, you could still change your mind," he said checking the app on my phone for the millionth time.

Cailin had contacted one of his friends at Vivint Smart Home who came by and installed my new security system. It came with exterior cameras, integrated lighting, locks, thermostat, and other additional security features, all connected to an app on my phone. He was even seriously thinking about getting me a trained Pit Bull or Rottweiler, but I told him I could not take care of a dog, not now.

"Cailin, we've already discussed this. I've stayed with Trish long enough. I don't want to wear out my welcome and besides, I need to be on my own again. I can't live in hiding forever and I don't want to."

"I'm not asking you to live with her forever, just until I know you'll be safe." A vision of the two of them sitting on his back deck, holding hands while admiring a beautiful evening sunset crossed his mind.

"Cailin? Cailin." I waved my hand in front of his face trying to grab his attention. "Did you hear what I said?"

"Huh? Sorry."

"I said I need to get the house ready to sell. If I'm going to put the house on the market, I've got a ton of things to do. The chimney needs repairing, there are a few boards on the deck that need to be replaced and stained, the gutters need to be replaced, I need to change out the flooring in the kitchen, plus I have to go through six years of junk and throw away a ton of things." I grabbed a notepad and started making a list of things to do to get the house ready to sell.

I continued to ramble although it didn't seem as though Cailin was paying attention to what I was saying.

"Or maybe I should have a moving yard sale. I've never planned a yard sale before, but I bet Mallory could help me with that and—"

"Move in with me."

"What?"

"Move in with me. Move in with me, Libba. I'll help you get the house ready to sell. I'll take off work next week and spend the whole week here repairing things. I can even get some of my crew to come over and help. We can have it ready by the end of the month. Come on, move in with me, Libba." He walked towards me and wrapped his arms around my waist.

"Cailin ... I don't know what to say." I took two steps backward and slowly sat down on the couch.

"Say yes. We already spend every weekend together anyway and I, I want you there. I want you to live with me." Cailin sat down beside me and placed his forehead against mine, taking a deep breath. "Libba, I know we've only known each other for a short while but I can't begin to tell you how strongly, how deeply, I care about you. From the first time we met, I knew what we would share would be different and it has been. It is. What I feel for you is something I've never felt with anyone before, and I can't imagine I ever will." He paused for a second. "Libba, I think I'm—"

I placed a finger on his lips. He closed his eyes and waited. I leaned in and kissed him softly, so softly.

I knew what Cailin was about to admit but I wasn't sure if I was ready to hear those words or not. True as it was, I knew he was right. What we had was different. How I felt about Cailin was far different from how I felt about Alec.

Cailin completed me.

He made my soul come alive, and with every day that passed I felt that bond between the two of us grow stronger and stronger, and I knew I was falling deeper and deeper.

I thought it was the same for him. I hoped it was. I thought I could tell in the way he spoke to me, in the way he looked at me, and especially in the way he touched me. His touch, just a simple touch, was more intimate than anything I ever thought possible.

With every touch it felt as though he passed a part of himself to me, as if our souls were connecting and becoming one. And every time we made love, when we would reach that point and climax together, I felt that same surge of electric energy that I felt the night he changed my tire, only now it was stronger, more powerful, more awake, more alive. Now it passed through my entire body as if it knew no boundaries, no limitations.

Cailin held the key that unlocked my soul. I never believed in people having a soulmate, nor given any thought to the possibility that one day I might find my own. I had never experienced or shared this type of feeling with anyone, nor did I think I could ever experience it with anyone other than Cailin.

And that's when I knew.

That's when I knew he loved me, and I loved him. That's how I knew I was *in* love with him, and how I knew that no matter what, I always would be in love with Cailin Wade.

"I love you," we said at the same time.

"But," Cailin knew there was more.

"I'm not ready to move in with you. Not yet."

When I decided to sell the house and brought up the topic to Trish and Mallory for a second time, Mallory told me that if I were serious, she knew someone who could be my agent. I was beginning to think that I could always count on Mallory to have a contact for any service I might need. I assumed it was because she was a single mother and as a single mother, Mallory was used to doing everything on her own, whereas I counted on Alec for many of the household and financial matters.

Mallory recommended a very reputable real estate agent named Johnny Calhoun. Johnny had a record of selling homes within thirty to sixty days and after the two of us spoke on the phone, he immediately came over the next day and made several suggestions for improving the house. He discussed the changes with Cailin who scheduled his crew to come over every day in order to have it completed by the end of the month.

After two weeks of working on the house, it was definitely taking shape and looked much better than I could have expected. Cailin's construction crew repaired everything on mine and Johnny's list, even fixing a few repairs that Cailin suggested, and I was almost ready to put the house on the market. All I had left was to sell the junk I had accumulated over the last six years.

I had my yard sale the weekend before the fourth of July. Trish, Mallory, and Olivia were coming over early to hang up the signs and help me organize all the things I had decided I wanted to sell, which seemed to be enough to stock an entire thrift shop.

Trish helped me place furniture ads on Craig's List and my bedroom furniture, dining set, and lawn mower was already sold and picked up. Martha had a friend whose daughter just graduated from Appalachian State University and was moving into an apartment. After showing her friend pictures of the living room set, her friend decided to purchase it as a surprise for her daughter. She was picking that up later in the afternoon, giving me plenty of time for my yard sale in the morning before it became too hot.

Mallory suggested grouping items by price and brought over several large baskets and boxes to keep everything organized. All the paperback books I was willing to depart with were placed in a large box, but I decided to keep my hard-bound collections. I had a ton of comforters, curtains, dishes, yard equipment, and other tchotchke items that Mallory said would sell very quickly if I priced them right. She also suggested selling coffee and donuts because, as she put it, "Men that are dragged out of the house for a woman to shop need a little encouragement to keep going, especially that early in the morning."

We were almost done setting out the items when our first customers arrived at six forty-five in the morning. Mallory was right. The man went straight to the coffee table that Mallory and Olivia were standing next too, dropped a single dollar bill into the jar sitting on the table, grabbed a donut, and poured himself a cup of steaming hot java. Olivia offered him cream and sugar, which he turned down, but thanked her all the same. The woman, presumably his wife, perused through my things and walked away twenty minutes later with a bag full of trinkets that I remembered buying on my honeymoon with Alec. At first, I thought departing with such items would cause me a little grief. The thought of getting rid of things from my past was a little unsettling, but as the sale went on, I realized I didn't need those material things after all. They probably held more bad memories than good ones and I decided that from here out, what I wanted most was to remember my new experiences with Cailin and my new-found friends.

There was a steady stream of traffic for the first two hours and my money jars were filling up quite nicely. Although I didn't really care how much I made from all the sales and I already decided that whatever was left unsold I would deliver to the local women's shelter, it was actually a lot of fun talking to all the patrons who had dropped by. To my surprise, I recognized many of them either from the grocery store, the mini mart, and even the antique stores I often frequented. A few inquired as to why and where I was moving, and some even offered their condolences and admitted they had heard about the attack and they didn't blame me for moving. It was weird to talk about my past and future plans with nearly complete strangers but somehow, while doing so, it gave me the sagacity that what I was doing and where my life was going, was as it should be. For the first time in a long time, I felt content. I was finally able to put my past behind me.

Cailin arrived around nine o'clock with breakfast burritos and orange juice for everyone. Playfully, he looked at Mallory and as he handed her a burrito he teased, "I'd tell you not to do anything I wouldn't do on your date with Mike tonight, but honestly, that leaves the door wide open for a lot of mischief."

"You're going on your date with Mike, tonight?" Trish asked, standing with her hands on her hips, tapping one foot on the ground. "And you didn't even SAY anything ALL morning!"

"I was waiting for the right time to bring it up," Mallory explained. "Thanks a lot, Cailin."

"Hey babe," Cailin joked, "just keeping it real."

"I suppose you knew about this too didn't you, Libba. Why am I always the last one to know?" Trish walked up to the three of us and snatched a burrito from Cailin.

"Sorry Trish," I said. "Mallory asked me not to say anything and I promised I wouldn't. Remember you asked me not to say anything about you and a certain individual too."

"Yeah but I've already told her about Robert!" Trish said, pointing a finger at Mallory.

"Robert? You mean Lieutenant LeBrecque? You and the Lieutenant!" Cailin burst out laughing and nearly choked on his burrito.

"I thought you knew!" Trish shrieked, then turned to face me. "You mean you didn't tell Cailin! Oh, great Libba, now I look like a fool!"

"Hey like I said," I defended. "You asked me not to say anything and I didn't."

"Yeah," Trish said, "but I thought you would at least tell your boyfriend. Geez!"

"Well, if I would have told Cailin, then he would have told Mike and then Mallory would have been the only one who didn't know." I explained. "Why didn't you tell me you told Mallory? Then I could have told Cailin and he could have told Mike and then everyone would know! And I wouldn't feel like I'm keeping secrets from everybody!"

"Calm down you two," Mallory interjected, "we have customers."

"You. Ugh!" Trish looked at Mallory like a mother scolding a child. "Give it up. I want details and I want them now."

Mallory shook her head.

"Okay. First, Mike and I *are* going out tonight but it's nothing romantic or formal or anything like that. We're just going out as friends and then I'm sure that will be the end of it."

"Why do you say that?" I asked.

Mallory took a small bite of her burrito and glanced at Olivia who was playing dress up with my old purses and summer hats. She seemed to choose her words carefully as she spoke. "Mike seems like a great guy but I'm sure he would agree that neither one of us want the children, Olivia and Noah, to get hurt if things don't go well between the two of us. Remaining friends is the logical thing to do. I would hate to break Olivia's heart ... or mine again," she added.

"Oh Mallory, is that what you're afraid of?" I always wondered why Mallory didn't date but I never attributed it to the fact that she had once suffered from a broken heart and was afraid to love again. She must have really been in love with Olivia's father. Poor girl.

Mallory nodded.

Even a wave of sympathy crossed Trish's face.

"My brother is a decent, honorable man Mallory," Cailin interjected. "He would never do anything to hurt you or Olivia. I know he cares about Olivia very much, and you too, for that matter. He's not one to date around or have one-night stands. He definitely believes in a monogamist relationship if that's what you're worried about."

"Oh, I know. I don't doubt that one bit. Perhaps that's what I'm afraid of." Just then Olivia came skipping towards us. "Olivia, look at you! Aren't you beautiful with that hat on!" Using her daughter as her scapegoat, Mallory placed an arm around Olivia and walked away leaving Trish, Cailin and me standing there with our half-eaten burritos.

No one brought up Mallory and Mike's date for the rest of the morning. At noon, Mallory's mother picked up Olivia and the rest of us loaded everything that didn't sell onto the back of Cailin's truck. Trish and Mallory went their separate ways, and Cailin and I drove to the women's shelter. Shortly after we arrived back at my house, Martha's friend came over to pick up the living room furniture. Once she was gone, I straightened up the house and stood in the middle of the empty living room. I couldn't believe I was finally ready to put the house up for sale.

As we were leaving, I picked up the last of my mail that I would receive at this address. My plans were to stay with Cailin for the weekend, and after the holiday I would move temporarily into a furnished condo. I wasn't sure how long I would stay there or if I would decide to rent or buy a new home, but for now, the condo suited my needs. Cailin and I had not discussed me living with him since our initial conversation weeks earlier. I think he knew I needed my space, but I couldn't help but feel like he was up to something.

On our way back to Cailin's house, I fingered through the pile of bills and junk mail I had grabbed before we left and came across a hand-written card addressed to Elizabeth Spencer. I knew of only one person who referred to me as Elizabeth and her contacting me threw me off guard. It had been four years since I heard anything from her, what possible reason could she have for contacting me now?

Carefully, I peeled back the envelope and pulled out the card. Inside, it read:

Dear Elizabeth,

I know I'm probably the last person you would expect to hear from, and I can't blame you if you don't want to talk to me. First let me say that I'm sorry for not keeping in touch with you after all these years. For reasons I can't explain on paper, I thought it was best that we distance ourselves from you and especially from Alec. Although I feared for you, I always thought you would be safe, until I saw the news.

I know the police are looking for Alec. I also know that what he is being charged with, while it may shock you, it doesn't exactly surprise me or Arnold. Alec's always had a temper, but every day I prayed that you would never find out just how bad his temper was.

I am sorry for what he did to you and I do hope you can one day forgive me for not being honest with you sooner. I thought that because of you he would change, that he would get better but perhaps not.

There are some things we need to talk about Elizabeth. I think I may be able to help with the search.

Please meet me at Woodland's BBQ, at noon, on Sunday.

Kathy Newsome

I thought about Mrs. Newsome's letter on the way to Cailin's house. I wasn't sure what to make of it or if meeting Mrs. Newsome was a good idea. She was never unkind to me, although she did always seem a bit distant, but I simply attributed that to her quiet nature. She and Mr. Newsome were such good foster parents to Alec, so I tried not to dwell on it much.

"I suppose I should meet Mrs. Newsome and see what she has to say," I said to Cailin once we were at his place. "Maybe she *can* shed some light on what could be going on with him."

"I don't know, Precious. What if it's a trap?" Cailin filled two glasses of wine and led me out onto the deck. "What I mean is, what if he somehow put her up to meeting with you but he really plans to come in and force you to leave with him."

"No, I don't think Mrs. Newsome would have any part of something like that. She would never do that to me, this much I'm sure of." The wine was good, so I took another sip.

Cailin adjusted the outdoor lighting and turned on some music, settling on a soft country station of the nineties. I was sitting sideways on the wicker loveseat and Cailin lifted my legs so he could sit next to me, placing my legs over his lap.

"How about we not talk about this anymore tonight? Let's just relax, have some wine, and enjoy the view," Cailin said as he rubbed my legs, softly massaging each. He bent forward to give me a kiss and as I faced him, I began to lose myself in his gaze. He placed a hand under my chin and leaned in, kissing me softly. He kissed my lips, my checks, my neck, then returned to my lips with more earnest than before. I melted into his kiss, kissing him deeply, enjoying the wine on his tongue as it flicked inside me. Again, I felt our souls melding into one, swelling then subsiding, only to swell again with the next heartbeat.

I sat up and Cailin grabbed me by the waist with both hands. He leaned back on the seat and positioned me on his lap, his hands on my hips as he guided me into place. I sank onto him and could feel him swell, harder and bigger, as we rocked up and down, kissing and sucking with each breath. I pulled my shirt over my head and his hands reached up taking off my bra with one fell swoop, still kissing and sucking, my heart swelling and subsiding. I grasped Cailin's shoulders, anchoring myself to him as I rocked up and down, up and down, swelling and swelling like white sea caps patiently awaiting high tide. Cailin was my ocean and I a ship, sailing gently in the night until finally reaching the edge of serenity.

Mallory stepped out of the shower and stood looking at herself in the mirror. Her dark hair was wet and water droplets hung from long ringlets of curls, like black icicles melting in the sunlight. She rubbed her stomach over a few silver streaks on her belly, stretch marks from giving birth to Olivia. She didn't so much mind them. They were small sacrifices that reminded her of the tiny life she had brought into this world.

She thought about what to wear on her date with Mike. It would be warm during the day but might cool down slightly after dinner and she wanted her attire to be appropriate for both places. They were going to an outdoor summer concert then driving up Valley Boulevard to Twigs Restaurant for an early dinner. She loved going to outdoor concerts but had never been to Twigs before and was looking forward to dining there.

She walked to her closet and pulled out a pair of skinny green casual slacks that she rolled up over her ankles. She paired the pants with a white and green-striped sleeveless peplum top, then slipped her feet into a pair of yellow yarn wedged sandals. She chose bulky light green earrings and gold chunky bracelets to complete her outfit and hopefully draw attention away from her bust. Mallory was average in height, but her thirty-four D bust drew more attention to her than she liked.

Mallory heard Mike as he pulled into the drive. She checked herself in the mirror one last time before locking the door and walking out. She stood on the steps watching Mike park the car.

Mike couldn't take his eyes off Mallory. He knew she tried to dress more conservatively and professional, but he thought there was nothing she could wear that wouldn't scream sexy, yet elegant, to him. He wasn't sure how she did it, but she did.

He got out of the car and walked towards her.

"Hi, Mike. It's good to see you," said Mallory, smiling as Mike approached.

He answered with a wave but continued walking toward her until he reached the steps, stopping two steps below her. He took another step, and they were now standing eye level to each other. Mike took a deep breath and slowly let it out. Since the first time he saw her, he thought, he was mesmerized with her ever-growing dark eyes. He smiled nervously and put out his arm, gesturing that she take it.

"You look stunning," he said partly raising one cheek and giving an approving half smile. "You ready to go?" he asked.

"Thank you. I'm ready," said Mallory. "Do you remember who's playing today? I meant to look it up but didn't have time."

"I never know who's playing," he said, opening the car door for Mallory. "Normally, Noah and I just ride by and if they sound good, we stop, and if not, we keep going. Ah … sorry. I meant to try to make this an adult only night and not mention Noah, but I've already messed up on that one."

Mallory giggled. "Don't worry, I thought the same thing, but it's okay. Before too long, I'm sure I'll slip up too."

They drove to the park and it was packed with people laying on blankets or sitting on lawn chairs. Even the park benches were taken.

"I brought a couple of chairs and bottled waters. They're in the back." Mike popped the trunk, then turned the engine off and got out of the car. He walked to the passenger side and helped Mallory out then went to the back to grab the chairs.

They found a spot near the edge of the playground and set up the chairs. The band was already playing. Kids were running around, a few older couples occupied the benches, and throughout the park, groups of friends, couples, and families seemed to be having a good time. Mike and Mallory talked some while the band played and after several songs the band decided to take a break. They were in the middle of a conversation about Mallory's job and how she thought she was ready for new challenges when Mike heard his name called and looked up to see Ginny, Jared, and Caleb heading their way.

Ginny explained that she was driving by when she spotted Caleb and Jared with a group of friends, so she pulled in to say hi and hang out a while.

"Where's Cailin?" asked Caleb. "I don't see his truck anywhere."

"Cailin and Libba are probably still cleaning out Libba's old house. She's putting it on the market soon." Mike took Mallory's water and helped her up from the lawn chair.

"Hey, Mallory. Love your outfit!" Ginny said taking her wrist and admiring her bangles. "These are gorgeous!"

"Hey, Mal," Jared said looking her up and down and spending a little too much time with his eyes lingering at her breasts. Mallory tucked a piece of hair behind her right ear and crossed her arms at her chest.

"Hi."

"How ya doing?" Caleb asked reaching out to shake Mallory's hand. "I'm Caleb. I don't know if you remember me from the hospital or not."

"Hi, Caleb, yes I remember you. And hi, Ginny. It's good to see you again." Mallory reached over to Mike and took her water, taking a few sips from it.

"Ginny's right, you do look great" said Caleb, quite complimentary. He looked Mallory in her eyes and *not* at her breasts. "Nice earrings by the way."

Mallory smiled and took another sip of her water.

Mike noticed the way Mallory seemed to blush when Caleb talked to her. He also noticed how she crossed her arms when Jared spoke to her. That jerk, always trying to bed someone; this was not the time. He didn't want Mallory feeling uncomfortable on their first date, but he also didn't want Caleb sharing her attention either.

"So how are Cailin and Libba doing?" Caleb asked. "I bumped into Cailin the other day and I wanted to ask about the guy who put Libba in the hospital and if he had been arrested yet, but he didn't have much time to talk so I never got around to it. I hope everything is okay by now."

Mike and Mallory explained the latest news and Mike couldn't help but notice how Jared seemed to be undressing Mallory in his mind right before his eyes. Didn't he know they were there together? He saw Caleb nudge Jared once when he made some crude comment and he thought he heard Caleb whisper that he needed to back off. Jared just ignored him, but Mike was sure Mallory had heard and was beginning to feel self-conscious. Growing up with Ginny, Mike knew she was used to Jared's foul mouth and probably didn't notice a thing, but not Mallory.

Mike looked at Mallory and gently grabbed her elbow. "I'm sorry I didn't notice the time, but we should be going. We have someplace else to be right now."

Mallory started walking back to the chairs and Ginny and Caleb turned to follow her. She grabbed her purse and Mike caught Jared starring at her as she bent over.

"Jared," he said quietly, looking directly into Jared's face. "You really need to stop looking at her like that. She's not that kind of girl and I think you make her nervous."

"Yeah, yeah, whatever man. Don't get so bent out of shape. Or is she your girl now?"

"I'm serious Jared," Mike said grabbing Jared's arm a little tighter than he meant. Jared jerked his arm away from Mike.

"I'm outta here dude." Jared turned shouting to the group, "See you guys later! I have someplace ELSE TO BE right now too!" And he stomped away.

Mike joined the others and started packing up the chairs.

"What was that all about?" Ginny asked as she watched Jared walk away.

"It's not important." Mike replied. "Mallory, are you okay? I know he makes your skin crawl."

"No, I'm fine," she said, then turned to look at Caleb. "Really, I'm okay. I've been around men like that before. I mostly ignore foul-mouthed men like that but if I need to, I can handle myself well enough."

"Either way, you shouldn't have to put up with it when we're around. Isn't that right, guys?" Caleb said, looking at Mike and Ginny. Then he softly looked at Mallory and smiled. Mike noticed Mallory's demeanor change as her dark eyes grew bigger and bigger.

"Yeah," Ginny said. "I'm used to him but that doesn't mean you should have to listen to his crap. Sorry hon."

"I know, but really, it's okay. Hey, why don't you guys come with us? We're going to Twigs for dinner." Mallory looked at Caleb. "You should join us, you don't mind do you Mike?"

"That would be great!" Caleb smiled.

"Ooh, Twigs is fancy," Ginny said. "I'm in!"

This was not the way Mike had imaged his first date with Mallory.

CHAPTER 17

NOT THE WAY IT WAS
SUPPOSED TO BE

"You don't really believe I'm going to let you meet her by yourself, do you?" Cailin was still pacing the bedroom as he had been the whole time I was getting dressed.

"Cailin, I haven't seen Mrs. Newsome in four years. It's going to be awkward enough for the two of us to see each other again, let alone her seeing me with my new boyfriend, and just months after getting a divorce. I really think it would be best if I met her alone. She might not be too forthcoming if you're there. You *can* be a little intimidating, you know."

Cailin thought about what I said. "Fine then. I'm taking you and sitting at the bar. You two can have your privacy but I'm not taking any chances."

"I'll agree to that."

Cailin and I arrived at the restaurant fifteen minutes early hoping to arrive first so I could get a table that was close to the bar. Mrs. Newsome was already sitting in the dining room when I walked into the restaurant. She was seated at a corner table slightly secluded and away from the rest of the dining area.

I sent Cailin a quick text to let him know she was here.

Mrs. Newsome had not changed much in the last four years. Her hair was still a mousy brown color, and she had a lot of gray that covered most of it. She wore it short and there were hints of waves in her otherwise straight hair. She had a strong cleft chin that she always slightly tilted up but now I could see that both her jawline and cheeks were faintly sagging due to age. She looked more fragile than I remembered, and I sensed a bit of apprehension about her, like she was afraid someone was watching.

I looked around and slowly made my way to Mrs. Newsome's table, fidgeting with my hands along the way. She looked up as soon as I approached. Neither of us was sure whether to shake hands or hug and after a few awkward seconds, Mrs. Newsome embraced me. A minute later, Cailin walked in and casually strolled to the bar. He seated himself as close as he could get to our table, ordering a coke and some nachos as he sat down.

Mrs. Newsome and I talked for over an hour and the whole time Cailin sat there listening. I wondered if he could hear everything Mrs. Newsome was telling me. If so, I'm sure he would want to be the one to find Alec and make him pay for everything he had done.

Mrs. Newsome told me that Alec showed up one night asking for twelve thousand dollars. When she asked him why he needed that much he refused to tell her, so she refused to help. She was going to call me to find out what kind of trouble Alec was in when Alec became furious and grabbed her. She tried to get away, but he snatched her by the back of the hair and threw her on the couch. He started yelling at her and that's when Mr. Newsome came running through the backdoor with a shovel and told him to get the hell out of his house and never come back. Mrs. Newsome continued, explaining this was the reason why they stopped sending Christmas cards and every day since she prayed that he never treated me that way.

I told her he had.

SOUL TO SOUL 227

Alec thought he learned to control his drinking since that awful accident four years ago. He never told anyone about that night, not even Libba. If Libba knew, he feared she would turn him in, and he couldn't let a woman do that to him. The fact was, he knew he couldn't tell Libba why he was in that area without telling her he had gone to see his foster parents to ask them for money. If he did, she would want to know why he was asking for money and if he didn't tell her, she would keep searching until she found out the whole story. No, it was better that he kept this to himself. After all, there were no witnesses.

He'd left the Newsomes' in a rage. If they had given him the money none of it would have happened. He was going straight home but instead, he stopped by the bar and had a few drinks. Just one or maybe two drinks, he thought, but the bartender cut him off after his second drink and tried to call him a cab. He didn't think he was too drunk to drive, and he knew he could handle his liquor, so he got into his car and drove away.

Alec remembered closing his eyes, just for a second, he thought, but then he felt dizzy and opened his eyes, realizing he was driving in the middle of the road. He remembered something in the road, a dear maybe, and he swerved the wrong way, crossing over the median. He never saw the other car until he was right on it. He jerked his car not sure if he swiped the other one or not. The other car swerved, hit the side rail, and crashed into a tree on the side of the mountain. When he got out of the car to check on the couple, they were dead. He panicked and ran. That's all he could remember of that night, which still haunted him.

Looking back, Alec knew where his drinking and drug problems came. How could he not? He was just like his father, who was like every other foster dad who had taken him in. They would make a little extra cash, blow the money on booze, then hit all their so-called children. But the Newsomes weren't like that. No, they were different, they were kind. They gave him his own room and bought him new clothes. Mrs. Newsome cooked homemade meals every night and he and Mr. Newsome tossed baseballs after dinner while Mrs. Newsome cleaned the kitchen. They encouraged him to read, to study, to work hard for good grades. They awarded him for straight A's but never punished him for bad ones, only encouraging him to try a little harder the next time. And they looked at him with compassion, something Alec never saw that often in his younger years.

Then the one time, the one time, he needed something, even asked for it on his own, they had failed him. And he reacted the only way he knew how, by hurting the two people who ever gave a damn about him.

For as long as Cailin could remember, Black Bear General Story was his favorite place to buy candy. When he and Mike were younger, their parents would take them there occasionally and let them each pick out a pound of candy, if they promised not to eat it all before the weekend was over. Mike could never keep his promise but somehow, Cailin could make his last almost the entire week. Mary Janes were his favorite, but he also liked Bit-O-Honey and Cow Tails. Mike on the other hand, liked everything. His candy taste was all over the board from candy sticks to coconut flags, from peanut brittle to pineapple taffy. For someone so calm and level-headed, the man had no control when it came to sugar treats. Mike liked everything sweet—candy, cakes, lemonade—it didn't matter as long as it was sweet. With his build, and nearly perfect dental records, no one would ever imagine he liked sweets as much as he did. Good genes must run in the family because Noah was just like him. So far, Noah never had a cavity and playing soccer kept the young boy active and the right size and weight.

Cailin, Mike, and Noah walked up and down the candy aisles

trying to decide what candy to get. Cailin decided immediately and filled his bag quickly with his three favorite treats. Mike and Noah took much longer.

"Just pick some candy for goodness sake." Cailin complained. "Here, give me your bag and I'll fill it for you."

"No way. I don't want a bag full of Mary Janes. Maybe I'm in the mood for Mallow Cups." Mike stared at the candy trying hard to decide.

"I want Skittles and gummies!" Noah said with much excitement. "And maybe some Hot Tamales!"

"Speaking of Mallow Cups," said Cailin. "How was your date with Mallory?"

"It was fine." Mike moved to the next aisle, placing a few pieces of taffy in his bag.

"Fine? Just fine? That's all you have to say?" Cailin was curious now. "You go on a date with Mallory and I *know* you have a thing for her, and you say your date was fine. Just fine."

"Yes, Cailin. It was fine. Just fine." Mike caught Cailin raise an eye to him, not believing him at all. He huffed and explained, "Okay, it started out great. We went to the park to listen to the live bands and we were having great conversation talking about all kinds of things. We laughed and laughed and talked and talked. It was the best time I've had in a long time, but then Ginny, Caleb, and Jared showed up."

"Oh no." Cailin's shoulders shrunk. That wasn't a good sign.

"Oh no is right. Jared is such a jerk. Such a stupid ass jerk! He's fine around us. You know that. We've hung out with him a million times since we were young, but I guess I never really paid attention to how degrading he can be towards women, or maybe, maybe he was never this bad and just started acting this way. I don't know. Either way, he just wouldn't stop. I know Ginny is used to that kind of talk, but Mallory?"

"Mike, I know what you mean," Cailin tried to console his

brother. "Mallory is a thoughtful and kind woman with a good heart. She's delicate and you like her, and you want her to be treated with respect, not just from you or me but everyone. I get it. What did he say to her? Is she all right?"

"He *always* says something to her. And he always stares at her … her … everywhere! The man has no shame. And it wasn't just Jared. Caleb kind of stood up for her a couple times, which was great believe me, but you know how Caleb is. He's that 'sweet guy that every mother wants for their daughters' kind of guy. And … I don't' know, it seemed like there was something between them. Now, I can't tell if she's interested in me or interested in Caleb."

Mike was silent for a second and Cailin wasn't sure what to say. He knew Mallory was afraid of starting a relationship and getting hurt or hurting the kids; she had said so the day of the yard sale.

"Maybe she likes both of you as friends. I mean, maybe she's not looking for a relationship right now. She seems to like the life she and Olivia have, and she could be thinking about Olivia and making sure neither of them gets hurt."

"Yeah, I know." Mike put a few more pieces of candy in his bag and twisted it. "Caleb and Ginny went to dinner with us. She invited them to join us."

Cailin knew Mike's mind was preoccupied with Mallory because he wasn't paying attention to what he was adding to his bag. He put Mary Janes in it.

"Oh. That's not good." Cailin took Mike's bag and picked out the Mary Janes replacing them with Smarties, Necco wafers, and fireballs. "Maybe after Jared, she was nervous about being alone with you, so she wanted more people around to lift her spirits, make her feel comfortable, and help take her worries away."

"You think she was scared to be alone with me? Like I would treat her like Jared?" Mike spit the last words out.

"No! No, I said that wrong. What I meant is, maybe she just

wanted company, like girl company, and she couldn't invite Ginny without inviting Caleb too."

"Oh? I didn't think about that. Maybe. But she and Caleb did talk, and laugh, a lot. She told me she had fun though, but she didn't let me to walk her to her door. She kissed me on the cheek before she got out of the car and ran inside."

"Knowing you, I know you didn't expect anything more on a first date than a kiss on the cheek. But I'm sorry about Caleb, Mike, and I'm sorry about Jared too. Really." Cailin handed Mike his bag of candy. "You don't have anything to worry about with Caleb. He's not the kind of guy to swoop in and try to take someone's girl, especially right in front of him."

"But she's not my girl, Cailin. We went on one date and now I can't even call it a date if you ask me." Mike looked around for Noah and spotted him eyeing the fudge.

They walked to the counter to pay for their candy and Mike called Noah over. "I'm okay though. I might call her in a few days to check on her and Olivia."

"Olivia?" Noah asked as he came back over. "I want to play with Olivia! Is she and Ms. Mallory coming over? Can we have a cookout and invite them over! Please, Daddy, please! Everybody can come. You'll come won't you, Uncle Cow?" Mike took Noah's bag from him and put it on the counter.

"Well, guess that's one way to get everyone together again," Cailin said as he added his bag to the counter. "And you'll get a chance to talk to Mallory without Caleb OR Jared around."

"Yeah." Mike thought. "Yes. That's a good idea Noah! A summer cookout sounds like a fine idea." Mike said, already planning his next move.

CHAPTER 18

CHEAP WINE
AND DORITOS

Saturday morning arrived and I needed to run to the store to pick up a few things for the pineapple casserole I was taking to Mike's for the cookout. I threw a load of laundry in the wash, grabbed my keys, and headed out the door. Cailin would be over in a few hours to take me to Mike's and then I would stay with him for the weekend. Walking to the car I had the strangest feeling that I was being watched. I stopped and looked around but there was only a lady jogging with her dog and no one else in sight. Alec was still out there somewhere, though I had received no news from Lieutenant LeBrecque in a while. I made a mental note to call him on Monday, or maybe ask Trish if she could call him to see if he had found out anything. Maybe after they talked, he would ask her out on another date.

I made my way to the store determined to only buy Ritz crackers and sticks of butter, when I found myself holding a box of Sociable crackers and staring at the squeeze cheese.

"I like the cheddar myself," said a female voice.

"Cheddar is the best." I turned and saw Ginny coming down

the aisle holding a bag of Doritos. We hugged and laughed and then I asked, "What are you doing here?"

"Just picking up a few things for a boring Saturday night. I have the night off and no plans so I thought I would sit around watching movies, drinking cheap wine, and eating Doritos."

"I've had those nights before. Sometimes they're just what you need after a long week. You're not working tonight then?"

"No. I was supposed to, but I hurt my hand last night and my boss wants me to take it easy for a few days." She raised her left hand, and it was then that I noticed it was wrapped in an ace bandage.

"What happened?" I noticed her forefingers were a little swollen too.

"Hurt it slamming a beer on the counter. Broke the bottle and had to have some glass picked out of my hand." She peeled a little of the bandage back and showed me a few red spots on her palm where the glass had apparently cut it. "This creep was hitting on the new girl and it pissed me off a little too much. I don't exactly have the best temper you know. I could work, but when my boss says I can have a Saturday night off with pay I'm not stupid, I'll take it!"

"I hear ya! You like working there, don't you?"

Ginny looked at her hand again. "I do. The pub is great, but you know me working there is only temporary right? I'm saving up for the AT. I plan to thru hike the Appalachian Trail next year," she smiled.

"Really! That's so exciting!" I exclaimed.

"Yeah." She grabbed a can of squeeze cheese and threw it in her hand basket. "Right now, I'm saving up, and next March or April I plan to leave. Then I can check it off my bucket list," she said, making a check mark in the air with her good hand. "After that I want to move and see if I can get a job as a trail guide or maybe be a mountain first responder or something. I have all kinds of certifications as a first responder and rescuer from college. I just haven't decided what I want to do when I grow up!"

"Ha! I think you'll have plenty of time to decide that when you're backpacking through the white caps! I hate to cut this short, but I have to run. I'm supposed to be making a pineapple casserole to take to Mike's and I've got to hurry and get it in the oven before Cailin picks me up." A thought came to me. "You should come over. Mike's having a cookout. You know he wouldn't care if you stopped by and I know there'll be plenty of food."

"Pineapple casserole, huh? I might have to go just to see what the hell that is!"

"You'll love it! Ritz crackers, pineapples, and cheese. I know it sounds gross but believe me, it's really good!" I told her. "I'll see you there then. Around six o'clock?"

"I'll be there."

We hugged and I made my way to the check out.

Soon after, I was in the car and about to put it in reverse when I saw a man at the corner of the store staring in my direction. He gave me an eerie feeling and I squinted to try to see him better. It looked like Alec, but I couldn't be sure. He was wearing a cap and sunglasses and it was definitely his build, but there was something slightly off about him.

I didn't know what to do. Surely, he wouldn't try something in the middle of the day in a public place. I thought about calling the police and staying put until they arrived but then a lady walked out of the store and right behind her was Ginny. The man started to move. Ginny was walking directly towards him.

I got out of the car and was about to yell for Ginny to run, when the man walked up to the other lady and took the bag from her. She handed him the car keys, and after he helped her into the car and put the bag into the backseat, he got in on the driver's side and drove away.

Ginny caught sight of me and waved then got into her car. I

waved back, feeling foolish and more jittery than I needed to be. The sooner I got back, the sooner Cailin would be over to pick me up, and the sooner I would be at Mike's having a good time with all my friends. Then, maybe, I would have some cheap wine and Doritos with Ginny.

Cailin picked me up, and on the way to Mike's house I told him about the strange feelings I had both before and after the grocery story. It was really starting to weigh on me.

"You're overreacting, Precious." He put an arm around my shoulder and pulled me closer to him. "But you're right, he's been quiet. There's no telling what he's up to or where he is. It's a small town though. If he's around, he'll be caught sooner or later."

"I have a feeling he's up to something and I can't shake it. What if he's been watching me and he knows about you and Mike, or Trish and Mallory? I'd never forgive myself if he tried something with one of them." I snuggled my head deeper into Cailin's chest inhaling the scent of him. He smelled clean with a hint of sandalwood and he made me feel safe in his arms.

We arrived at Mike's just as Trish was pulling up. She was with a guy I'd not met but he looked like someone I'd seen before; I just couldn't place him.

"Who's that?" asked Cailin.

"I don't know," I replied. "But I guess Trish is over Lieutenant LeBrecque. Oh, and I forgot to mention, I ran into Ginny and invited her. She said she'd come."

"That's fine. Looks like it's going to be a party!" Cailin helped me out of his truck handing me the pineapple casserole I had made.

"Hey, Trish!" I yelled as Cailin and I walked over to her.

"Hey, guys! This is Andy. Andy, this is Libba and Cailin. Cailin is Mike's brother." Trish winked at me as she introduced her new fling.

"How's it going?" Cailin reached a hand to shake Andy's.

"Nice to meet you," I nodded and smiled.

"Uncle Cow!" screamed Noah running out of the house and straight into Cailin's arms. He turned to stare at Andy. "Who are you?"

"Noah. Remember your manners." Mike came walking out of the house shooting a stink eye at Noah. He extended a hand to Andy and introduced himself, then gave Trish and me a quick hug.

"Come on back," Mike said. "I just fired up the grill."

Trish and I set the table. I was about to get the scoop on Andy when Olivia came skipping around the side of the house and Noah took off to play with her. Mallory followed carrying a big picnic basket with pink fabric around the rim, and Ginny was behind her holding a bottle of wine in her good hand.

Behind them, Caleb was carrying a six pack in one hand and a big bag of Doritos in the other.

Mike barely noticed Olivia as she ran up to him and gave him a big hug around his knees. He was too busy noticing Mallory and the way her long dark hair fell against her milky white cheeks. She was absolutely beautiful. The contrast of her dark hair and light skin was like coal on snow. The sight of her made a hard knot form in the middle of his throat and made it difficult for him to swallow. Olivia squeezed harder bringing Mike back to reality.

"Well look at you, Olivia," said Mike. "I mean Miss Dorothy."

Olivia was wearing a Dorothy, from the Wizard of Oz, Halloween costume complete with ruby red slippers. She even had her hair in two pigtails, one on each side of her chubby little cheeks, which were splashed with the tiniest bit of pink blush.

Mike bent over to swoop Olivia up in the air then gave her a big hug before putting her back on the ground. He put his hands into his pockets, looked up, and that's when he noticed Caleb. *What was he doing here?*

"Mommy said I could wear it if I promised not to get it durty," Olivia said.

"Then we shall see to it that you don't get dirty." Mike said to Olivia, but it was too late. She took off running with Noah, kicking the soccer ball, and getting grass on her ruby slippers.

"Olivia, your shoes are getting dirty!" Mike yelled but it was no use. He'd have to clean them up for her before she left.

"Hi, everyone!" Mallory said as she put the basket down on the table. She looked at Mike and gave him a shy smile. "I hope you don't mind but I brought a few things," and she proceeded to pull out citronella candles, plate coverings made out of decorative netting, antibacterial hand gel, a salad, two types of salad dressings, as well as wooden hand tongs for the salad, and what looked like a seven-layer dip.

"Dang Mallory, you have everything but the kitchen sink in there!" Ginny marveled looking at all the things Mallory pulled out of her basket.

"Overachiever. You get used to it after a while," Trish said. "She's always prepared for anything."

"And here are the chips," Caleb said as he put several bags of chips on the table and Mallory pulled out a bowl to put them in.

"Hope you don't mind but Ginny invited me over," said Caleb, shaking Mike's hand.

"Nah man, it's cool," said Mike. "You know you're always welcome." Mike turned to check the burgers on the grill before his disappointment could show. He didn't mind at all that Caleb was there, as long as he didn't take all of Mallory's attention like the other night at dinner.

Trish introduced Andy to Mallory, Ginny, and Caleb, and everyone became engulfed in conversation while snacking on chips and dip. They found out that Andy worked at the stables that

Trish had gone to with Lieutenant LeBrecque when they visited the winery. She bumped into him at the mall a few days later, exchanged phone numbers and they have talked to each other ever since.

"Do you own any horses of your own?" asked Mallory as she stood up slightly to glance at the kids who were now sitting in the middle of the makeshift soccer field.

"I wish," said Andy. "Right now, just taking care of the horses at the stables is enough. I get to ride them when I lead the trail rides and that's a few times a day, so I get to do what I love and get paid for it. Plus, I get tips so it's not too bad."

"Would someone mind getting me a plate from the kitchen so I can put these burgers on them. Oh, and the cheese from the fridge," Mike interrupted, then grabbed the hot dogs and started placing them on the grill.

"I'll get 'em" said Cailin, standing up and kissing Libba on the top of her head. He ran into the house and came back a minute later with only a plate.

"Mike, I couldn't find the cheese. You sure you have some because I looked all over the fridge and didn't see any."

"Did you check the door? That's where I always keep it." Mike said as he took the plate from Cailin.

"Of course, I did. I know that's where you keep it but I'm telling you I couldn't find any. Go have a look for yourself. I'll get the burgers off the grill."

Mike walked in the house and came back a minute later with an *uh-oh, I screwed up* look on his face.

"Umm, I don't suppose anyone would mind running to the Food Lion and grabbing some cheese? It appears of all the things I could forget, that was it."

Caleb stood up. "I'll go. I'm blocking everyone anyways with my truck. Anybody want to tag along?"

Mike noticed Caleb looking straight at Mallory as he said this, but also noticed that Mallory wasn't paying any attention to him. She was busy talking to Ginny and Andy.

"I'll go." Trish stood up and grabbed her wristlet. "I'll get a case of beer. Anybody need anything else?"

"Can you get one of those small bottles of Gatorade for the kids to split," Mallory said. Then she yelped and immediately placed one hand on her chest. Libba saw the goose bumps starting to appear on her arms. "Oh! Excuse me. I must be getting the hiccups."

Mallory looked at Trish and Libba, her eyes growing like golf balls as she did so. Both of them knew Mallory too well to pretend not to know her yelp was nothing as simple as a hiccup.

"Mallory, is everything all right?" Libba asked, grabbing Cailin's hand and squeezing it. He looked at Libba as if he could sense she was scared.

"Yes, of course." Mallory yelped again. "Trish be ... Caleb drive carefully, won't you?"

"No worries. I haven't been drinking." Caleb turned to walk to his car.

Trish looked at Mallory, then at Libba, then back at Mallory. She nodded her head and turned to follow Caleb.

Cailin looked at Libba then whispered in her ear. "Umm, what's going on?"

Libba turned to whisper in Cailin's ear. "Mallory yelps like that when either something really good or something really bad is about to happen. And the last time she did it, she got goose bumps on her arms just like now." Cailin glanced at Mallory and saw the goosebumps still there. "That was when we had the cookout at Muirfield Manor, and you remember what happened that day."

"You mean you think she can sense when Alec is around? You think he might be near?"

"I don't know but I've had a strange feeling all day and now

Mallory seems to be yelping her warning signs. I just don't have a good feeling about this. Stay close to me, promise?"

"I won't let anything happen to you, you know that." Cailin placed an arm around Libba and kissed her softly on the lips. "I'm here, Precious."

"Get a room!" Ginny teased.

Mike was close enough to hear what Libba had said to Cailin. He walked over to Mallory, who was now standing away from everyone watching the kids as they resumed their soccer game. He stood behind her and rubbed her arm. She turned and looked at him.

"Mallory, you're freezing. Are you okay?" Mike moved to stand in front of her. "Tell me what's wrong."

Mallory looked at Mike and crossed her arms, then started to rub them as if trying to get warm.

"I don't know if something is wrong, I just know that something *isn't* right."

"Did you have a premonition or something?"

"A premonition? Do you believe in such things?" Mike shrugged his shoulders. Mallory looked deep into his eyes and she thought she saw something flicker. "I don't get premonitions unless its three seconds before I knock over a glass of milk or something like that and then it's too late." She smiled at Mike. "For some reason, I make those ... hiccup sounds and then, then, either I get the chills and goosebumps when something bad is about to happen, or my heart starts racing and I get butterflies in my stomach when it's something good. This time I got goose-bumps and I'm afraid for Trish, and Libba too. Something is about to happen, but I don't know what or when, I just ... know."

"Trish will be fine. She's with Caleb. And Libba is right here with Cailin so you know she's all right. There's nothing to worry about. I won't let anything happen to you either. We're all safe. Please don't worry." Mike placed a hand on each of her arms and rubbed them. Mallory closed her eyes and Mike couldn't resist, he kissed her on her forehead. He started to take a step back, but Mallory grabbed him by the elbows making him stop. They stood there staring at each other and then they heard someone's cell ring. The cell rang a second time and Mallory turned in time to see Libba grab her phone and swipe it.

Trish was calling.

"Libba, we just saw Alec! He's heading North on Valley Road!"

Mike and Cailin jumped into Mike's car and took off towards Valley Road. Mike gunned the engine, the tires of his car hugging the curves of the road. Within minutes they spotted Alec, who had veered off, hitting a mailbox, and going into a ditch.

Cailin jumped out of the car and ran towards the car Alec was driving, but Alec was already out and running up the side of the mountain. Cailin chased Alec on foot running up the mountain behind him. When he was just inches away, Cailin dove at Alec's feet, tackling him to the ground. They struggled but Cailin was too strong for Alec to get away.

Alec swung at Cailin but Cailin caught his fist in the palm of his hand. With his other hand he punched Alec, swinging his fist up and into Alec's nose. There was a *crack* and immediately blood began to gush out. Alec screamed with pain and turned on his side. Cailin turned Alec onto his back but Alec flung his arm in the air, catching Cailin by his elbow and swinging it back. He then swung at Cailin knocking him a few inches away and in that short amount of time, Alec was able to flip himself over and get to his feet, kicking Cailin in his stomach.

"This is how I did it to Libba, Cowboy!" Alec roared, blood dripping from his nose as he kicked Cailin in the stomach, once, then twice.

Alec lunged to kick Cailin a third time, but he was too slow. Cailin grabbed his foot and twisted hard and fast. The force made a sharp *pop* and again Alec screamed in pain. Cailin yanked Alec by his foot pulling him closer. Alec fell to the ground scrapping his back as Cailin dragged him across the bare ground. Cailin punched Alec in the face, left cheek, right cheek, left cheek—once, twice, three times ...

"Cailin! Stop! Enough, stop it!"

Mike stood ten feet away from Alec and Cailin. He watched his brother pound on Alec this whole time. As much as he wanted Cailin to beat the life out of Alec, he couldn't let his brother continue fighting someone who was no longer able to defend himself.

"STOP IT, I said."

Cailin held his fist in the air ready to strike one more time.

"Cailin, if you continue to beat him when he's not able to fight back ... you're no better than he is," Mike said. "I can't let you turn into someone like that Cailin. He's not worth it."

Mike walked over to Alec who was lying still on the ground, blood dripping from his face, his ankle twisted in an angel indicating that it was broken. He took off his belt and wrapped it around Alec's hands, binding them together.

Slowly, Cailin sat on his knees. He looked down at his hands and saw the blood dripping from them. His face turned as pale as a ghost.

Cailin spoke very quietly. "I don't know what came over me. I probably would have killed him if you hadn't stopped me."

Mike looked at Cailin with pity.

"I just kept seeing him in my mind hitting Libba over and over, and all I could do was hit him back. I don't know—Mike, I didn't mean to ..."

"I know Cailin. I know." Mike rested a hand on Cailin's shoulder. "It's over now."

Mike pulled his cell from his back pocket and called Lieutenant

LeBrecque. He then opened the trunk of his car and grabbed an old rag and handed it to Cailin.

"You want me to call Libba for you?" he asked.

Cailin took the rag and began wiping his hands, not answering Mike's question, just wiping as if trying to erase any reminders of what he had done.

Finally, he said "I don't think I can talk to her right now. I need a few minutes."

Mike walked a few steps away to give Cailin some space but kept an eye on him and Alec. He decided to call Mallory to let her and everyone else know that they were okay, that they found Alec, and Lieutenant LeBrecque was on the way. Cailin might not want to talk to Libba right now, but Mike needed to hear Mallory's voice.

Mallory told Mike they were on their way and should be there soon. Trish and Caleb had returned shortly after Mike and Cailin left and after a few minutes of arguing, Caleb and Andy agreed to drive her, Trish, and Libba in the direction they had seen Alec going. Ginny stayed behind with the kids.

A few minutes later they arrived, mere seconds after the police and EMS. They got out of the car and watched as Lieutenant LeBrecque parked then motioned for them to stay where they were. Mallory and Trish stood on either side of Libba, who stared at Cailin, large tears forming in her eyes. When he looked up at her, the tears made their escape and she lunged toward him only to be held back by Trish and Mallory.

"Cailin!" she screamed. "Cailin!"

"Keep her here," Caleb said to Trish and Mallory. "I'll go see what I can find out, but it might not be safe for her until they take Alec away."

They watched as Caleb approached two EMS men who were now working on Alec, while a third was dabbing at a cut on Cailin's face. After a few minutes, the EMS lifted Alec onto a stretcher and Caleb headed back to the car. Libba couldn't help herself. She took off running straight towards Cailin even though Lieutenant LeBrecque was still questioning him and Mike.

She landed on her knees directly in front of him, her hands shaking as she did her own examination of his hands, his face, his body.

"I'm okay, Libba. Really, I'm okay," Cailin said, trying not to touch her with his bloody hands.

"I was so worried," Libba cried. "I was so worried you might ..." She didn't finish her sentence.

"I know. I know. I probably would have if it weren't for Mike."

Libba looked up at Mike and then to Lieutenant LeBrecque. She stood up facing the lieutenant but then turned and watched as Alec was loaded into the ambulance. He was muttering and seemed to be regaining his consciousness.

"What will happen to him now?" Libba asked the lieutenant.

"They'll take him to the hospital, and I'll make sure a guard is put on watch outside his room. I'll go by later to question him. I'm sure he'll go through a psych evaluation too ... Hard to tell what will happen after that." Lieutenant LeBrecque looked over to where Trish was still standing with Mallory, Caleb, and Andy. He looked at Trish for a long hard second, then wrote something in his notebook and turned to Cailin and Mike. "I'll give you guys a few minutes, but I'll need you to come straight down to the station as soon as possible."

Mike nodded. Lieutenant LeBrecque shook his hand and then walked away. Another police car had arrived on the scene and the Lieutenant spoke to the officers a few minutes before leaving and following the ambulance down the hill and out of view.

Trish and Mallory started walking towards them, but Mallory stopped when she noticed Mike approaching. He walked up to Mallory and stopped within arm's reach. He looked at her and shook his head. "You were right. You knew something was about to happen." He shrugged his shoulders and gave a small chuckle. "Noah would probably call that your superpower."

Mallory looked at Mike and couldn't help herself. She closed the distance between them in two steps and hugged him tight. His arms automatically wrapped around her and he buried his head into her curls. Mike was so shaken that he couldn't speak, so he let Mallory's embrace comfort him and for Mike, it was exactly what he needed. At that moment, he could feel Mallory's heart beating as fast as his, but slowly, slowly, both their hearts began to pace with one another and together they found a gentle rhythm as one.

CHAPTER 19

SOUL TO SOUL

An hour after we arrived at the police station, Ginny walked in carrying Mallory's picnic basket filled to the rim with food. She had called Martha, who immediately offered to come over and watch Noah and Olivia so that Ginny could meet up with us and make sure everyone was okay. Mrs. Stanley helped Ginny pack up the burgers and chips and then started cleaning up to busy herself. When Ginny left, she said Mr. Stanley was balancing Olivia on one knee while he and Noah battled over video games. No doubt he was bound and determined to beat Noah at FIFA soccer if it was the last thing he did.

Cailin and I were sitting at Lieutenant LeBrecque's desk waiting for him to come back from the hospital when Ginny approached us with two burgers neatly wrapped in parchment paper. Neither of us had an appetite so she left it on the desk just in case we changed our minds.

Trish and Caleb jumped up and started ravenously going through the basket to see what Ginny had brought. I could always count on Trish to have an appetite, no matter what kind of drama had transpired. I noticed Mike and Mallory shrug their shoulders too, as if to say, "why not" and together they walked over to Ginny to peak through the basket.

Cailin barely said anything to me on the way to the police station or since we had arrived. I supposed he was in shock but honestly, I really couldn't tell what he was thinking. He had gone straight to the restroom and washed his hands but kept looking down at them as though he had missed a spot. I couldn't take it any longer. I turned to him and took his hands in both of mine.

He tried to pull away.

"Don't" I said, very softly. "I want to look at the hands of the man who saved my life."

"What?"

"These hands have saved me, Cailin. More than once. You used these hands to change my flat the first time we met, remember? These hands held mine when I laid in the hospital, unconscious and barely holding on to reality. These hands have caressed me and made me feel more loved than I have in years. And now, now these hands have helped capture someone who can never hurt me again. Don't be ashamed of these hands Cailin. These hands are strong. But they're strong in a good way. You did nothing wrong. And I'm grateful for you."

I pulled his hands to my lips and gently kissed each one then brought them to my heart and closed my eyes. I felt a soft little shock of electricity and opened my eyes in time to see something pass through Cailin's eyes. Did he feel the same shock as I? He pulled me to him and kissed me, then released his hands from mine.

"These hands could have killed him Libba." He said stoically. "I was so mad, I really think I could have killed him with my bare hands."

"But you didn't," I said.

"Only because of Mike."

"No, because of you," I corrected. "You have more self-control than you think Cailin. I should know," I said as I leaned my bottom into him a little more closely and gave him a sly smile, trying to make light of the situation.

He wrapped an arm around me and pulled me closer to him, then reached over and grabbed the two burgers Ginny left on the desk and handed me one. I tried to eat yet could only manage a few bites.

After a while I turned to look at Cailin. He was holding the burger in one hand, but his eyes were staring straight up at the ceiling. I wondered what he was thinking and knew he didn't feel like talking. I closed my eyes just wanting to rest them for a few minutes. I was so tired, but I had so much on my mind that I couldn't relax. It was hard to believe that just a few months earlier I was married to Alec, a man that I now realized I never really knew. Or had I, but I never realized or rather I never noticed, that he was changing right before my eyes.

I always thought I was an observant person. People watching was supposed to be my hobby, yet I never paid enough attention to my husband to see that something was troubling him, to see that we were drifting apart, to see that he was drifting into an abyss. Had he given me any signs? Would I have noticed if he did? I knew the answers to both questions, and it was no.

For the longest time I was absorbed in my work and my career. I went into the office early and normally stayed late. I was always the one to take on more assignments, meet with new clients, take on the extra report, start a new company initiative. It wasn't until I met Cailin that I had lunch with someone who wasn't a coworker or potential client.

I thought about Alec and how things were between us those last few months. And then I remembered.

I remembered the gas receipt that I questioned Alec about on a day that I thought he was out of town. He said I had my days mixed up because there was no way he could have gotten gas if he wasn't in town. Right?

I remembered the empty liquor bottle I found in the recycle bin the morning I accidentally put the trash in the wrong bin. I had to run back in the house and grab a step stool so I could put it in the correct bin before the city picked up the trash that morning.

I asked Alec about the empty bottle that night before we went to bed. He gave me look of absolute callous and I couldn't understand why it had upset him so much. We got into an argument about trust that night. I don't remember everything that was said, but I do remember the pain ... and the fear? Yes, the fear.

That night he frightened me. That night he threw a boot at me. I sat very still as it whizzed by me, going right between my head and the lamp on the side table. That night he raised the back of his hand to me, and again, I sat very still. Waiting. But he didn't strike. That time he didn't strike and that night I cried myself to sleep.

It all seemed so long ago yet really, it wasn't. And now, here I sat with Cailin by my side and Alec in the hospital most likely facing a long time in prison.

Cailin was so different from Alec. Besides their physical differences—Calin was tall and muscular while Alec was of average height and lean—they were also different in their mannerism and the personalities they exuded. Where Cailin was confident, Alec was cocky. Where Cailin was humble, Alec was hollow.

Every time I was with Cailin a part of me seemed to wake up from some deep lost part of me that I never knew existed. Every time we touched, it was as though my soul lit up, pulsing with a soft electric surge that pulled me closer to him, pulled our souls closer to one another. I might not be sure how I got here, but I knew here, with Cailin, was where I wanted to be and where I wanted to stay.

A door opened and then I heard footsteps and opened my eyes to see Lieutenant LeBrecque walking towards us. Mike and Mallory started walking towards us and so did Trish. Ginny, Caleb, and Andy stayed seated in the corner of the room where they had gathered to eat.

Lieutenant LeBrecque told us that Alec was going to be evaluated by a police psychologist who would determine if he was mentally stable enough to stand trial. He added that by the looks of things, it was his personal opinion that Alec was also suffering from alcohol addiction and would be hospitalized so that he could have time to detox and start to recover from his injuries.

"He's talking kind of crazy if you ask me, like he has bipolar disease or some kind of Schizophrenic disorder but I'm no doctor," said Lieutenant LeBrecque. "I'm still going to charge him with attacking Libba, the hit and run of Everett McPherson, and the kidnapping of Jennifer London. He won't be able to hurt you for a long time, Libba. I can promise you that."

"Thank you," I said. "Really, thank you for everything."

"Oh, don't thank me, I'm just doing my job. These are the real heroes," he said, gesturing to Cailin and Mike. "Why don't you gentlemen come with me so I can get your statements and you can be on your way. I know you've been here a long time so let's try to wrap this up so you can all go home."

Cailin and Mike gave their official statements to Lieutenant LeBrecque and we were allowed to leave. Back at Mike's house, I talked to Mallory and Trish for a while before Trish and Andy left. Andy offered to take Mallory and Olivia home too, but Mallory insisted that even though her nerves were a little shaken, she was okay to drive. She just wanted to get her and Olivia home, safe and sound, and then go to bed. I watched as Mike carried a sleeping Olivia to the car, but I couldn't hear what they said. Mike kissed Olivia as he strapped her in the car seat, then I saw him walk Mallory to the driver's side. She got in and rolled down the window and Mike stood there talking with his hands in his pockets. I saw him bend over and stick his head in the window and I think he gave her a kiss on her cheek, but I couldn't tell.

Secretly, I hoped he did. Something good had to come out of this day.

I rode with Cailin back to his place. Neither of us really spoke to each other on the way home and I found myself staring out of the window watching the trees as we passed them by, making our way up Shulls Mill Road to Cailin's secluded spot in the mountains.

We pulled into the driveway and Cailin cut off the engine. He grabbed my bag from the backseat and together we walked into the house.

"Mind pouring us a drink?" he asked as he walked to the bedroom to put down my things.

I went to the wine cabinet and was about to pour us each a glass of red when I decided we might need something a little stronger. Instead, I poured us each a glass of bourbon and handed Cailin one as he walked back into the room. He swung it back in one gulp, poured another glass, then walked out onto the deck. I followed, sipping and watching him as he took a spot on the bench we always shared together. I sat facing him and tucked my bare feet under his thighs then waited. I knew he would talk to me when he was ready.

We sat there listening to the stillness of the night when finally, he took a deep breath and spoke.

"Libba ... I would never hurt you. I would never lay a hand on you and hurt you like he did. I know I lost control today Libba, and I'm so glad you weren't there to see ... but I will never be like that around you. I *never* want you to see me like that."

"I know that, Cailin." I took a sip of my drink but didn't take my eyes off him.

"I know you say that Libba, but I mean it. I promise ... no, I swear ... I will never do that to you. I need you to know that

Libba." Now he turned to stare at me in my eyes. His eyes searched mine to make sure that I understood what he was trying to say.

"I do know that, Cailin." I leaned forward and placed a hand on his leg. He looked at me with solemn eyes.

"I heard yours and Mike's statements Cailin, and what resonates with me is that neither one of you said Mike had to hold you back, which tells me that you stopped on your own accord. YOU stopped yourself Cailin. Not Mike, but you. He may have said something that made you think about what you were doing, I don't know I wasn't there, and I don't need you to tell me all the details," I said quickly. "But whatever happened, you stopped yourself, which tells me you have control over your feelings. You have control over the type of man you want to be. You know the difference between what is right and what is wrong, and you choose to do what is right and what is good. His life was in your hands Cailin, these hands remember."

I put my drink down and grabbed both of his hands in mine as I continued. "You chose to let him live. And I don't think you stopped for him, but for us. For you and for me. So, if you can do that Cailin, if you can do that, then I know you would never hurt me. You haven't lost yourself Cailin. You haven't lost your soul. I know, because it's right here." I took his hand in mind and brought it to my chest where I flattened his palm to my heart. "Your soul is right here Cailin. It's a part of me now and my soul is a part of you. We'll get through this Cailin. Together, soul to soul."

"Soul to soul. Yeah ... soul to soul," he said, and for a long while we sat there holding each other's hands, his thumb rubbing the top of my hand.

After a while, the tension in the air began to dissipate and I could tell Cailin was beginning to relax away the day and let go of all that had transpired in the last few hours.

Turning to face me again, Cailin smiled that wicked smile

of his and I knew all would be okay. "Guess what?" he asked. "I think Muirfield Manor should be finished soon."

"Really!" I exclaimed. I was so happy for him. He had put so much hard work into restoring and decorating it.

"Yeah. There are a few things left to do and then of course I need to get final inspections done, which hopefully with Mike's connections, shouldn't take long. Otherwise, I think it's safe to say I'll have it all done …" he took a second to think about it, then added, "maybe the beginning of October I guess."

"That's wonderful news," I said. "Then what? I mean what's the plan going forward?"

"Well, I guess I need to hire someone to manage it. My original idea was simply to buy it and restore it, and then turn it into a bed and breakfast. I never really thought about all the devils in the details." He paused for a second then continued, "I need someone who can take the reservations and manage the books. I'd prefer someone who lives there, so they would always be around to greet the guests and take care of things, you know? Someone who would get up early and make breakfast for the guests, maybe hold high tea," Cailin chuckled at that. "But of course, host happy hour in the early evening, maybe serve dinner. You know, bed and breakfast stuff."

He looked at me and I know I was grinning from ear to ear.

"What?" Cailin asked. "Why are you grinning, what are you up to?"

"I know the perfect candidate," I said, and I leaned in to give him a big kiss. I scooted over to climb onto his lap, and he placed his hands under my thighs, sliding his hands up to cup my butt. I kissed him deeply, slowly, and with every breath I could feel him harden more and more under my lap. He stood up holding me in his hands, and I wrapped my legs around his waist as he carried me back into the house and into his bedroom.

Cailin spent the rest of August at Muirfield Manor. He worked nearly nonstop, determined to have the place finished before the official start of autumn, when the leaves would begin to change color. He imagined hosting a fall festival on the lawns as the grand opening but decided he would let the ladies and the new manager take care of those arrangements.

One day while working at Muirfield Manor, he received a call from Lieutenant LeBrecque. As he hung up the phone, he texted Mike to meet him at the police station.

"Thanks for coming out. Have a seat," Lieutenant LeBrecque said as he shook Cailin's hand and then Mike's. He gestured to the two chairs in front of his desk and closed the door behind them. "I've been reviewing Alec's files, and something's been bothering me for a while, so I did some investigating, but I wanted to have everything in order before I spoke with you boys."

"What's this about?" Cailin asked as he positioned himself in front of a chair but didn't sit down. Mike sat in the chair next to him and looked at Cailin as if to say, *sit down and maybe he'll tell us.* Cailin finally sat down but continued, "Don't tell me he found a loophole and is being set free."

"No, definitely not. Nothing like that. I've been going through his files to make sure we have a strong case to put him away for a long time. I did some digging and apparently, he's more of a reckless driver than we thought. He has a history of motor vehicle violations, see for yourself." Lieutenant LeBrecque pushed a few papers forward so Cailin and Mike could see the list of violations. The list noted dates of various incidents dating back to the years Alec was probably in high school—speeding tickets, parking tickets, a minor fender bender, and a citation for running a red light. Lieutenant LeBrecque's name was next to the one for the fender bender. Mike pointed at that one and looked up at Cailin.

"Yes," Lieutenant LeBrecque said. "I gave him that ticket. I don't remember every person I pull over and honestly, I don't remember this one either but seeing my name there ... well something about that kept nagging at me and I didn't know why. But now I do." He paused and looked at Cailin and Mike to see it they had figured it out yet.

"This is right around the time our parents were killed in the car accident." Mike said. "What, maybe a week or so later?"

"Eight days to be exact" said Lieutenant LeBrecque. "And look at the make and model of the car, and specifically, the color of it. I read through my notes. I wrote that his car had damage on the side and when I asked about it, he said he hit a deer and still needed to get his car repaired. You can see my notes at the bottom of the page."

Cailin flipped through the pages until he got to the one with the details of the infraction. He skimmed the page quickly, reading the notes at the bottom.

"It's the same color as the one that hit our parents." He looked at Mike, then at Lieutenant LeBrecque. "You think Alec was driving the car that killed our parents?"

"What?" Mike grabbed the papers and read through them quickly. He looked up coming to the same conclusion as Cailin.

"I think he did," said Lieutenant LeBrecque. "We can question him, and we will of course. You have my word on that. But unless he confesses, I don't think there will be enough evidence to charge him with, but I wanted to let you both know that I'm going to try."

Cailin was angry, so angry. He wanted to scream. He wanted to hit someone. He wanted to hit Alec but then he thought about Libba. How could he tell her that after all Alec had done to her, to them, to find out that he was also responsible for the death of his parents ... that would be too much for her to bear. Would Libba still want to be with him? Would she look at him and always be reminded of the pain and loss her ex-husband had caused him?

Mike looked at Cailin who was still sitting, a mixture of anger and anguish on his face. Mike figured Cailin was thinking of Libba. How was he going to tell her this?

"Thanks, Lieutenant," Mike said. "I think we need to think about this for a while. It's a lot to take in right now and quite frankly, until you have all the details it's just hearsay and assumptions. Though I clearly agree that it does appear he did it. Let us know what you find out please and we'll be in touch." With that, Mike tapped Cailin on the leg. "Come on. There's nothing we can do about this right now. They'll find the evidence to tack onto Alec's charges or not. Either way, it's not going to bring back Mom and Dad, and Alec's going to jail anyway. I've accepted that Mom and Dad are gone. We've accepted it for a while now. We don't need this to consume us any longer."

They left Lieutenant LeBrecque's office, neither speaking until they reached their cars.

"I don't think I'm going to tell her. Libba, I mean," Cailin said.

"It's up to you, bro," Mike said. "But I think you should. I know she's going to be overwhelmed knowing her ex-husband may have killed her current lover's parents but she's a strong one. It's bound to come out sooner or later and it will be better if she hears it from you and not anyone else. You know that."

"Yeah, you're right," Cailin said. "Can you believe it though? After all this time … what if he confesses. What if we finally hear what happened to Mom and Dad." He paused. "Honestly, I don't know if I even want to know."

"I know what you mean," Mike sighed. "I know what you mean."

Mike stuck his hands in his pockets like Cailin had so often seen him do when he was in deep thought, hung his head down, and slowly walked to his car. Cailin knew he had a lot of thinking to do too, so he decided to head back to Muirfield Manor where he could clear his mind and hit something with a hammer. Or better yet, split some wood with an axe.

Back at the manor, Cailin decided to spend the rest of the day working in the yard. He had hired some landscapers who were now working in the East lawn, laying out a rock garden and planting bushes. He figured they wouldn't be done any time soon, so he went to the West garden to work out his frustrations. As the sun began to set, Cailin caught sight of one of the landscapers, Manny, walking towards him.

"We're all done, sir," Manny said. "My guys are putting away the last of the equipment but if you want to do a quick walk through before it gets dark, we can."

"Sure thing. Perfect timing in fact." Cailin put down the axe and tossed the last piece of wood over to the pile that had quickly accumulated.

"This looks really nice," Cailin remarked when he saw their work. "I think it's just as my girlfriend imagined, too."

Slowly, he walked around the inlaid fire pit admiring the design of the stone ground surrounding it. The patio space was about thirty feet in diameter and had four low back Adirondack chairs around the pit, plus a built-in concrete bench off to the side. The area wasn't huge, but it was large enough for several guests to sit and still have enough room to walk around comfortably.

The landscapers had laid down the mulch and planted a few small evergreen and juniper trees around the patio. Gem boxwood bushes and maiden grass provided low varieties of greenery and were interspersed along the side of square pavers that led from the patio to the lush grass. He had requested lavender and clover honey plants in honor of when he first met Libba and thought she smelled as sweet as lavender and honey; those were delicately placed in just the right place to add a splash of color.

Another patio that held more traditional furniture and a few tables sat parallel to this one and was connected by two oversized, flat, round boulders. These, the men had fashioned from a huge boulder that once sat on the side of the house and had obstructed the view from the front yard. With the rubble that had amassed from the destruction of the boulder, Cailin had requested a rock garden be constructed in the back of the garden. He thought he might place a water feature in it, maybe with a solar light of some kind, but that could wait until later.

"Nice, very nice," Cailin repeated as he slowly took in the entire scene of the East lawn.

"You know, sir, when you said you wanted an inlaid fire pit I wasn't sure if I would like it. You know, 'cause most of the time people want a raised pit, not one in the ground, but I think it works in this space." Manny stood next to Cailin, nodding his head in approval.

After a few minutes of small talk, Cailin and Manny walked back to the front and shook hands, and Manny drove off. It was getting dark so Cailin decided he should probably leave to meet up with Libba. He knew she was hanging out with Mallory and Trish after work, but she said she might swing by later and he wanted to get home and shower before he saw her.

Cailin was sitting on the couch when his cell rang.

"Hey, you," he answered, as he grabbed the remote to mute the TV. He took a sip of his brandy that he'd been nursing for the past half hour.

"Hey. You sound like you've had a rough day. Everything okay?" Libba asked.

Cailin thought he would tell her, had every intention of telling her, but when it came down to it, he just couldn't. Not tonight anyway. He would tell her, just not now. "Just a little tired. I worked at the house today," he said, stretching and trying not to yawn too loudly over the phone. He sat up now and was beginning to wake up a little.

"Yeah, how's it going? How's the back yard?" she asked with a touch more enthusiasm than usual.

"Libba, you're going to love it. It looks pretty awesome. I think it's just what you wanted, and the rocks looks great. I think I need to put up some fairy lights though," he teased.

"Uh huh," Libba smiled into the phone. "Maybe you can find a statue of a fairy sitting on a lily pad and hang up a sign that reads Welcome to Libba's Pad," she giggled.

"Have you been drinking?" Cailin asked. "You're sounding a little giddy."

"Giddy! That's funny!" Libba laughed. She was definitely a little tipsy.

"Liiiiibba," Cailin teased, stretching out her name. "Do I need to come and get you and put you to bed?"

"Umm, bed sounds good." Cailin could imagine her licking her lips on the other side of the phone. "But no. I'm good. I'm staying with Trish tonight because yes, I have had a bit more to drink than I planned but that's because we were celebrating."

"Celebrating? I take it we have our manager then?"

"Yep. It took a bit of convincing but eventually, okay after about three Blue Hawaiians, she started to get excited about it and then she said yes. She made a list"

"A list?" Cailin interrupted.

"Yes, a list. You know how she is. She has to develop a website, research reservation software. I don't know … she started listing a whole bunch of stuff." Libba took a deep breath. "In other words, she's in her element."

"I'm sure she is. She'll do great." Cailin stood, took a final swig from his glass and walked to the kitchen. "I imagine she needs to give notice at her job but that will give me time to get other things ready for her. Did she say when she could start?"

"No, but she did say she would talk to her boss on Monday and work something out. You do realize she's never even stayed in a bed and breakfast before. I think she should probably go and stay in one just to get that real-life experience and maybe see how things are run at other establishments. It might be a good little vacation for her too, before she starts working for you. Orrrr," Libba stretched this last word out. "WE could go and stay in a little bed and breakfast and have someone wait on us for a weekend."

"Umm, that would be nice." Cailin was beginning to miss his precious fairy. "You sure you don't want me to come and get you? I could order in some breakfast. We could sleep in and pretend we're at a bed and breakfast."

"I can't. I promised I would stay here. We just ordered pizza and are about to start binge watching the Halloween movies. Can you believe, Mallory has never seen any of the Halloween films? Not even one and there's like what, ten? Trish wants to have a Halloween marathon. You know how she gets. I doubt we make it through the second one, but I think Mallory has to at least watch the first one. It's such a classic."

"Okay, well on that note, I'll let you go. You girls have fun." Cailin smiled. "I'll call Mike in the morning and tell him the good news."

Mallory walked into her office and slowly closed the door behind her. She hung her jacket on the hook on the back of the door and walked to her desk, softly running her fingers along the top. She sat down and opened a bottom drawer. Pulling her handbag from an oversized laptop bag, she placed it inside the drawer, then pulled her laptop out and sat it on the desk. She powered it on, and while she waited for it to start, she slowly took in the room, the light fixtures, the color of the walls, the view from the window. This was her office, her new office. She never had her own office before, and it was so huge. Opening the desk drawers, she found a small box containing her new business cards. She opened the box and put her hand over her mouth in delight as she read what it said.

She could not believe she was the new innkeeper and business manager of Muirfield Manor. What was she thinking? She left the comforts of the law firm she had worked at for years only to eventually move into an old house where she would be expected to not only act as an innkeeper and tend to the needs of house guests, but also run a business and manage the everyday upkeep of a bed and breakfast, all while trying to make a profit. Did Cailin and Libba really think she could do this? Of course they did or Cailin would never have offered her the job. She had been thinking about making a change, challenging herself to do something different and step out of her comfort zone, but this? She wasn't sure, but surely if Cailin and Libba had faith in her, she too, would have to have faith in her abilities.

Mallory had never managed a bed and breakfast before; for that matter she never even stayed in one until two weeks ago when Trish booked her a stay at a place she had once visited. Trish said the proprietors were very friendly and would probably be willing to give Mallory a few tips on what the B&B business was like.

"Ask them to be your unofficial mentor Mallory," Trish had

encouraged her. "They are such good people and I know Diane would be honored to take you under her wing."

Trish was right. Diane and Paul, the owners of The Floating Rose, were certainly down-to-earth, good and decent people. Diane had told Mallory that she had no clue how to run a B&B when they first opened the doors of The Floating Rose. Sam inherited it from an aunt who had died and didn't have any children of her own to leave it to in her will, so he became the new owner. They almost sold it, but something told her not to. Diane started reaching out to folks she thought could help her. One person led her to another and the next thing she knew she was running a B&B. Diane told Mallory, "If you can run a tight household, you can manage a B&B. You just might have to clean a few more toilets."

She thought about her little weekend getaway. Technically, it was a reconnaissance mission so she could gain insight to the hospitality industry, and even though she spent most of her time learning as much as she could from Diane, she was able to enjoy a few simple pleasures of her own.

Olivia stayed with Mallory's mother at least once per month, but this was the first time Mallory went out of town without her daughter. She loved Olivia with all her heart, but she had to admit, being waited on and not having to cook dinner, plus having someone else bake and serve her chocolate chip cookies was sinfully relaxing.

Mallory thought about her new position as the manor's Innkeeper and Business Manager. What a big difference from working at the law firm. That position had come by happenstance and not because she dreamed of working in a law office. She had advanced twice in the few years she worked there and made a decent living for herself and Olivia, but honestly, she never thought she would work there forever. She wasn't a lawyer, and she didn't want to be, but she also wanted to be more than an administrative professional. Yes, the corporate world was beginning to wear on her, and she knew this was a great opportunity.

Besides, Mallory had a knack for hospitality, formal training or not. She majored in business management with a concentration in accounting, so she was confident in her ability to handle the books. Plus, she enjoyed cooking and entertaining and had a way with planning meals such that everything was ready at the same time, so she wasn't really worried about cooking and serving guests either. Cleaning the house would be no problem, nor would it be hard to keep up with inventory, she thought. So why was she so nervous?

She decided she would embrace the challenge and do the best she could. That's all that Cailin had asked of her anyway. He had told her to run it like she would her own business and he just wanted to be a silent owner but if she needed anything, he was there. She knew he meant it and she aimed to be successful.

Mallory had five short weeks left to prepare for the grand opening and she knew the time would fly by before she could blink. She had to get the website up and running first so they could start booking reservations. For that matter, she needed to learn the reservation software, figure out the accounting process, come up with a marketing campaign to attract guests, figure out breakfast menus, order supplies, and plan a grand opening for who knew how many attendees. Plus, she needed to give each room a theme, decorate it, have it photographed so they could go on the website, and … she was becoming overwhelmed.

Mallory took a deep breath and remembered what Cailin told her. "Don't try to do everything by yourself. I hired you to man-age, that means delegate and oversee, not work yourself to death. Get help, hire a staff. Whatever you need."

Cailin had given her a company credit card, which had a higher line of credit than she ever heard of. They had discussed the budget for the open house and Mike was helping with inviting people from the community since he seemed to know everyone anyway. Of course, Cailin, Libba, and Trish would help however they could, but they also had their regular jobs to think about. This *was* her regular job now. Oh dear.

She went to her laptop and opened her email. She had two unread messages. One was the usual *Hello and Welcome to Outlook.com* email that she saw come through after installing the software the night before and the other was from Mike. She opened it and read:

> Hi, Mallory. Welcome to Muirfield Manor! I know you're going to do a great job and I just wanted to let you know that if you need anything, don't hesitate to give me a call. Regarding the list of attendees for the open house, I've gone through some of my contacts and have about twenty-three people to invite so far. I think I can finish this list fairly quickly, probably in the next couple days, but how do you want me to send to you? Word or Excel? Also, are your plans to send formal invitations to some like the mayor and city manager? Just wondering, because if so, I can provide addresses, emails, and phone numbers. We can talk later. Call me. Mike.

She decided to respond to this later and flagged a reminder for one hour. She did not want to seem too eager to reply, plus she needed time to take everything in. Mike would understand.

She went to the tab with her To Do list and started to read through the long list of items. She added a few more, prioritized them, and gave herself deadlines, then decided she could not do any more without coffee. She decided she would explore the kitchen and get to know this house a little better, then she would start reaching out to her own contacts for help. She might have five weeks before the big day, but she was determined to have everything ready and in place in four. But first, coffee.

CHAPTER 20

THE WOMEN OF MUIRFIELD MANOR

I stood next to Trish and Mrs. Stanley on the front porch of Muirfield Manor. I was amazed at how everything had come together in such a short time. From Cailin offering Mallory the job in August to now, they—Cailin, Mike, Mallory, Trish, Ginny, and even the Stanleys—had somehow managed to complete the renovations at the manor and help open it for business in less than three months, start to finish.

I had to admit, Cailin and Mallory did most of the work, but I liked to think, no I knew, that I had a lot to do with it, too. It was a group effort, really. I had reached out to some of my connections from *Nostalgia Remembered*, who gave Mallory some rather good discounts in exchange for including their logos on the signage. Mrs. Stanley's friend, the one who bought my furniture for her daughter, said her daughter worked as an intern for a local news station. She had arranged an interview with Cailin and Mallory to be featured in their Exploring Small Businesses segment and the grand opening was also featured on the Community Calendar and Newcomers Guide. Once people heard the news and the signs started going up, Trish and I were constantly busy helping Mallory with arrangements that we both took a week of vacation from work to focus solely on preparing for this very day.

I scanned the front yard, noticing how surreal it all seemed. I let myself become submersed with the sweet smell of fresh baked goods, the slight breeze from the October wind, the laughs from Olivia and Noah playing with their friends. I closed my eyes, looked up to the sky, and took a deep breath in gratitude. I was finally where I was meant to be.

Opening my eyes, I noticed more people were beginning to arrive. I observed how some had dressed up to attend the grand opening while others dressed in casual workout clothes. Several sets of families came, as well as couples, teenagers, a few shop owners from Main Street, and many people I had never met before. I recognized the waitress from The Ridgeline restaurant where Cailin and I went on our first date; she was standing in a crowd with three other women. Then I noticed a young couple with a baby that couldn't be more than six months old. The girl looked familiar and when she turned and glanced at me, she waved and I recognized it was Natalie, the girl from the garage where I took my car to repair the tire. Natalie had initially told me about Cailin and Wade Brothers Construction and compelled me to talk to him in the first place. Who knows, if it weren't for Natalie, I may have never started dating Cailin. I needed to remember to speak to Natalie before they left and decided I would send Natalie a baby gift as my way of thanking Natalie for encouraging me all those months ago.

"No way!" Trish exclaimed.

I turned in time to hear Mrs. Stanley finishing a story about her husband's latest escapade while fixing a leak under the kitchen sink. He hit his head so hard that a huge bump formed on his forehead almost immediately, hence the reason why he wasn't at the grand opening.

"There's no way a hat could fit over that bump!" Mrs. Stanley laughed. "Poor man. He did have quite a headache at first but he's much better now, gets a little dizzy when he stands up, so I told him to stay home."

"Do you think he'll be all right at home by himself?" Trish asked.

"Oh sure," Mrs. Stanley waved her hand like she was waving away a fly. "He's probably watching TV. I left him a sandwich and soup. He'll be fine."

I smiled and greeted two people as they approached the front door. I handed them a brochure and opened the door so they could enter.

Inside the house, Mallory introduced herself to guests and offered tidbits of information about the manor's historical nature and how Cailin had restored it without losing any of its original integrity. I checked in on her a few weeks ago, and Mallory clearly was embracing her new position as innkeeper and business manager. Today, however, Mallory was simply acting as hostess, a role that perfectly suited her.

To look at Mallory, one would think she had lived at Muirfield Manor for years and was simply hosting a family reunion. She really did fit in with the atmosphere and the manor seemed to accept her as a mistress of the house. In fact, though it might sound strange, I knew the manor accepted me and Trish as well.

I remembered how comfortable I felt in the manor gardens, as if they were calling me and welcoming me home. I had a vision for the design and told Cailin about it one day and he made my vision come true. He even once commented that when we walked through the gardens, the plants seemed to bow in reverence for their fairy queen. It was a peaceful space where I had started a nightly yoga practice having spent most of my evenings there with Mallory and Trish preparing for today's event.

Trish, too, seemed content at the manor. She regularly spent her time here as well and was constantly snapping photos and posting them on Instagram, #MeAtTheManor #MuirfieldManor. In just a few short weeks, Muirfield Manor formed a huge social media following due to Trish's marketing efforts.

As it happened, Trish was a big help to Mallory with getting the manor up and running. We found that Trish was great at all things marketing, from designing the website and marketing collateral to attracting followers on Twitter, Facebook, and Instagram. In fact, it was Trish who came up with a rather aggressive social media campaign that at first Mallory was a little skeptical of, but it had ultimately proven to work better than Mallory could have imagined. The manor was completely sold out of reservations for the first three weeks except for one night when there would only be one couple staying. The rest of the month all the rooms were booked and the next month was beginning to fill as well.

With Trish's help, Mallory hired all the vendors she needed to organize the grand opening, from the guest list to the signage, to the caterers, to the promotional giveaways. Trish had even given Mallory an events checklist—of course, Mallory was ecstatic to get this list—that spelled out every detail to plan and implement a successful event.

Trish said she liked helping Mallory with the marketing needs for Muirfield Manor. She had ideas for guest accommodation packages that she and Mallory would discuss later. Mallory was excited to hear about Trish's ideas and mentioned she had a few to toss around of her own to get Trish's feedback. They made a great team, and Mallory told me that she was secretly thinking of offering Trish a job as the Manor's marketing consultant.

Yes, I knew Muirfield Manor accepted Mallory, Trish, and me as parts of its heart and soul, and I could see a future for all of us right here.

Trish and Mrs. Stanley continued talking so I turned my

attention back to the crowd where I spotted Cailin. He and Mike were greeting people as they came through the little white picket fence at the front of the yard. The front parking lot filled up quickly and people were now parking on the side of the road. Trish mentioned that some people were parking at the public lot and walking down. It was a huge turnout.

Cailin greeted an older gentleman in a tan suit and accompanied by a small, light brown Border Terrier wearing a black and red checkered wind jacket. The small dog sat still as Cailin and the man shook hands and briefly spoke. Cailin then turned to me and pointed, and I noticed the older man was Johnny Calhoun, my real estate agent. Johnny waved, and started to make his way towards me.

"I'll be right back," I told Trish and Mrs. Stanley, and started walking off the porch. They stopped talking to see where I was going.

"Hey, is that your real estate agent?" Trish asked as she followed me down the stairs. "Awe, he has such a cute little doggie!"

"Yeah, that's Johnny!" I exclaimed. "I hope he has good news."

Together, we walked through the lawn meeting Johnny near the small footbridge covering the pond.

"Hi Johnny, how are you?" I said, stretching my hand to shake his.

"Libba Spencer," Johnny said in his slow southern drawl. "I'm fine. Question is ... how are you, my dear?" He reached into his pocket and pulled out a dog treat. The dog looked up at Johnny, wagging its tail and prancing on its paws.

"That's such a cute little dog you have, Johnny. May I pet him?" Trish asked as she bent over the dog.

"Sure, but be careful, this one's pretty ferocious!" Johnny laughed as he handed Trish the dog treat, and she squatted to play with the dog.

"What's his name?"

"HER name is Bonnie," said Johnny.

Trish laughed. "Seriously, you named your dog Bonnie. Johnny and Bonnie!"

They all laughed, and Johnny gave Trish a few more treats to feed to Bonnie.

"Libba, I have some good news for you," Johnny said. "Remember the two men that came by last month and wanted to buy the house but wouldn't commit to anything because one of them was waiting to hear about a promotion at work?"

"Yes, I do. Did he get the job?" I asked.

"Well ... no, but he did get another job. He said he was ..." Johnny looked up at the sky as if trying to remember word for word what he was told, "tired of waiting for his company to make the move, so he made it instead."

"Good for him," interrupted Trish.

"Exactly!" Johnny said giving Trish more treats for Bonnie. "Anyway, the tall one, Kevin, he stopped by and asked to see the place again, so I met them both out there. They called a little while ago with an offer so I thought I would swing by and share the news personally. I hope you don't mind me barging in on your big day here, but I didn't want to wait too long to tell you."

"No, Johnny it's no trouble at all. In fact, that's terrific news!" I gave a little jump and clapped my hands.

Trish stood and smiled. "Congrats, Libba! I'll let you two have some privacy then. Johnny can I get you a lemonade and some cookies? Mallory's white chocolate macadamia nut cookies are out of this world."

"Well ... I've never been one to turn down a good cookie, isn't that right, Bonnie," he said, and Bonnie sat like a good dog, then lifted her paw to shake his hand.

"She's so cute!" Trish said as she patted Bonnie on the head, then she turned to walk towards the house.

"This is exciting," I said. "Am I going to like their offer?"

"Oh, I believe you'll be very happy with the offer," he said.

We sat down on a nearby bench and Johnny pulled out a note-pad from his pocket. Cailin saw us and excused himself from the family he was talking to and came over to join us.

"Good news!" I jumped up and gave Cailin a big hug. "I just sold my house."

"Really! No Way!" Cailin picked me up and swung me around in a big circle, giving me a kiss as he set me back on the ground.

"Today must be a day for good news because that man I was just talking to," he pointed to the family he just left, "he's the developer that's renovating that old strip mall just outside ski mountain. Off the record, he said we won the job! They're going to email all the bidders on Monday announcing they selected Wade Brothers."

"Congratulations," said Johnny.

"Congratulations, honey!" This time it was my turn to give Cailin a kiss.

"All this kissing going on," Johnny joked, "You two might want to get a room in this bed and breakfast right here."

At that, we both laughed.

Mike appeared and looked at Cailin, "I know you're waiting on Ginny to arrive, but Mallory wanted me to see if you were about ready to make your speech."

Just then, Trish returned with Johnny's lemonade and cook-ies. "Well, looky there. If it ain't Ginny and Andy."

They turned to see Ginny and Andy coming in their direc-tion. Cailin whispered to me, "I thought Andy had a thing with Trish."

"That ship has sailed," I whispered back. "Trish told Andy she wasn't really into him and told him he should hookup with Ginny. I think they've been going out for a while."

"Really, how did I miss that? I just talked to her like yesterday. She didn't say anything."

"You snooze, you lose," I teased.

"Hey, guys!" Ginny waved and smiled as she and Andy approached. "Big day for ya, Cailin." She winked and kissed him on the cheek, whispering something in his ear that made him look slightly nervous, then she gave Trish and me each a hug.

Cailin and Mike both shook hands with Andy, and I introduced Johnny to everyone.

"I'll let you kids do your thing," Johnny said, as he picked up Bonnie to leave. "Libba, you give me a call tomorrow and I'll get everything ready for you, okay?" With that he waved goodbye and left.

"Well, let's get this show on the road," Calin said. "I have a speech to make."

Everyone gathered on the front lawn of Muirfield Manor, waiting for Cailin and Mallory to make their appearance. I looked around, again amazed at all the people that had shown up. I realized then that the Wade brothers—having grown up and lived here all their lives—knew nearly everyone in the community. Of course, they did. I had lived here six years and didn't know half as many people. I decided that would change, yet in reality, it was already changing.

I had branched out more and more over the past six months, making new friends, and making a name for myself in the community. It didn't hurt that my boyfriend was well-known. When people saw the two of us together, someone always approached us and Cailin would introduce me. It was a regular occurrence. Now that the town knew Cailin was the owner of a new bed and breakfast, even more people approached him. He told people to contact Mallory so often that I started carrying a handful of her business cards with me to pass out whenever someone mentioned Muirfield Manor. I had a feeling Muirfield Manor was going to be a successful venture and not only would Cailin benefit from it, but so would the town of Blowing Rock.

"May I have your attention please," Cailin said, standing with Mallory on the stairs of the manor's front porch. "Welcome to Muirfield Manor!"

Everyone on the lawn cheered and clapped as Cailin and Mallory waved to the crowd.

"I think I know most of you here today but just in case, my name is Cailin Wade." He gave a wave to the crowd and when he found me, he winked.

I blushed under the attention.

"I want to thank all of you from the bottom of my heart for coming out here today to support the grand opening of Blowing Rock's newest bed and breakfast! You know, when I bought this place over a year ago, I had no idea if today would even happen. At first, I wanted to just restore it but as I was working inside this ... this old beauty," he paused and turned to look at the scale of the house. "You're gonna think I'm crazy, but I swear she told me to share her with others. I think this house wants to be filled with love and laughter, with the smell of good food. With good people.

"I put a lot of care into restoring Muirfield Manor and that's why having the right person to live here and continue with my promise to share her is so important. And I think—no, I know—I found the right person to do just that. Ladies and gentlemen, it gives me great pride and pleasure to introduce to you the mistress of the manor, Miss Mallory MacDonald."

At this, Olivia and Noah jumped up and down cheering as loud as they could as the rest of the crowd applauded Mallory.

"Thank you, Cailin. Wow, thank you, everyone." Mallory clasped her hands to her heart and gave a little prayer. "Well, I wasn't expecting an introduction like that, but I can promise you Cailin—and to everyone here—that I will do my best to keep the spirit of Muirfield Manor alive. Today wouldn't be possible without the help of two of my dear friends and I'd like to recognize them if you don't mind."

Mallory waved for me and Trish to join her on the stage, then said, "May I introduce Libba Spencer. Some of you may recognize Libba as Cailin's better half," she teased. "And this is Trish Knight." Mallory wrapped her arms around us, giving us each a hug.

"Libba and Trish were a tremendous help getting the manor ready, getting the grounds ready, and simply helping me to stay organized, and sane, for these last few weeks. I genuinely don't think I could have managed all of this without their help."

Mallory positioned herself so that she was facing both of us. To my surprise, Mrs. Stanley came walking out of the house with two huge bouquets of flowers, handing one to Trish and the other to me.

Mallory spoke again, "Libba, Trish, thank you for everything you've done not only to help Cailin and me with this grand opening, but also for being the best friends a girl could ever ask for. Cailin may have called me the Mistress of the Manor, but truly, WE are the women of Muirfield Manor."

The three of us hugged and laughed and Cailin came back to the makeshift stage.

"Ladies and gentlemen, the Women of Muirfield Manor!" he screamed into the microphone.

Ginny put her fingers in her mouth and gave a loud whistle, and the rest of the crowd cheered and applauded.

"I believe we have a band ready to play in just a few minutes but before they do there's one more thing I'd like to say before I turn everyone lose." Cailin nodded his head towards Mrs. Stanley and gently padded his front pocket. Mrs. Stanley touched Mallory and Trish lightly on their elbows, gesturing them to the side of the porch. She must have wanted to make sure only Cailin and I shared the entire view of the front porch. I looked at the crowd and noticed Mike take his phone from his pocket and hold it up, either to take pictures or to record. I wasn't sure.

When I looked back at Cailin, tears began to form in my eyes as he knelt down on one knee. "Cailin what are you doing?"

"Libba, my Precious. From the moment I first saw you, you captured my heart. Every day we are together, you capture a piece of my soul. I have waited a lifetime to find you and the rest of my life I freely give to you, if you would do me the honor of becoming my wife. Libba Spencer, will you marry me?" Cailin opened a little gray velvet box and presented his mother's ring.

I looked deep into Cailin's eyes and with all my heart and with all my soul, I knew he was the one for me. My mind flashed through the past several months—the first time he held my hand, him making me blueberry pancakes, sitting outside the sandwich shop, the first time I stepped inside Muirfield Manor, him sleeping next to me in the hospital, his hands ... his hands. He was always there for me, through the good and through the bad, and I absolutely knew the answer.

"Yes, yes!" I cried. "Yes, Cailin. I will marry you!"

As Cailin slipped the ring onto my finger, I knew he too felt that familiar electric surge spin through us both, filling our hearts with true love and joining us, soul to soul.

The End

EPILOGUE

L ibba sat cross legged in the middle of the garden of Muirfield Manor. She had finished her yoga practice but remained on her mat, reflecting on the past year of events that led her to this very spot. Her mind had wandered, but now she needed to focus on the song she would sing to Cailin tonight at their engagement party. After he proposed, everyone was hanging out at the manor and Ginny brought up the night she first met Libba. She asked if there would be a karaoke band at their reception and if so, would she and Cailin sing and would everyone else get a chance to sing, too, because as Ginny had stated, "hello, karaoke is my jam." Then she insisted that Libba needed to sing a song to Cailin at their engagement party because Cailin had sung to her on their first date.

Libba claimed to be a horrible singer; however, Trish said Libba was constantly singing at her place and she had a really good voice. After much lamenting and a lot of peer pressure, Libba agreed to sing a song and the day finally arrived when she had to go through with it. She knew she had to pick a song that was within her vocal range but also cool enough for Trish to approve. She narrowed it down to a recent song by Taylor Swift or an oldie but goodie by Shania Twain, except that she wasn't sure if she could pull either one of them off. She would just have to do her best and try not to freeze on stage.

She entered the manor through the back door and grabbed a bottled water from the main kitchen. Since before the manor opened, she was coming here on a regular basis helping Mallory get ready for the grand opening. Now that the manor was open, she continued to practice her yoga in the garden every day after work, and sometimes the guests would even join her. Mallory asked if she would be willing to teach a class every now and then, maybe even open the class to the public but Libba wasn't sure if she wanted to make that step. She didn't mind if people joined her occasionally, but she really came for the serenity the garden brought her. It soothed her soul after a long day of work, settled her mind, and relaxed her body. Plus, she got a chance to hang out with Mallory or give her a hand with happy hour if Gwen, the new night concierge, had the night off. Normally Trish would join them, and occasionally when Cailin and Mike would come over to help, Mallory would whip out her Color Street nails, and the girls would do their nails together while the guys entertained the guests. Mallory made it a point to always have on hand Stella Rosa wine and bags of Doritos, too.

Mallory had hired Gwen to work three nights a week and every other weekend. Having Gwen around was a huge help, especially now that business was picking up. Not to mention, with Mallory being a single mom and running a twenty-four-hour bed and breakfast, she was busy during the day and wanted to be able to spend time with Olivia in the evening. Secretly, Mike expressed to Cailin that if she continued to work so much, she would never have time to date—"if she wanted to that is"—and suggested he hire someone. Cailin agreed and brought it up to Mallory one afternoon. *It would be especially helpful during happy hour and for late check-ins,* Mallory had agreed, so she posted an ad on Facebook and after interviewing five candidates, she hired Gwen.

Libba tapped on the office window and peeked inside the room where Mallory and Gwen were meeting. "Sorry to bother you but I wanted to let you know I'm heading out now. I'll see you later at the pub."

"Of course, no problem," Mallory smiled. "I'll be there."

Libba drove to her condo practicing both songs on the short drive home. She knew which song she would sing. She just hoped she wouldn't embarrass herself.

As she showered and got ready for the evening, her mind reminisced over the past nine months. Cailin was there every step of the way. Their love had grown quickly but it was stronger than anything she ever felt, and she was certain that this time her marriage would last forever. She didn't know how she would have managed the last few months without him but then she realized, Cailin only attributed to part of whom she had become.

It was her friends—Trish and Mallory—who also helped her through those hard times. It was the two of them that she cried to when Cailin was away; it was the two of them that she laughed and got drunk with and shared sometimes crazy, sometimes heartfelt stories with; it was the two of them who encouraged her to go for her heart's desire and find her soulmate; and it was the two of them that helped her become the person she wanted to be. The person she was now. They were her best friends, and she knew, like her love for Cailin, not every day would be perfect and not every day would be easy but no matter what, their love and friendship would always prevail.

Libba sat back in her chair and watched everyone around her. This was her new family—Cailin, her mom, Mike, Trish, Mallory, Ginny, Martha, Louis, and even Caleb—and they were all here celebrating her and Cailin and the new life they would soon be sharing together. She imagined her and Cailin continuing the tradition of going to the Stanleys' the first Friday of every month; going to Noah's latest sport fad, which transitioned from soccer to flag football; and having cookouts at Mike's house or perhaps Muirfield Manor. Every scene that flashed through her mind was filled with talking, laughing, eating, drinking, and simply having fun and enjoying life.

Ginny moved to sit behind Libba who was sitting between Cailin and Trish. Libba and Trish swerved their chairs to face her and then Mallory scooted her chair over too.

"Libba, I know I've told you before that Cailin and I grew up like brother and sister and so I'd like to say, welcome to the family." She leaned in and gave Libba a big hug, then she looked at Trish.

"Trish, you know you're the reason why me and Andy are together, but I wanted to tell you something and I hope you're okay with it."

"You're pregnant!" Trish leaned forward in excitement.

"Oh. No! But I'm glad to see you would be happy for me if I were. No, I wanted to tell you, tell you all actually," and she looked at the three girls before her. "Libba, remember I told you I wanted to hike the Appalachian Trial," Libba nodded. "Well, Andy and I have decided to thru hike it together. I finally told him it was on my bucket list and it's on his, too!"

"That's wonderful, Ginny!" Now it was Trish's turn to give Ginny a hug. "Really, I'm happy for you."

"Yeah, that's great news," Mallory said.

"Congratulations," said Libba. "I'm actually glad he's going with you because I really didn't want you going by yourself. When do you leave?"

"That's the thing. Hopefully, we're back before you and Cailin get married so I was hoping you picked a date."

"Oh. I'm sorry but no we haven't. I can assure you that it will be a while though. Besides," Libba grinned, "we couldn't get married without one of my bride's maids."

"You mean ... you want me to be a bridesmaid!"

"Of course, all of you—and Trish before you even ask, I haven't decided who will be my maid of honor yet."

"It'll be me," Trish and Mallory both said at the same time. They looked at each other and laughed.

"Libba has plenty of time to figure that out," Mallory said, looking over Libba's head. "But right now, I think she has a song to sing."

Cailin was standing behind Libba and she knew it was time. She turned to face him, and he kissed the top of her forehead.

"You ready?" he asked. "You're not going to bail on me, are you?"

"I'm a woman of her word, Cailin Wade, and I'm ready. Question is, are you ready for me?" Libba turned and walked up to the stage.

Cailin moved his seat slightly in front of the rest of the group, purposefully doing so that no one could see his face when Libba started singing. Ginny moved and took the chair Libba had occupied as Mike returned with another round of drinks for everyone. He sat down in Ginny's now empty seat, positioning it on Mallory's left side.

"Do you know what song she finally settled on?" he whispered.

"No. She's been singing all sorts of songs when she comes to the manor and Trish was right, she really does have a lovely voice. I can't wait to hear what she picked."

The lights dimmed and Libba walked on stage.

She planned her outfit perfectly, knowing Cailin would only have eyes for her. Libba wore a winter-white long-sleeved laced top tucked into a periwinkle tulle skirt that had jagged edges like a fairy's dress. Her light pink heels arched her legs just enough to show off her muscles. She stood in the middle of the stage with the light shining down upon her long blond curls. Immediately Cailin was under her spell. Indeed, she looked like a fairy, his precious fairy.

When the music began and Libba started singing, the whole room went still. Even the wait staff stopped to stare at Libba and listen. Her voice was beautiful and Cailin was entranced by the sound of it. He'd heard her sing a little here and there, but she never opened her heart to sing like she was doing tonight. For him.

Mallory saw how Cailin watched Libba, mesmerized in her every move. She yearned for someone to look at her that way but feared it would be a long time. The Stanleys were looking at each other and then Martha leaned her head on Louis' shoulder. Mallory turned to look at Mike to find him looking right back at her. She quietly hiccupped, but this time no goosebumps. Her heart started to race, and she felt the flutter of little butterflies in her stomach, yet all the while Mike's gaze did not wane. He touched her hand and a warmth spread through her.

Mike leaned in like he was going to kiss her but then he stopped. Still, he never stopped looking at her. Mallory wasn't sure if he were going to kiss her or not, but then she decided if he wouldn't kiss her, she would make the first move. Mallory leaned in and placed one hand on his cheek. Slowly she inched forward until their lips touched, softly. She raised her other hand to his face and kissed him deeply until her heart slowed and the butterflies drifted away.

Libba saw Mallory reach over and kiss Mike but she continued to sing to Cailin. She had finally decided on *From this Moment On* by Shania Twain because she felt the lyrics ran true for everything she felt for Cailin, and the new life she was starting with him.

> *I give my hand to you with all my heart*
> *I can't wait to live my life with you, I can't wait to start*
> *You and I will never be apart*
> *My dreams came true because of you*

From this moment as long as I live
I will love you, I promise you this
There is nothing I wouldn't give
From this moment on, oh ...

When Libba finished the song Cailin rushed to the stage, kissed her, and twirled her around in his arms. Trish and Mallory too ran on the stage, Mallory holding Mike's hand and dragging him on stage with them. Another song started and Libba, Trish and Mallory stood beside each other and started dancing. They had practiced this dance routine for the last few weeks to surprise everyone tonight. They danced and danced, laughed and laughed, and when the song ended, everyone in Murray's Pub jumped to their feet and applauded the Women of Muirfield Manor.

CPSIA information can be obtained
at www.ICGtesting.com
Printed in the USA
BVHW071052180421
605248BV00011B/349